The Scattering of Stars

K.L Lawlor

Dedication

Mum, for believing in me when I didn't believe in myself. This series wouldn't exist without your constant support, love, and unextinguishable excitement. Thank you.

Sam, for being my rock during my lowest moments. Your unrelenting support got me through this monster of a project. You're the best.

Pronunciations

Names:
Nylani (Nigh-LAH-nee)
Damirius (Duh-MEER-ee-uhs)
Uvalaris (OO-vah-LAH-riss)
Uvariss (OO-vah-riss)
Soleresos (Soh-LAH-res-OHS)
Umos (OO-mohs)
Cecilaena (Seh-sihl-lay-nuh)
Uvalaar (OO-vah-lar)

Places:
Kohrmiir (CORE-meer)
Marrduni (Mar-DUNE-ee)
Yalarepsos (Yah-lah-REP-sohs)
Autriel (AW-tree-ehl)
Doxdel (DOCKS-dull)
Corrof (CORE-off)
Ula'Rae (OO-lah Ray)
Dororra (DOOR-or-rah)

1

Nylani

The sun beats against my back as it reaches its peak in the mid-afternoon haze that graces Kohrmiir. The farm town is settled on the southernmost part of the county, Marrduni, so the heat is always unbearable here. The nights aren't much better.

Chatter from nearby workers fills the stagnant air as I walk. The expansive fields that surround this tiny town are always busy. The people wake at dawn and fall at dusk. I hear a laugh from one of the larger guys - Talro, I think - that echoes across the flatlands. That reminds me, it's Friday. An early end tonight to make way for the long-awaited gossip that people can't seem to get during the rest of the week.
I groan internally. I hate gossip. It doesn't do anything besides stir the pot in communications. And I need communication to live.

The gravel crunches under my boots as I head for

the Tanned Tankard, steeling myself for the constant babbling that will no doubt erupt when I open the door. The Tanned Tankard tavern is the main tavern for the people here. Sure, there's The Merry Drip, but the larger size here invites more people.

The chipped, sun bleached orange paint does little to ease me. Neither does the garish sign that crowns the tavern. But, I must do what I can to fit in here. My appearance is enough for most people to turn me away. I've kept the facade up enough to make people like me, so a few more hours shouldn't hurt whilst I prepare to leave. I can hear the prattle and laughter already as I reach for the handle, my scarred hand gripping the metal doorknob tightly enough to leave an indent in my palm. I suck in a deep breath, forcing my shoulders to slack. I need to relax.

The door opens and I'm slammed with the sound of a full floor of giddy people blathering away. I wince. Then I force a smile on my face as I step in, taking note of the people that are in my immediate vicinity. Large, muscular farmhands, as well as their housewives, all sit amongst their friends immediately in front of me. Cold drinks are in their hands, the condensation pooling onto their sunburnt skin. Orus –people of bovine ancestry-, orcs, humans, and the occasional elf all sit in equality here. That is the way of Kohrmiir.

In a dark corner near the bar, I see the usual drunkards that have claimed the spot, pleading with the barmaids for another drink. They slump their shoulders into each other, becoming a multi-headed amalgamation of heavy-lidded, grinning jokesters. If you had never had a conversation with them, it would be frightening. But, I know them, and they look about as harmful as drowsy puppies to me.

The familiar ringing of the bell above me announces my arrival, much to my dismay. Heads turn to see who entered, and I'm overloaded with gestations of greetings. Voices cheer, hands are shaken, and heads are nodded as I empty the doorway. I soften my face to hopefully show warmth to them; the last thing I need to look like is rude. A voice from the bar calls my attention, and I'm grateful to have an excuse to beeline away from the comradery.

"Just yer usual, Nylani?", the barkeep, a portly man called Kavda, asks, a steaming pot already in his meaty hand. I nod, pulling my lips up into a smile. I hope it's convincing, but I can't muster the energy to try too hard today. I find the familiar table in the farthest corner of the tavern, emptied and awaiting me. I heave a sigh of relief. I slump into the rickety wooden chair, my sunkissed, battered arms resting on the soothingly cold round table. Within moments of sitting, a young, raven-haired barmaid approaches me, weathered teacup in hand. I don't recognise her immediately - a new face I've needed to account for - but as she approaches I force my smile again.

"Here you go, ma'am," she squeaks, gingerly placing the steaming cup of homemade tea in front of me. The billowing steam moistens my face almost immediately. A pleasant change from the dry heat outside. I notice the youngster lingering awkwardly beside me. She sways on the balls of her feet, fidgeting with the hem of her skirt. I swallow a grumble. Instead, I simply look up, locking eyes with the wide brown ones that seem aghast I've noticed her.

"Uh... Um." She stammers. The longer I look, the younger she seems. Is Kavda hiring children now? "Is there anything else I can get you, ma'am?" An eyebrow quirks almost immediately, out of instinct. "No," I respond curtly. She recoils a little, like a child that's been hit. Shit. "Thank you," I add quickly, trying to soften the blow as much as I can. It seems to work, as I notice her shoulders relax. A voice calls for "Maddie!" and the girl whisks away into the gaggle of people once more.

As soon as her back is turned, I release a held breath. I need to be more careful of my tongue. I feel my face relax back into neutral, which, unfortunately, shows as an uncaring deadpan. I've been told I always look like I'm in a foul mood when I look like this. It's helpful to diminish unwanted attention, but unfortunately a foul face doesn't bring many customers. Apparently a sullen, scarred elf isn't approachable.

I sip my tea. The herbal concoction has a slightly sweet taste to it; the way I like it. Kavda may be many things, but inattentive isn't one of them. That's why I can rely on him to send word my way when someone needs help. I glance up at the barkeep. He smiles and nods in my direction. I smile back, a genuine one this time. It's barely perceptible but I know he sees it.

Hours pass as I stay in the isolated corner of the tavern, with the same young barmaid refilling my cracked cup once it's empty. The large arched window that sits beside me documents the slow descent of the setting sun, the sky becoming dappled in light pinks. The tavern is bellowing by now; everyone has finally finished their day's tasks and have retired here for the early eve. Children are rushing by, their parents too busy with idle chatter to notice or care. Screams of elation ring in my ears, making me wince and cover them.

Thankfully, no one seems to notice me. I huddle further into the corner, willing the shadows to encompass me. My shoulder presses into the wall, the cool stone a reprieve from the stifling air in here. I turn my head to the window, the settling sun sinking behind the flatlands. The crops and flora that cover the fields are smothered in a golden glow that gives them an ethereal shine. The world seems almost magical outside of this window; the farms look like paintings, the colours bleed into each other like watercolours merging onto a damp canvas. My eyes drift to the large lime tree that dominates the Ranerra's orchard. The stippling golden hue drifts through the leaves, the limes that hang there turning into gilded, mystical fruit. The deafening commotion around me begins to fade away to nothingness. My vision blurs, and I can feel myself get sucked into my memories. Back to my home.

In an instant, I'm back there. In the behemoth of a backyard that I grew up in. The sensation of the grass tickling my bare toes feels so real I swear I can feel it within my boots. Roses, peonies, tulips, and many more of their kin are scattered around me in the forest of a garden. They gently sway with the breeze, their linen petals fluttering erratically.

At the bottom of the field, I can see the gigantic guardian of an apple tree that rested on an upturned layer of earth at an angle. It seems to almost loom over the tiny blooms that laid before it. I remember walking towards the gargantuan tree, staring up at the nearly ripe red apples that hung teasingly low. I touched the bark of the tree. It had become an elegant braid of the different sections of trunk intertwining amongst itself over the many decades of its extraordinary life. I remember being fascinated by it, my tiny unmarked hands ran over the rough exterior with glee.

My eyes followed the intricate binding of the bark, which ended at its branches that stroked the sky; the tips barely touched the clouds that glided past. The memory quivers a little, and I'm transported to the meadow just ahead of the tree and its mushroom-addled grove.

I remember reaching for a flower. It had looked so soft, its petals like the softest silk in the entire Empire. Nothing I had seen before could compare to the beauty that I saw before me. The budding flower had midnight blue petals, like the deepest depths of the night sky. Tiny, curious fingers reached out to touch them, but... It goes blurry. Like trying to adjust your vision after being dunked into the ocean. Speckled light seeps through, but everything else goes out of focus.

Did I help it bloom? The image of those navy petals expanding and displaying the white speckles of the inner core swims by my mind. But... no. That doesn't feel right. A still image of the flower in full bloom - a gorgeous starry night sky in its petals as the centre resembles a crescent moon - imprints itself in my visual. But the image is grainy. The edges are fuzzy. Is it a real memory, or a thought I want to be real?

A sudden snap to the image of an electric current running down my tiny arm replays in my head. A spark shot out of my fingertip, blood dripped onto the grass below me. The spark zapped at the head of the bud, and ran all the way down to its roots. It wilted within seconds. I remember how hard I cried, both in the shame of destroying the flower, and the sudden pain I had experienced. This makes more sense. I'm used to destroying things. That's my specialty.

I'm thrusted into my body again. The constant babbling in the tavern doesn't seem to die down at all. I need to ground myself. Deep breath in. Deep breath out. These memories are always so jarring. I look at something, anything, to try to distract myself. I focus on the once-white cup in my hands. The warm tea feels cold against my sweating palms, though the tea is trickling steam. I take a deep gulp of it, the earthy flavour running down my throat. Deep breath in. Deep breath out. I look at my hands.
Deep, gnarly scars sink into the walnut skin of my

hands. Thin, needle-like lines surround and overlap the harsher scars, and run up to my forearms. I begin to trail them. From the back of my hands up to my forearms are covered in these skinny tears, with much more garish slashes interrupting their lattice-work design. The deeper wounds have split skin apart, exposing darker flesh beneath that has mostly healed in ugly scars. It really was no wonder why people were scared of me when I arrived here.

I look at my scars with disgust. With frustration. It's my fault they're there, after all. My magic is unpredictable, unruly. White-hot energy courses through me all the time, searching for ways to explode out in a violent manner. Whenever my emotions run high, or when my mind slips, a whip of electricity is guaranteed to lash out at whichever unlucky fool is nearby. Mostly, it's me.

Nothing compares to my first real scar – it coiled itself around my right forearm and sunk so deep it nearly touched bone. The pain was unlike anything I had ever experienced before. Almost unlike anything I have experienced since. The pain and agony consumed me whole that day - roughly fourteen years ago - and I don't think I'll ever forget it.

Fire erupted around me. My beautiful garden was aflame and had turned to crisp beneath my bare feet. All I could see around me were the oranges and reds of the fire, there were no shapes within the flames. Just the burning, consuming wall that engulfed the world around me. Smoke filled my lungs, my ribs ached with each heavy, aggressive cough. I tried to move, but fear kept me frozen. Then the piercing rip of my arm made me scream.

Blood covered me. I can remember the slick stickiness that smothered my small hands. The metallic stench of my own blood clung to me. Then I collapsed to the ground. My mind was swimming, but I tried to crawl with my good arm. I'm sure I was crying, but I can't remember fully. The pain in my arm was too much for prepubescent me. I dug into the earth, dirt mingling with my blood. Soot covered my clothes and face, making it hard to see. A scream rang my ears. A woman's scream, I was sure of it. I couldn't hear what she was saying, but I recognised the voice. Another piercing scream rang out within the fire, and then silence followed. I tried to yell, but my throat was choked with smoke. I clung desperately to the ground, like the cool earth would save me. I continued my laborious crawl.

Finally, the doors that led to the kitchen came into view through the blaze that encapsulated me. I saw her then. The woman who screamed. Silver - no, brown. No, it was definitely silver, hair covered the woman's face that laid on her back in the kitchen. Her hair was contaminated by her own blood. It was haunting. The faceless, ethereal woman had burned into my mind from that moment on. I was lifted away, screaming and crying against a brutishly large arm. And that was the last I saw my gorgeous garden. And the woman who screamed.

Gasps and an eruption of giggles yank me out of the memory. I suppress a gasp, not wanting any prying eyes on me. Thankfully, the women on the table beside me seem far too engrossed in each other to care. Deep breath in. Deep breath out. The women – roughly the same age as me – are all giggling and gossiping loudly amongst themselves. They seem almost like school children, their titters and snickers fill the tavern, despite there only being five of them. Their rosy cheeks expose how much alcohol has already been drunk, with the full glasses showing how much more will go. I lower my eyes, looking at my refilled cup. Hm. Odd. I didn't notice anyone passing by. I hope I didn't look too disoriented.

Whispers of escapades with some of the muscular farmhands catch my ears, but it's an easy enough task to tune the erratic women out again. Their continual screeches break the barriers of my mental peace, the shrill pitch strumming my eardrums recklessly. How annoying. I turn back to my tea.

The piping heat in my throat is somewhat soothing. I lean back against my chair, careful not to topple it from the uneven cobble slabs. Cusping my cup under my chin, I tune into the conversations beside me. If they're not going to quieten, I might as well see if there's anything of value there.
Unfortunately, nothing of substance - just who's sleeping with who - until a shocked gasp pierces the idle chatter. Hushed whisperings of, "Is that Damirius?" and "Gods, he looks so much better with a tan..." drift past. I scoff. They're all as bad as each other. The chatter finally ends, with everyone now turning their attention to the light mauve tiefling that has just entered the room.

2

Damirius

All eyes are on me as I open the tavern door. As the only tiefling in this godsforsaken, bigoted village, I stick out like a sore thumb. Unfortunately, the rumours do little to deter the feeling.
My name is whispered in every corner of this backwards, archaic town. Gossip narrates the story of a 'devilish man that ravishes in the aches and yearnings of every being he comes across'. Apparently, no man, woman, nor amorphous creature seems beyond my seductive grasp. Or so it's been said. Though, I will admit that my unbuttoned blouse does little to dissuade the rumour. The wide collar really accentuates my chest, the cream compliments my gorgeous lilac tone.

I suppose, though, that even though they talk about me negatively, it's better than not talking about me at all. Better for business, and such. Especially when they try to 'warn' newcomers about the 'big, bad tiefling' that will 'seduce your children'. I scoff at the thought as I continue through the tavern, staring them down as they stare at me. They have no qualms at painting me the villain, yet they all crawl to me when night arrives. It's almost guaranteed that at least two will try to trail me when I leave tonight.

A young barmaid greets me as I walk towards the bar. She must be new as she smiles genuinely as I talk to her. Instinctively, I fiddle her long, ebony hair. I can see the old man behind her glare at me. I twirl it around my finger. She giggles innocently, and I know I've caught her.

I grin, the smugness pointed towards the port bellied geezer. "An ale, my dear," I coo to her, watching the barkeep as I talk. He glowers from behind her, but doesn't say a word. He knows better; what with all the dirt I have on him. I drop my hand, letting her wave of raven hair slip out of my hand as she darts to fetch my drink. I notice her round, freckled face grow redder and redder as she stumbles past the old man. He gives me a pointed glare, so I step away. With my back to the bar, I'm able to get a better view of who's inside the tavern. People are either staring straight at me, or looking away. Like that can shield them. I smirk to myself. They're all so pathetic.

I continue my walk across the tavern floor, calculating each step as I watch their reactions. The clacking of his heeled boots echo through the unnerving silence. Some people genuinely jump at each tap. It's almost amusing. They act so high-and-mighty when in public, but they have no guts to actually say anything. They forget I have knowledge of their deep desires until I'm within view.

The walk around the tavern floor is arduous, but not for me. I like this game of cat and mouse I have to play. If I lose, there's nothing they can take. If they lose, their pride is forfeited. And that seems to be worth a lot here.
I glance at each table, quickly enough to have a general idea of who sits there, but not long enough to make eye contact. People shuffle closer together, making it clear I'm not welcome. I don't stifle my laugh. Their shoulders draw closer to their reddening ears. Then, finally, I spot a table with an open chair.

The self-appointed town hero, Nylani, sits there alone. Slumped against the wall, looking out the window at the shifting late noon sky. We've never had an actual interaction, but I know enough about her from the constant praise she receives. It's frustrating. She's consistently at their servitude and gets praised; I am, too, and all I receive are dirty looks and ridiculous rumours. She's no doubt heard them too, which is why she won't even look my way as I stride over to her table.

I loudly pull the chair away, announcing my arrival, and still she doesn't turn. I sit, get myself comfortable and rest my arms on the dinghy table, watching her every move. Still, she doesn't register that I'm here.

What is with her? Is she deaf? Or just horrifically rude? Whichever it is, I don't like it.
She silently sips at her tea, eyes locked on the setting sun. I cough drily, hoping that would be enough to get her attention. Her grey eyes flick over to me. So she is just rude. Nice to know. I swallow the rising indignation I feel in my throat, and smile as wide as I can at her.
 "So, what brings a lady like you to a place like this?"

Even I cringe internally at that; it has slipped out so fast I couldn't catch it. I keep my smile there, trying to play it off as intentional. I can almost hear the disinterest as she rolls her eyes at me. Still, she says nothing. A moment goes by. And another. My smile has finally dropped. How bothersome. How did she manage to get this hillbilly town to sing her praises?

I sit back in my chair, folding my arms across my chest. If she won't answer, I'll just sit in her silent company, I decide. Either she goes first, or we can get a conversation going. She has found someone just as stubborn as her, and I can guarantee I will emerge victorious in this baffling battle. Finally, she turns her head to look at me. I cock an eyebrow, anticipating a response. Those terrifyingly light eyes bore into me with a hardness and grittiness akin to cement. Against her olive skin and angular proportions, those eyes don't seem to match her genetic palette. They're far too light and rounded against everything else.
"Tea."
Her voice was so soft I almost didn't catch it at first. It takes me a moment to actually comprehend what she said, with the help of her gesturing

towards the half empty cup she holds. Her impatience is clear. A blush starts to creep up my neck, the heat threatening to extend towards my cheeks. I clear my throat, squaring my shoulders. "Right." I have to clear my throat again. It feels like a lump is sitting stubbornly on my voice box. "Yeah, their tea... It's really good."

I groan inwardly. Fuck. Shit. And piss on it all. This conversation is dying quick. I'm used to stubborn assholes, so why is she causing me so many issues?! I can't figure it out. I look around the tavern, trying to find something - anything - to keep this conversation afloat.

Now that I'm seated, people have resumed their chatting, drinking, and perpetual noisiness. It almost seems as if we're invisible in this gloomy corner. I slowly turn to look back at this miserable elf, only to find her already staring back at me. A chill runs down my spine. Those eyes almost shine in the darkness that the candelabra above has casted her in. They seem to almost peer into my soul. And they don't like what they see.
My stomach twists into a giant knot, threatening to make me hurl. I want to leave, but my legs won't let me rise. Those intimidating, ghostly grey eyes

keep me seated; her scowl accentuated by the two large scars across her face. One splits her right eyebrow, and travels down to her cheek. The other dashes across the bridge of her nose and curls just under her left eye. I notice her gaze lift to something behind me, and almost instantly her appearance suddenly softens.

The cold glare I was receiving suddenly disappears as the blushing barmaid from before saunters over. She carries a large tankard of the plainest, cheapest beer the tavern could offer in her delicate hand. A demand from Kavda no doubt. He's probably spat in it too. She sets it in front of me, and I can't stop myself from immediately raising it and drinking hungrily. Spit or no, I need this drink.

The heat from outside, combined with this aggravating woman, is enough to make a man drink themselves into a stupor. It amazes me that she's renowned in such high regard with an attitude like hers. But, when I set my glass down, I see her smiling. Smiling! And laughing!
The woman who just sat silently and glared at me, is laughing alongside the barmaid who brought my drink to the table. I flush my confusion and amazement down with another swig, listening to

the two women chatter idly. Nothing of importance; just standard chatter about the commotions on Fridays and how bothersome the summer heat is. I have to hide my smirk in the drink. She truly is just one of them. A stubborn, superficial hypocrite.

I place my glass down, keeping my eyes on the barmaid. I smirk up at her, feeling victorious as she bites her lip to stop herself from giggling. Now that I'm actually studying her, I can appreciate her appearance; a typical natural beauty - dark hair, dark eyes. Freckles that adorn her rosy cheeks, and a small mole on her neck. She was definitely easy on the eyes, at least.

Me staring at her seems to make the human blush harder, and I notice the elf on my table folds her arms and huffs. I have to stifle a laugh. Typical. She's the jealous type. My grin widens. I run my tongue along my fangs before winking at her. She practically glows a brilliant tomato red. I sometimes forget just how easy it is to get at the hearts of the more naive, innocent ones. I chuckle as the poor youngling scurries off, attempting to look busy and failing miserably. I have to bite my bottom lip to stop my laugh from exploding outwards.

I turn my attention back to the scowling elf. I can't help but grin at her disapproving glare. She really is just like the rest of them. A stubborn fool too cowardly to see past the facade.

"So, Princess, anything else that draws you to the countryside, apart from tea?" I drawl out. I push the condescending tone as far as I can. Her eyebrow twitches. I grin.
"What did you just call me?" she grumbles. I can't help but chuckle. Gotcha.
"Princess?" I continue the charade. Her jaw tightens and I feel invigorated. "It's a nickname for a special lady that radiates elegance and intellect such as yourself." My grin widens unnaturally large. I can't contain myself. Seeing her fight with herself is almost too good to be true.

She heaves a sigh and she leans back in the chair, her thumb and index finger pinching the scarred bridge of her nose. I rest my chin on the palm of my hand, watching her inner debate clear on her face. I'm surprised it worked so well, considering how easily she managed to block me out at first. But, I won't complain.

"Work," she grumbles. I tilt my head to the side,

waiting for her to continue. She doesn't follow the cue.

"Work? What type of work?"

She groans at my question, as if wanting her one-worded answers to be enough. But it won't be. Not while I'm controlling the conversation. I raise an eyebrow, waiting for her to answer.

She sighs, clearly annoyed that her stubbornness doesn't phase me. I let a small, sly smile show. "Anything. Killing beasts, retrieval requests, heavy lifting. Whoever's paying, I'll do it." Her voice, when truly neutral, was quite delicate; a slight tilt to the end. It's quite melodic, actually. And this is possibly the longest I've ever heard her talk. I can feel my smile stretch further.

Suddenly, her hands slam against the tabletop. Startled, I jolt backwards in my chair. She rises from her seat, and even while standing, I can still see the top of her head. However, her glare is what makes me feel small. Her intense stare makes me shrink, and suddenly I feel like a stumbling schoolboy.

"Well," she says, her voice suddenly icy, "as fun as this has been, I have a ride to catch." She walks away, not even bothering to look back at me.

Though, I wouldn't want her to. My jaw hangs open gormlessly. I'm sure I look like a fool.

I glance over to her abandoned cup, the drink continuing its skittering trail of steam upwards to the ceiling. Her complete disinterest in me, or even just the battling communication, was nothing I had ever experienced before. I've had arrogant clientele before. I've had rude clientele. I've had clientele that refused to communicate in any way other than constant bickering.
But she wasn't clientele. She was just a person.
A person that didn't like me very much at all.

The sudden cling of coins draws my attention. The diminutive elf was already by the front of the tavern. She's turned towards the bar and is flicking coins to the bar staff. But not just any coins. The sparkling glimmer of silver reflects off of the candlelight above. Actual silver.
I need to join her. Follow her, for all I care. That kind of money is hard to weasel out of people, and she uses it as chump change. My family - Mama, Papa, and all my siblings - could be fed for a week off just one of those blasted coins and she throws it away to a portly man in the middle of nowhere.

She reaches the door and I'm on my feet. I glug the remainder of my drink and it dribbles down my chin. But I don't care. And I especially don't care about the stares that follow me as I dart for the door. My feet pound against the uneven floor and I zip around patrons who yell. But I don't care. She's my ticket out of here, and I'm not wasting this opportunity now.

"Hey! Hey, wait!", I yell, tumbling out of the tavern. I grab her left arm, hoping to grab her attention. She spins around to face me, her free hand raising into the air. And I do one thing I never thought I'd do. I fall to my knees.
"Take me with you," I plead, suddenly aware of how breathless I am. "Please." I look up at her, trying to read her face. If she's surprised, she hides it well. Then, she scoffs at me. And my stomach drops.

"Who said I'm taking anyone anywhere?"
Now it's my turn to groan. Frustration rises in me, and I blurt out, "I've been wanting to get out of this dreary town for ages. You're my ticket out of here!"

She rolls her eyes, I can feel her anger rise and radiate off of her. "Who says I'm just going to let you join me?!" she declares. She snarls down at me. A wave of desperation rolls over me, slumping my shoulders. I'm so close. So close to getting out of here; away from the snide jeers. The rumours. The hostility.

And then, a thought appears. An insidious, venomous thought. I have to hide my smile.
"So, the honourable and noble Nylani, saviour of Kohrmiir, refuses to help a patron in need?" I drawl. Her piercing eyes look at me, bewildered. I rise from my knees, not taking my eyes away from hers. "Oh dear. What will the people say?"
I lean over, my face right in front of hers. She frowns, and I can't contain my grin any longer. She seems to study me for a moment, the pair of us standing there in palpable silence. Her frown dissipates, leaving her unreadable. Damn it.

"You honestly believe the people will be mad that I didn't help you?"
That stung. It's true, but still... Having the townspeople's opinion broadcasted so openly hurt.

I steel myself, edging my face closer to hers. "They don't need to know it's me," I force a cocky smirk. I lean into her ear, revelling at how awkward she looks from our close proximity. "I'll have you know, I'm an exceptional liar."

That, itself, was a lie. But she doesn't need to know that. I pray it'll be enough. All I want to do is get out of here. Once I'm away we won't ever have to see each other again. I stare at her, waiting for her move in this aggravatingly long dance. With a grumble, and an accusatory hand on her hip, she scowls up at me.

"Fine. You can come along. But if you die, it's on you." She jabs an aggravated finger into the middle of my chest, before she turns on her heel. I rub the offended spot, a mild throb aching in my sternum. Wait.
"Dying?! Who said anything about dying?!" I yell. Where is she taking me?!
She ignores me, continuing her trek through the streets of Kohrmiir, without even looking back at me. I follow, realising we're walking the roughly laid cobblestone path that heads to the stables by the entrance gate of the town.

As we walk, the presence of this miniature woman seems to be a beacon for people to drift towards her. Everyone seems to appear out of nowhere to talk to her. Anything from general chit chat to thanking her for her help and servitude. I chew the inside of my cheek, biting back spiteful remarks. No one seems to notice me as I walk beside her, and for that I'm grateful. If I was given a glance, I don't think I'd be able to hold back any of the accusatory thoughts that are swimming in my head.

I start to trail behind her, wanting to separate away from the continuous stream of people that keep showering her with praise. She's twisting and turning, making sure everyone gets a moment of her attention. How conceited. She ruffles a child's head, clasps someone's hands as they shake hers. The bubbling bile of anger threatens to rise as I watch her arrogant ballet of chivalry down the street. Finally, the people begin to dissipate and we can walk in relative quiet again. Her pace quickens, her eyes set ahead and furrowed. I haven't even said anything - why is she angry at me now?! I have to take longer strides to keep up with her march. Finally, we stop at the stables. I look up and see Farmer Mack atop his chestnut horse. The size of the young horse always strikes me as comical against Mack. The man is roughly the size of a child, his head remarkably large against his withered frame.

He always seems to have a permanent hunch, his shoulders sit just under his large ears. The tips of his ears and forearms have a permanent case of sunburn, whereas the rest of him stays pale by his large, brimmed straw hat. His chin juts out far enough to make the rest of his face squash around it, and a tooth on his lower jaw protrudes past his lips, brushing the tip of his bulbous nose. Despite everything, Mack was probably the only nice person in Kohrmiir. At least, he's been nothing but cordial with me.

The tiny elf yells up to him, "Hey, Mack! You ready to head off? We're ready to go if you are."
She raises a hand, gesturing who 'we' means. I lift my brows. Didn't expect such comradery already. The elderly man slowly lifts his head to look at me, a courtesy nod pointed my way. I nod back. I'm glad the geriatric, old guy just sticks to his farm. At least someone doesn't listen to rumours around here.

"'Course ah can take ya', Miss Nylani, ma'am. Always ready fer a ride on lil' ol' Hazel!" He calls back, his protruding tooth making him whistle as he talks, "Jus' hops aboard the back an' get comfy. It's a long ride." He pats the shiny, silky brown coat of his companion that dwarfs him. I have to stifle a laugh; his hand is tiny against the muscular build of his tamed beast. Said beast huffs gently in response to her master's affection.

"Just a second. Need to go grab my things in the Inn," she calls up to the farmer. Then she turns to face me. Her smile immediately drops. "If you have anything left here, get it before we go. Because once we're moving, I'm not walking back just because you forgot your coin purse." Her tone is harsh, though I shouldn't be surprised. I pull the best smirk I can. Gods, this is tiring. I shrug off my small satchel bag, dangling it from my fingers.

"Everything I need, I carry in here, ma'am." I make sure to sound as sardonic as possible. She huffs before walking across the street towards the inn. A bleached, pale sign hanging above it announces its name of "The Sunset Inn". I can't help but roll my eyes and scoff. She's going to make this entire ride difficult. I just know it. The hacking sound of a cough catches my attention. I spin around, seeing little old Mack watching me carefully.

"Miss Nylani there is a truly kind soul, youn' man. But she won't take kindly to yer talkin' down ter her like tha'. Be prepared for a mighty shock," the old man chuckles, his beady eyes glinting mischievously.

I raise an eyebrow, inviting the old timer to explain, but he simply smiles and shakes his head. I contemplate for a moment. If she truly is a kind soul, she definitely doesn't like showing it. I nod to Mack for his advice, anyway, appreciative that he at least spoke to me kindly.

The sound of crunching gravel catches my attention. I look up and see the elf, carrying a large, brown haversack on her back. It looks incredibly worn, with fraying strands of fabric around the hem of the sack, and the leather straps around her shoulders bleached from sun exposure. She walks past me without much regard, and heads straight for the wagon that Mack's horse is strapped to.

"Come on!" she yells to me as she begins to climb into the wagon. She makes it look so easy, considering the opening is almost eye height with her. "If you don't get on, we're leaving you behind."

With that, I quickly stride over to the rear of the wagon. I watch her pull herself up with immense ease. Great. This is going to be embarrassing. I throw my bag inside the wagon and try to pull myself inside. It's a lot harder than it looks. My arms shake from the exertion, my stomach sore from tension. I finally manage to haul myself inside, and spot the tiny elf sitting atop a small mound of hay, smirking with amusement.

I grumble, but it only seems to make her sardonic smile grow. I kick hay in her direction, grinning as it splats her straight in the face. She has to spit some out of her mouth. I make a small pile to rest my rear on, and collapse with as little grace onto it. I let myself sink into the hay, bemused at the sight of my travelling companion having to pull hay out of her hair. The wagon slowly wheels across the bumpy cobblestone road as the horse starts to move, beginning the trek out of the village I had the displeasure of residing in for the past year.

3

Nylani

The road of the Whispering Valley feels like it's stretching into a limitless stream. We've been on the road for hours now, the sun now half-hidden by the horizon. The gentle clip-clop of Hazel's hooves have been creating a continuous metronome of time passing by. I try to block it out, but the silence that has settled in the wagon makes it hard to ignore.

I settle myself into the hay, watching the scenery crawl past me in a slow, arduous glide. Endless, rolling flatlands of empty fields slide along as the carriage gently rolls by. Groups of birds fly past overheard, families rushing to the safety of home before nightfall. The occasional shrubbery and gathering of trees break the blandness of the flatlands, but the only other things I can see are the swaying blades of grass, and the occasional weed amongst them. With the sun nestled behind the hills in the depth of the horizon, the sky has now been painted in dark blues and purples. Fireflies begin to rise from their sleeping spots and illuminate the night surrounding the wagon. A firefly lands on my knee and I blow a gentle gust to get it moving again.

From what I know, the Whispering Valley got its name from some superstition that was spread through travellers that rode the path. Apparently, whatever was said on the path would drift to the Hushed Harbour that lay at the end of this long, dreary road. The rumour seemed to solidify into truth when travellers encountered the residents of Hushed Harbour. The isolated and begrudging manner of the townsfolk, helped spread the paranoia that they knew of all the travellers' secrets shared on the path to their secluded home. I believe they were just quiet folk and hated having tourists visit their loch. I know I would.

Anyway, it became accustomed for voyagers to stay silent, or simply make idle chit-chat to fill the time of travelling. It was discouraged to talk in depth to fellow passengers for fear of something slipping their lips and haunting them for the entirety of their time at the Harbour. The thought makes me shiver; as much as I don't believe in superstitions and such, I'd rather not be needlessly tormented by anti-social fishermen.

Unfortunately, it seems as though the stowaway in my wagon was also not one to believe in superstitions, and loudly proclaims a need for conversation.
"So, I guess we should introduce ourselves properly now." He pipes up, his voice deafening in the quaint silence around us. "Since we're adventuring together." He adds, grinning at me.

I'm sure he believes he's antagonising me. If anything, he's just giving me a headache. I look up at the sky, not wanting to see that shit-eating grin any more. Stars have begun to appear in the periwinkle sky.
"We're not adventuring together. You're tagging along, and I'm going to a job." I don't mean to grumble, but I'm so bloody tired. And his persistent chattering isn't helping. I don't have the energy to match his enthusiasm. Besides, it's true. He just wanted a ride out of Kohrmiir. I've got a task ahead of me.

"The name's Nylani." I finally relent, the perpetual prodding of his expecting stare causing my patience to snap. "I already know about you, Mr Damirius Haldwin. The infamous, promiscuous tiefling that harrowed Kohrmiir with your relentless flirting."

A small grin flickers across my lips, but I squash it down. I don't need him thinking I'm flirting, too. I can recall the constant bickering and gossiping that happened within the tavern on countless nights; some whispers were louder and angrier than others. However, all accusations pointed towards the smug tiefling sat across from me in the tiny wagon. If there was anything the two - or more - offended parties would agree on, it was that it was all Damirius' fault.

"Nice to know that the baseless rumours even got to you, Princess," he remarks. He sounds sour, but a devilish smirk pulls at the edges of his lips. "Nice to know it's not entirely baseless," I instinctively retort. I don't want to bicker with him, but he brings it out so easily. It's infuriating. "I saw you relentlessly teasing poor Maddie." The poor, helpless girl was like putty in his hands. All he had to do was smile at her and she almost buckled to her knees before him. I glance at him, finally taking him in properly.

Like most tieflings, he adorns a set of horns atop his head. His curl around his skull, though, like a crown. The ends abruptly jut away from each other, creating a sharp tip. His auburn hair curls around the horns, and falls just past his right brow. I can see the boyish charm that could potentially make a few women swoon, but there's not enough to warrant an entire town crumbling to its knees because of him. It's curious, but I pick no further. Realistically, it's none of my business.

I look past the half wall at the end of the wagon. The small farm town of Kohrmiir had already faded away from view. Farms were replaced with endless meadows, fields, and barren lands. Perhaps the myth of the Whispering Valley deterred people from ever settling here. I suppose it would make sense, given the wide berth people give to Yalarepsos. Even with the ancient ruins now covered in moss and wildlife, no one will touch it due to the legends of souls that supposedly haunt it.

It takes me a moment to recognise the silence that encompasses us. If it's tense, I can't sense it. Not that I care much, anyway. Silence gives my head peace for once. And I want to lap up as much peace as I can. I slump further into the pile of loose hay and slowly sink into it. The cushioning of the compact hay is bearable, at least. Still, it's better than just lying on bare wood. I drift my eyes upward, watching the fireflies that fill the sky. It has now darkened to a deep navy blanket, the endless fabric of space wrapping around the world. I can see the two moons in the sky now. They slowly, methodically, rotate around each other in their eternal dance. Legends depict them as lovers, but I've never been certain. Aren't lovers supposed to be crazed - obsessed, even - of their counterpart? If so, why do they continue to stay so far apart?

Out of the corner of my eye, I can see the blasted tiefling's head tilt slightly to the right to face me. His hand props up his chin, his elbow deep in a pile of hay. I suppress a groan; he's going to start talking again.

"You know, you look better like this. Seriousness doesn't suit you."

I can't muster the energy to scowl at him any more. Instead, my eyes lazily glide to his direction, cocking my eyebrow. "Don't be mistaken, tiefling. I can still throw your ass off this cart. I'm just resting between jobs." I sink further into the hay, my eyes closing as I finally let myself rest.

I can hear him chuckle. It's almost guaranteed there's a stupid grin on his face. There's a rustling beside me. I think maybe he's sitting up now.

"Well, you're definitely chattier." He muses. "Why didn't you talk this much beforehand?"

It takes a lot to suppress my laughter. "Easy," I manage to choke out, "You're annoying." I can't help it. A laugh erupts out of me. I open my eyes to see his childish pout. He sulks, arms folded over his chest. The sight makes me laugh harder. His sulk doesn't last much longer, and he falls into a fit of laughter too.

"Well," he manages between giggles, "That solves that, then."

I look up at him, confused. "What?"

"I was starting to wonder if you could actually laugh." He states, that infuriating smile making its reappearance on his face. "Turns out you actually can."

I roll my eyes. "And it turns out that you're actually funny." I remark. His smile wavers. Now it's my turn to smirk at him. I close my eyes again, nestling back into the hay. I feel victorious. I hear him chuckle to himself, and my smile doesn't seem to want to leave yet.

It's been so long since I've felt this way. I almost forgot what it was like to laugh. To jest. Not take everything so seriously. But I won't admit to that, least of all to him. I would never hear the end of it on this horrifically long ride. I can hear him moving around. I crack an eye open to watch him, curious. He settles into a bed of hay, watching the sky. My eyes open fully as I look upwards, too.

The moons are in the middle of the dark canvas of the sky, one close to the world, slowly spinning in a waltz with a much smaller one that resides to the left of it at the moment. If we were to sit and watch them all night, we would have a full view of their slow transition. The smaller one, Soleresos, rotates around their larger counterpart, Uvariss. Uvariss does their own rotation, and slowly the two replace each other's spaces.

"Do you believe in them?" Damirius asks into the air, his eyes fixated on the moons, "In the Lovers of Uvalaris, I mean."

The story of the Lovers of Uvalaris had been a well-worn fable within the elven community, from what

I know. According to the books I was allowed to read, elves are thought to be the oldest race to walk this plane, making the story of Uvalaris one of the oldest legends known.

From what I know, it's said that in the Beginning, when the Old Gods were still creating the world, Autriel, there was an agreement that there should be only one moon to caress the skies. However, they couldn't decide which. Should they go for the large, gorgeous orb of Uvariss, or the much more humble, glistening stone of Soleresos? However, as the fates would have it, the two sentient moon goddesses adored one another intensely. They fought with the Old Gods, begging and pleading to be wed to another instead. But, the Old Gods refused. Their plan was to pair one of the moon goddesses with the sun god, Umos.

The moon goddesses defied the Old Gods, and with as much care and gentleness as two masses of stone could carry, they collided together to form one unique moon – Uvalaris. The collision left the larger moon, Uvariss, blinded but the pair were finally together. And how they loved to dance. They filled the night sky with their laughter and beautiful swirling dance. The crater left in Uvariss was filled perfectly by the petite Soleresos, making the dance a beautiful display of how love is infinite, despite the pain you may endure.

However, the Old Gods were angered. As punishment, the two lovers were ripped apart. They were separated by just enough space between them to see each other, but to never feel the others embrace again. They are now forced to spend an eternity apart, staring at each other from millions of lightyears away. After many sorrowful years, the two began to enjoy their new dance. The story always confused me. If they were in love... wouldn't they destroy everything in their way? That's what love is... right? Carnage to keep the one you love close?

I feel his eyes on me. He's waiting for a response. I shake my head, pulling myself out of my thoughts. I clear my throat.
"No. I haven't for a while." It's not a lie. Many obstacles in my life have rid me of my faith in any Gods that may or may not be out there. I look at my hands.

"Why? If you don't mind me asking." His voice is uncharacteristically soft. It surprises me, and I think he notices. He chuckles gently. This laughter isn't pointed, or sarcastic. It's like we're both on an inside joke, but I don't understand the punchline. This isn't the man that ravaged a simple countryside. I watch him carefully. Is this a trap? The harsh tension of suspicion fills me.

"When did you become an expert on elven folklore?" It came out harsher than intended, but I can't risk a trap. He needs to be at arm's length. "Well, since my adoptive mother is half-elven, I guess."

Shit. Shit shit shit. He laughs again, the roaring belly laughter filling my ears and drumming into my head. My stomach drops. I was not expecting that. "Oh…" Is all I can muster. "Uh.. Sorry." My brain falters, his laughter the only thing it seems to process.

"Don't worry yourself, Princess," he chokes out. He's holding his stomach from how hard he's laughing. "I'm quite open about my family."

4

Damirius

Memories of mother and father surface to the front of my mind. Lorenzo, Arwyn, and little baby Myra come forward, too. Thinking of them makes my smiles effortless. I love them all more than anything in the world.

The sound of Mama's voice fills my ears for a moment, the reminder of 'make sure to get something to eat!' in her melodic tune. I can't help but smile wide. She was always worried about me. About all of us. I pause, the feeling of being stared at causing me to look up. Grey eyes bore into me, but not with their usual contempt. This time her eyes were wide; like a child hanging on to your words as you tell them a story.

The undivided attention is almost unsettling. It wasn't even more than a few moments ago that she couldn't stand to look at me. But I shrug the feeling away. It's actually quite nice to feel listened to. I wrap my arms around myself, hugging my torso as I sink deeper into the pile of hay. It's scratchy against my skin, but it's better than freezing in the chill air.

"From what my parents have told me, I was dumped on their doorstep in a blanket and not much else," I state matter-of-factly. It's easy to feel disconnected to it; I was an infant. I have no memory of it. But to see the young elf's jaw drop reminds me that not everyone sees it that way. I can't help but laugh.

"It's alright," I reassure her. "You should have seen them when it was time for 'the talk' about it. They tried to explain that it was hard, if not impossible, for elves and dwarves to produce someone like me." I feel myself smile at the memory. "I figured as much, by that point anyway. Not to mention I was the only tiefling in the area."

I laugh again. The image of poor Papa wringing his large, stocky hands in his lap trying to talk biology to me sticks in my mind. Never good with his words, but always, always trying to get better. That talk really was a struggle. For the pair of us. "My mum is half-elven, my dad's a dwarf. After raising me, they seemed to enjoy taking in the rag-tag children with no parents, so now I have eight other siblings."

"Eight?" was her only response. She seems to struggle imagining so many children.
Her wide eyes seem almost horror struck; it's almost like she's never even been near a child. I snort a laugh. "Yeah, eight. Human, elf, orc; doesn't matter to them. They'll take anyone in."
She seems more amazed with each minute detail I give her. It's almost alluring, having someone take an interest in this side of me. I've never had someone - aside from family - really care about the real me. Though people didn't really care for the exaggerated version that I created for people to fling themselves at, either. It's almost a relief, not having to keep up the facade. I didn't realise how exhausting it was to keep it up. I feel myself fall further into the hay. I finally feel relaxed.
"Well, what about you? Any siblings?"

"No," she states, quietly. "Just.. Just me. And my cat." Her eyes drop to her lap, her hands clasping together. The hay encompasses her, like a giant, scratchy, blanket. She looks so much smaller now.

This is new. I've never seen her look so... young before. It's almost sad. She starts fidgeting with her fingers, and looks back at me. I go to speak, but my voice catches in my throat. I cough, hoping to clear it. Thankfully, my voice returns. "What was your cat's name?"

"Kuju." She responds, her voice so quiet I have to lean closer just to hear her. She's picking at her nails.
"'Kuju'? Like the elven word for 'tiny'? Really?" I grin. Her face lightens at my jest and I smile wider.
"I was a child." She retorts, scoffing at me. Her remark feels half-hearted, her grin betraying any faux annoyance she was trying to portray. I can't help but laugh. The sound of her quiet giggle joins me.

Slowly, the laughter dwindles, and silence encompasses us again. It's not uncomfortable, this time. There's mutual acceptance in the air now, instead of quiet contention. I sigh gently, absorbing the tranquillity around me. I gaze languidly at the neverending plains that surround us. Fireflies illuminate the sky. It looks like they've become temporary stars, the volume of them almost squashing the light of their static siblings. The

emerald fields have darkened to a deep, dark green. The sea of grass that surrounds us sways in the current of cool, evening air.
Above our heads, an oil lantern gets lit. The miniature, weathered hand of Mack quickly retreats from the flame. A soft ebb of the light grows in the lantern, creating a steady source of warmth that emanates above me. It's comforting. I become entranced with the flame flicker and dance in its glass cage, teasing the moths that gather to soak in its warmth.

My mind wanders, curious at what this 'job' is that Nylani is embarking on. I've heard tales of her battling beasts and ridding bandits, but they sounded fanciful. Surely there was no way a single person - let alone someone who barely reached my chest - would be able to beat such adversaries with ease.
"At least if you end up having to fight a giant baby, I would know how to soothe it."

I groan. My hands cover my eyes, embarrassed. It had blurted out; a quick quip to fill the silence. My cheeks burn a brilliant purple, I can feel the heat radiate off me. To my surprise, I can hear Nylani laughing. Her laugh is hearty; a bellowing that

derives from the deep pit of her belly. It was by no means a dainty laugh, but it was heartfelt. Real.
I can't help myself, and I laugh alongside her. The sound of our uncontrollable laughter fills the progressively chilling night air. An immense wave of relief washes over me. At least they can enjoy the moment together. There was no mocking undertone to her laugh, just pure delight. I find myself laughing harder, delighting in watching her smile encompass her face.

"Well," she wheezes out, "I've not had to fight a giant baby yet." Another laugh tumbles forth. "But I'll keep it in mind."
"Thank you kindly," I reply, a fit of giggles spilling out as I slump back in the wagon.
"Maybe I should let you tag along for the job," she smirks. "Just in case."

Lying on my back, I stare at the dark sky, counting the stars before me. Everything in me eases. Like I'm floating in warm, soothing waters. How can I feel comfortable with a stranger? A stranger that a few hours ago couldn't even give me the time of day. It's confusing; I feel so at ease around her. But I barely know her. I won't deny it, it's a welcome feeling, regardless. It's been so long since I've had someone make me feel so at ease. I glance over to her. She's staring at the sky, too. She looks relaxed. Her eyebrows aren't creased, and her lips aren't twisted into a frown. A warm stir settles deep in my gut. How odd.

I slowly turn my head back to look at the sky, watching the celestial waltz above me. The moons take centre stage in the ethereal theatre; the delicate Soleresos almost within arms reach of Uvariss' crescent. Their supernal glows seem to yearn for each other, the edges of their light barely caressing against one another in the deep emptiness of space.

I remember how Mama used to speak of the moons; always in deep respect and admiration. Her voice would be full of sorrow each and every time she recounted the story, almost as if she were mourning it herself. It made it hard to not join her grieving each time the story was retold. Mama's heart was always the largest thing about her. I wrap my arms around me again, imagining Mama's tiny arms swaddling me like when I was a child.

An hour or two passes in silence. It's such a stark contrast from Kohrmiir; it was no wonder travellers found this road so unnerving. The silence would be almost maddening to anyone. Though, I find myself oddly at ease within it, for the first time in my life. Every aspect of my life thus far has been encapsulated in the noise of others; either by my siblings at home, or the people of each town I visit. But now, I find the quiet unusually peaceful tonight. It's like I'm able to breathe at full capacity for the first time after an intensive run. My body feels relaxed - rejuvenated, even – as I soak up the quiet buzzing of nighttime. The gentle illuminations of the oil lamp and moons act almost as nightlights, coaxing me to sleep. My eyes begin to droop, the promise of slumber only a few more rocks of the wagon away. But then, the familiar, whistling voice from the front calls back to us.

"Uh, miss Nylani, ma'am," Mack begins, "is there any chance yer could take the reins? Ah'm starting to fall asleep up here." A nervous chuckle follows, he almost sounds embarrassed to ask. I crack an eye open to glance at Nylani, who is smiling softly up at him.

"Of course, Mack." She responds, "It's only fair you get some rest, too."
The wagon begins to slow, the old wheels creaking in protest of their travel being paused. I watch her clamber out of the wagon once it's stationary. She makes it look so easy. She hops onto the saddle with ease, too. Was there anything she couldn't do? It definitely doesn't seem like it.

Mack hauls himself into the wagon. I didn't anticipate him to be so small, but here he was, in all his diminutive glory. He must have felt me watching, as he looks at me and gives a big, toothless grin. I smile back at him, shuffling closer to the wall to give him space.
"Ah'm no' tha' big, me boy!" He cackles. I laugh, positioning myself back where I was.

"Sorry Mack, you looked larger off your horse," I joke back. He smacks my arm as he parks his bony rear end into a pile of hay, promptly falling in with as little grace as possible. We both fall into a fit of laughter as hay flies between us, sticking to our hair and skin alike. Finally, we settle in the hay as sleep pulls my eyelids closed.

5

Nylani

An endless, serpentine road stretches out before me; no determinable end lay ahead, much to my irritation. I want to know what exactly I'll be facing. The letter I got was too cryptic to make any sense of anything. I sigh quietly. Hazel snorts in response. I chuckle to myself; it seems as though we share the same thought. This is going to be a long ride.

My hand grazes Hazel's side gently as we push forward. I can't help but chuckle as her skin ripples from my touch. I think it's tickling her.
I've always preferred the companionship of animals over people. Their simplicity is admirable; and they're always forthcoming with their intentions. Humans and other humanoids, though? Not so much.

I can't stop the grimace that overcomes me; a

sudden throbbing ache pulses against my temples. It seems as though the countless tasks I undertook in Kohrmiir have finally decided to take its toll on me. My body feels a thousand times heavier; my head sinking into my shoulders as we continue our incessant trek.

Truthfully, I'm glad to be out of there. The people had become reliant on me. It was draining. And annoying. When it comes to fieldwork, I can understand the 'all hands on deck' approach. However, the simple retrieval tasks or simply reprimanding misbehaving children, could have been done by themselves. Whether it was due to laziness or not, I could never tell. And now, I never will.

We continue our slow hike along the winding road. The darkness of deep night begins to envelop the small hay wagon, the chill of eve edging its way to me. I can see the thin cloud of my own breath whisper along the non-existent breeze. The gentle ebbing warmth from the oil lamp above grazes against the tips of my ears and shoulders. Thankfully, though, I don't need much to be warm - the heat of my chaotic magic keeps me from shivering. I suppose it needs to be good at something, right? I squeeze my legs into Hazel's sides, hoping it'll be enough to soothe the shivering horse. The mare gives an appreciative huff, and I can't stop my smile.

"Feel better, girl?" I ask, mostly to myself. It's clear she's relishing in the minute warmth I can give her. I look upwards, watching the moons that hang above us as my fingers run through her silken soft hair.

The moons hang low in the night sky, with Soleresos' glistening almost making her larger in appearance. Her glow expands around the waves and ripples of space, the blackened silk splattered with sequin stars. Soleresos stands out like a bedazzled gem; despite being the smaller of the two, she refuses to be diminished. Her partner rests closely beside her, the larger, crescent shaped moon sparkling with glee. The pair are almost touching. The smallest sliver of night separates the goddesses and their mutual yearn for one another. A quiet rustle from beside me pulls my attention away from the silent theatrics of a thousands-year old romance.

I gently press my heels against Hazel's sides,

stilling her as I scan the area around us. I can't see anything. The deep shade of night makes it hard to decipher anything in the endless rolling hills around me. The shrubs and hedges that scatter the fields vanish within the dark, and any potential people that hide within them. I take a deep breath and settle myself. After a moment, I relax and try to think logically. I doubt anyone would want to stay here – aside from the occasional bush or tree, there's not much place to hide. And the lack of consistent cover would make it hard for anyone to stalk someone riding the road, much less a group with plans to ambush. The open fields would give away most threats almost immediately.

However, with how dark it gets around these parts, it could be possible that they would use that to their advantage. I huff impatiently at myself. I really am my own worst enemy. Reluctantly, I decide to keep a continuous watch; if for nothing else but to soothe the nagging feeling that I'm not alone. Swivelling left to right, I strain my eyes into the deep blackness of night, watching the nothingness with a fanatic intensity. I'm sure Hazel snorts a laugh at my ridiculous display.

Hours pass, and no threat has made itself known.

I'm not sure if I should be relieved or not, though. I continue my robotic, monotonous patrol, even as the feeling of unease begins to wash away. The evening crawls onward, the night seeming as endless as this awful, perpetual path. The sound of Hazel's clip-clopping pace is the only noise that fills in the empty air around us. Buzzing firefly wings fill the undertones of night, and the rustling of grass makes my ears twitch and keep me alert, much to my dismay. I rake my fingers through Hazel's mahogany locks, desperately trying to soothe myself. I wasn't sure if Hazel enjoyed it or not, but since I hadn't been kicked off yet, I'll assume it doesn't bother her. I've seen Mack get dropped for less.

A rumbling, growling snore makes me jump. I whip my head around, the slumbering forms of the men behind me barely ascertainable in the flickering light above my head. I stifle a laugh, ashamed of my own panicked behaviour. I am safe. I turn back around, confronted by Hazel's large, unjudging eyes watching me. I stroke her head, silently thankful for the concern. She sighs at my touch before she turns and continues to trot. The occasional guttural grumble of the dormant men rupture around me, before the sound of them turning in their sleep and returning to a quiet snooze replaces the loud disruption. It's only in the rare moment of silence that I realise I no longer enjoy the lack of noise like I used to. I used to revel in it; yearn for the busy world around me to cease and allow the absence of noise to blanket the world around me. Silence was safe. Now, however, I can't stop myself from wishing to hear the two men laugh. Or even just continue to snore like grumbling bears. It's much more comforting. Noise meant I wasn't alone. And alone is the last thing I want right now. But I need to keep my guard up. For their sake, as well as my own.

I look at my hands, the familiar network of scars eliciting the usual wave of disgust and shame. I'm a danger to others, as well as myself. I glance behind me again, taking in the lanky, purple moron that has spread himself across the wagon floor. His awkward limbs stick out at impossible angles. I chuckle quietly. He's completely nonsensical, but his seemingly kind nature makes it hard to dismiss him. I shake my head, forcing my smile to disappear along with the memories of his roaring laughter.

It could be a trap, I have to remind myself. I sigh

heavily. A moment passes, and I find myself hoping that I'm wrong. The miniscule bud of hope grows in my chest, the odd sensation catching my breath for a moment. It would be nice to have a friend, for once. But I can never be sure. I squash the feeling down instantly.

The hours pass with little ease, and I find myself restless. The absence of noise creates a suffocating, oppressive sensation over me. I shift in the saddle, extinguishing the rising apprehension that desperately tries to claw its way through my chest. It's quiet. Too quiet. And I can't sense anything around me. Why can't I sense anything around me? It's frustrating. And daunting.
Hazel puffs and it rips me out of my erratic thoughts. It seems as though I lost the track of time as I stayed buried in my thoughts.

The colours of the night sky start shifting to a pastel pink and lilac, replacing the deep navy as the sun begins to rise. Slowly, the colours inch across the horizon, reluctant to rise for a new day. I can sympathise; I wouldn't want to wake to a cold, barren landscape either.

The lightened atmosphere slowly awakens the world around me, calling nature from its slumber. I can hear birds chirp pleasantries to each other as clouds appear to scatter the sky. The chill that settled during the night eventually seeps into the earth, the tension in my muscles finally dissipating. Squirrels pitter down trees to rummage in the foliage below. A rustle from behind notifies me of the two men finally rousing to see the early morning awaken.
"Good sleep?" I call to them, stunned by my own chipper tune.

'Never trust a kind person,' a familiar, tense voice had once told me. *'Kindness lets you underestimate them. Kindness fools you into trusting them. Kind people are the cruellest of all.'*

I can feel myself shake. Those intense, glaring blue eyes burn into the back of my mind. A shaky breath leaves me and dissipates into the cool morning air.

"Slept like a baby," Damirius responds, a goofy smile plastered on his face. I feel myself relax at the sight of his dimples. Suddenly, he yawns. I join. Tiredness yanks me downwards, the heaviness of my head making me crumple. I'm grateful when

Mack gives Hazel's rear a gentle tap, causing her to immediately slow to a stop.

"Thank yer, Miss Nylani," the older fellow mumbles, rubbing his beady eyes as he trundles to Hazel's side. "Yer should get a quick nap." He nods, apparently agreeing with himself in his half-daze. "Then we'll stretch our legs a bit, I think."
"Sounds like a plan," I agree, my exhaustion coercing my eyelids to close.
"Off ye get, Missy. Time for you to go night-night." He chuckles, tapping my leg.

In a swift movement, I tuck and roll off of Hazel's back, thudding into the wagon. The hay catches me, coddling around my chest in a warm swaddle. My limbs stretch out, suddenly alleviated from the tension the night instilled in them. Hazel huffs, apparently irritated at my impromptu acrobatics.
"Sorry girl," I call to her, snuggling further into the makeshift bed. "It was the fastest route."
I hear Mack chuckle, followed by the sound of Hazel resuming her clip-clopping metronome. Sleep rapidly overcomes me, and in an instant, my consciousness shifts to the realm of dreams.

6

Damirius

The tiny woman sprawls out like a cat basking in the sun. I can't help but chuckle. I find myself watching her; her lithe form steadily rising and falling as she sleeps. She's a contradiction to herself, I muse. She's arrogant and accusatory, yet playful and kind, too. It's hard to know where I stand with her; one moment we laugh, and the next she's as stiff as stone.

During my time working so *intimately* with others, I had presumed I had people figured out. People either used you or wanted to be used. If you thrust them somewhere uncomfortable, that would reveal their true intentions. But, she seems uncomfortable everywhere. I snicker quietly to myself at the thought of her chagrin smile, the tightness around her lips regardless of who she smiled at. Tension sits on her shoulders, regardless of how relaxed she appears. I hadn't noticed earlier, during our walk through Kohrmiir, but after being with her for a few hours, it was getting easier to spot now.

My body slumps against the wall of the wagon, and I pick the hay out of my clothes. I take a large gulp of the fresh, crisp air and let my body relax. The crinkling of shifting hay draws my attention, catching the slumbering woman stir in her sleep. She rolls onto her side, knees folding to her chest in a tight ball. Her hair drapes over her face, unravelling from her loose braid.

She stirs again. Holding my breath, I try to not disturb her sleep. She tosses to her other side, her hair flying away from her face. Now that I can see her face again, I notice how her eyebrows have pushed themselves together. Her body seems tense, her face frowning as she grasps aimlessly at the hay below. It looks like she's having a nightmare. Slowly, I rise in the wagon, my eyes never leaving the restless woman. She continues to toss and turn in her sleep. Fistfuls of hay follow her erratic writhing. I reach out for her instinctively, wanting to soothe her. I pause. Why would I want to soothe her? Is it because she reminds me of Rallo? I remember the tiny orcish hands that would grab at me, just as she scrunches hay beneath her fists. His dense brows furrow the same way hers do now. The quiet moments of me stroking his bronze locks to settle him pops into my mind and my hand reaches forward to bring comfort to the unsettled elf.

Suddenly, a yell shakes the wagon. The roar rings my ears and I fall onto my back. A thunderous crackling fills the world around me. The air feels alive - dangerous, even. Flashes of blinding light snap around me, filling my vision with nothing but horrifyingly bright whiteness. I squint my eyes, hoping that maybe I will be able to see something. Nylani!

I scramble across the wagon floor, desperately trying to feel for her in my temporary blindness. My hand grabs her shirt, the thin material soaked in sweat. The brightness fades and I can finally see her, lying helpless as she writhes, screaming in pain. I grab her arms, trying to pull her up. Her eyes stay scrunched, tightly shut.

"Nylani?!" I bellow over the cacophony of thunder around us. "Nylani!"
"Get off of me!" she screams, twisting out of my

grip. She flops to the floor again, just as another flash of lightning slices across her chest. She howls in pain. More flashes of lightning scatter around, bursting from her chest. All at once, she becomes blindingly bright, then dull and blood spattered. Involuntarily, I step back, worried about the razor sharp bolts that rapidly appear and vanish.

"Nylani, it's me, Damirius! What are you doing?!" No response. She continues to squirm and scream as lashes of lightning burst out of her. They seem to rip out of her like white-hot ribbons, splitting her skin open and whipping the air around her. Fear washes over me; my legs feel numb but they hold me upright. I try to move them closer to Nylani, but they suddenly become leaden and impossible to move. The wagon sways violently, the horse shaking it in fear. I grip the edge of the wagon like my life depends on it, and I genuinely believe it does.

I look behind me to Mack, desperate for help. From what I can see - which isn't much - his face stays stoic and in control. His leathery hands grip the reins tightly, correcting the mare when she tries to buck and thrash. He steadies his horse, his matured hands caressing her sides as she finally settles and lets out a loud huff. The wagon remains still, as if waiting for Nylani's fit to be over. I look over to the hollering, twisting form of Nylani, unsure of what to do. I turn back to Mack, noticing the look of concern in his beady eyes that likely mirrors my own. I search his face, questioning him silently on what to do. He seems to be asking the same. Great. We're both clueless.

Her screams pierce my ears. Her thrashes become more violent as more streaks of lightning rip out of her. I force myself to turn back around. Her face drips with sweat and tears. Her eyes stay scrunched closed, almost to the point that you wouldn't be able to see them underneath her brows. I take a hesitant step forward, fighting against the mountainous weight of my legs. Then, an arc of stray lightning pillars out from Nylani's chest and slices the side of the chestnut horse.

Everything goes in slow motion. The mare rears up and whinnies loudly. Mack yells as he grasps at the horse's mane. The beating of my heart is loud enough for me to hear it. My grip tightens, my knuckles white and my nails sinking into the old wood. I think I'm screaming, but I can't be sure. The only thing I can hear for certain are the loud snaps and cracks of electricity that explode beside me. Mack turns to look behind him and his darkened face illuminates from the brilliant white eruption in the cart. Another arc of lightning smacks the sky and crackles right next to my ear. The wagon begins to turn vertical, before slamming back down into the ground. Then the world increases its speed.

The horse gallops. Wheels wobble. We veer off road. A wheel snags a bump. The wagon tips. My body gets tossed high upwards. And I crash back in. Air gets shunted out of my lungs. I groan in pain. Solid wood pushes against my cheek. The cart slams right. I hit the wall. We level out. My back hits the floor. Another scream. Another flash. Yelling surrounds me. Am I yelling? I don't know. Thud. Thud. Crash! We slam against a tree stump. I'm in the air again. My vision blurs as I flip rapidly. My feet follow my head. I don't know which way is up or which is down. My arms flail. I try desperately to grab something. But there is nothing to grasp.

A flurry of colours speed past me, before my chest slams into something hard. My egs fling behind me, my heels almost smacking against the back of my skull. The force pushes me further through the dirt, the harsh ground ripping my skin. Then, everything ceases.

My body crumples in the grass, the cold earth somewhat soothing. Warm liquid trickles from somewhere on my face, though my arms ache too much to merit wiping it away. My limbs risk stretching out, sinking deeper into the now upturned grass. The softened underbelly of the soil appeases my wounds, pacifying the welts I can feel grow over every inch of me. A moment passes. No screaming or cracks of electricity.

Tentatively, I push my palms into the dirt, quietly relieved that there doesn't seem to be any broken bones. Finally, I push myself up, shaking as I rise to my feet. I look around, noticing how far away from the dirt path we had gotten. It would be at least another half an hour before we get back on track. I groan, rubbing the back of my neck. Every inch of me aches, but I choose to ignore it for now. For now, I need to find the rest of the group.

I scan the immediate area around me. Grass, shrubs and a smattering of trees surround me, though it's the dips and rises of the hills that hide everyone from my view. The expanse of the valley is immense; they stretch far into the horizon, and probably even further beyond that. Then, the huge, awkward horse steps into view, her whinnying booming around the silent landscape. Cautiously, I start to trek towards her. My hands cusp around my mouth, magnifying my voice as I scan the area whilst I walk.

"Mack! Nylani!" I bellow, "Are you okay?"
A response comes quickly, much to my relief.
"Yeah, ah'm alrigh'!" The familiar whistle of Mack calls back, "Jus' got ter Hazel. Yer seen Miss Nylani?"

I pause, quietly thankful to not have to calm the horse. I look around. "No, haven't seen her."
"Well, don't worry 'bout me!" The old man yells over the barren fields. "If you fell ou' round there, it's likely she did too."
I finally spot the man's diminutive hand caressing Hazel's snout. The top of his bald head barely crests over the top of the wild grass.
"Alright, I'll keep looking." I turn around, looking at the field behind me. Hopefully I can do it without being sliced open.

Glancing around, there seems to be no sign of her. Despite the open, barren fields, she appears to have vanished into thin air. I grumble quietly. Where could she have gone?
Almost as if to answer my silent question, I hear a barely audible groan farther ahead of me. My eyes scan the ground ahead thoroughly, but there's still no sign of her. I continue marching forward.

Wild bushes litter the immediate vicinity around me, with the odd tree spreading between groups of them. Another weak moan trickles out from somewhere nearby; the whinge louder than before. Then, a worn leather boot appears, sticking out of a thorny bush a few feet away. I proceed closer, cautious as I get within arms length of the bush. The worry of her sparking again sinks into my stomach. I try to swallow the hard lump in my throat. I watch intensely, hunched beside a nearby shrub. No movement, besides her breathing. My knuckle raps against her leather boot. She groans in reply.
"Please," the bush grumbles, "get me out."
I suppress a laugh, the image of the noble Nylani now a crumpled heap more amusing than I had anticipated. A giggle manages to choke itself out,

but I force it into a heavy sigh. She seems embarrassed enough.

I look down at her, a tangled mess of twisted limbs and wild hair greeting me in the sunken branches of the thorn bush. Pointed barbs jab her at all angles, her skin lacerated in multiple areas; though, I can't differ between ones that happened before or after her fall. She looks up at me with her wide, tear soaked eyes; a pang of pity strums my chest. I inhale a deep breath, anticipating the stings of multiple cuts as I plunge a hand in. The thorns mark my skin as my hand dives in, grabbing her wrist. I yank her up, surprised by how little she weighs as she flies up with little difficulty.

With her now standing in front of me, I can finally see the havoc she wrecked upon herself. Her hair is a tangled nest, her face and body covered in smatterings of blood. It trickles from her shoulders, arms, and her stomach. Even her leg has been lashed. Puddles of blood stain her clothing, the thin material clinging to her skin. My hand still holds her - loosely - but enough to notice her tremble. My eyes examine her face again; tear soaked, blood spattered, and drained.

"What was that?" I ask, exasperation clear in my tone. Any anger that had arisen from being thrown into the dirt has quickly dissipated. All that is left is the confusion and lingering tension that a wild horse ride would leave behind. From the look of her stressed, dreary face, it seems clear that she hadn't anticipated the frantic morning. She looks at me, her eyes frantically searching me as if hoping I'd have the answer. Her shoulders sag, almost defeated, when she realises I'm just as confused as her. She looks behind me, presumably at the direction of the path we diverted from, before turning her attention to the trees immediately around us. She pauses. Her mouth opens and closes, like a fish out of water. She seems to be struggling to find the right words.

"I..." she starts. She pauses again. Her face scrunches up. "I can't control my magic." She finally splurts out. She looks away from me entirely, like she's ashamed.
"I can tell." I immediately respond, though I try to sound as tactful as possible. "But you've controlled it before. I mean, this is the first time I've seen it." She seems settled by this reminder. She takes a

deep breath. "What set it off?" Immediately, her breath shudders again.

"A..." she sucks in a breath. "A nightmare." Her head falls, staring at the floor. "Stupid, right?"
"Not at all," I softly utter. Instinctively, my hand goes to reach her, but I stop myself. I pin my hand to my side. "So, the nightmare spooked you and your magic went crazy?" I ask, hoping that my non-judgemental tone helps to soothe her. Her head stays downward, though her demeanour continues to relax. The familiar sensation of calming my siblings overwhelms me as I watch her fidget and hug herself; she reminds me of too many of my previous foster siblings. I have to stifle myself. I doubt she would take being likened to a child very well.
"Yeah..." A shaky breath shivers out of her. "I'm sorry."

Impulsively, my hands cup her cheeks, and I lift her head up to look at me. Her eyes, whilst wide and bewildered, are also full of tears that threaten to fall. A thumb wipes at the corner of one of her eyes, picking up a swelling tear and wiping it away. No longer does the stoic, intimidating woman I once thought I understood stand before me.

Instead, all I can see is a frightened, trembling girl. If I didn't know any better, I would imagine she's terrified of her own shadow. Shaking hands start to reach up to my own. To hold them or bat them away, I don't know. I embrace her tightly, much to my own surprise. Tiny hands grip the back of my shirt.

"I'm so, so sorry," her voice quivers, "I didn't mean it." Wetness sinks into the thin silken material of my shirt, and her shoulders tremble as she begins to cry.
A tremendous ache pangs my chest. I stroke her hair softly, cusping the bottom of her skull for a moment before resuming. My other arm wraps around her protectively, holding her upright as she sinks further into my chest. We begin to sway amongst the gently waving grass. Instinctually I begin to shush her tenderly in her ear, like a mother soothing a fussy baby, and find myself feeling relieved as I feel her shaky breath steady.

Finally, I pull away. Looking down, I see her looking back up at me, a small, wet smile on her lips. We begin our slow walk back to where I had come from. After a few moments of us walking side by side in relative silence, she places a hand against my arm. Though, the rest of her stays a step or two away from me. I risk a quick glance at her, noticing how her face points everywhere but me. I turn away, not making any remark. Clearly, she needs a bit of comfort. And I'm happy to provide it. This is much nicer than most things I've done for a while.

"Ah! There ya are!" Mack suddenly calls out. "How are ya fairin'?" The question is pointed to Nylani, who immediately releases my arm.
"Rougher than usual, unfortunately," she calls back.

We continue our slow walk back to the miniature man. But then Nylani stiffens and stands frozen beside me. I look back at her, her eyes wide and pointed at something ahead. I turn back around, following where her eyes have fixated themselves. I look at Hazel, and a cut that I can only presume to be the aftermath from the magic that hit her.

The large slice - roughly the side of my forearm - arcs across the horse's stomach to the top of her hip. Thankfully, though, it's no wider than a papercut. Thin trickles of dried blood stick to her skin, creating small clumps of sticky, matted fur. Despite the wound, she seems fairly calm. She continues to graze out of Mack's tiny hand. However, Nylani seems to think otherwise, as her hands fly to her mouth, tears falling. I just about manage to catch her before she crumples straight to the floor.

"I'm so sorry Mack!" she cries, "I'm so, so sorry! I- I didn't mea-"
Mack raises a wrinkled, leathery hand. Nylani tries to choke out another apology, her heavy sobs stammering her speech. The old man shakes his head, and this manages to silence her completely.

"Ya ain't got nothin' to apologise for, ya hear?" He responds. His stern voice is betrayed by his warm, comforting features. In all my time in Kohrmiir, I have never known him to raise his voice; I doubt I was about to hear it now. "I know ya ain't did it on purpose." He continues, arms folding over his hunched chest. "It ain't ya fault them powers of yours are jus' too darn hard to control."

He stops, waiting for a response - an argument, maybe? He smiles a gummy, near-toothless smile when none appears.
"If ya really are that upset by spookin' the poor girl, ya can flip the wagon back up. Ain't no way I'm

lifting that beast by myself." He chuckles, mostly to himself, I think. In an instant, Nylani leaves my side, tears and emotion wiped away as she begins to inspect the overturned, but otherwise still intact wagon.

7

Nylani

Silence hangs between us. The now upright wagon resumes its trek across the dirt path, gently bumping along in the warm summer sun. It took the better part of an hour to correct the damage I created. Thankfully the wagon didn't have any sustained damage; it was just lopsided and a wheel had popped out of place. The hay that littered Mack's wagon had sprayed along the hillside, leaving the cart barren for the first time in my near half a year I had worked alongside him.

The shame keeps my head hung low, even though I know that neither men - nor Hazel - were angry at me. Hells, they're not even upset. However, the humiliation holds a heavy weight on my mind and keeps me hyper aware of each action I make. I fear that any sudden movements could kickstart a belated horror from any one of my companions. I tuck my knees under my chin, keeping my arms locked around them. If I stay as compact as possible, no wayward snaps will have enough room to spread to any of them. Right?

Suddenly, a grumbling from the pit of my stomach interrupts the tense silence. Great. The pangs of hunger twist my stomach, the torsion intensifying the longer I try to ignore it. Eventually, I relent and slowly unfurl myself. Keeping my limbs as far away from the tiefling sharing the wagon with me, I loosen up. I turn behind me to rummage through the tattered haversack. I stay as quiet as I can, ransacking the depths of the bag blindly. Finally, my hand grabs the familiar paper bag of pastries that managed to worm itself to the bottom.
"Are you hungry?" I ask Damirius, voice quiet and cautious. He jumps a little at my voice and my stomach sinks.

"Don't worry about me, Tiny." He responds, a warm smile on his face. "I have something in here, somewhere." He rummages through his own, much smaller, messenger bag. I hold my breath. Worry scatters my reasoning as the unease makes me feel anything I do could send him running in fear. Holding my sack of pastries, I watch as Damirius' face sours whilst he delves into his bag. All he retrieves is a handful of various nuts, decorated with the lint and debris from the bottom of his bag. Impulsively, I thrust one of the pastries into his face, surprised by my own spontaneity. He looks at me, eyebrows raised. Then his eyes wander back to the pastry in my hand. A shy smile creeps along his face as he slowly takes the pastry from me.

"You don't have to, you know," he mumbles.
"I know," I barely whisper, "But... consider it a formal apology."
He barks a laugh, startling me, before he finally accepts the food and bites into it. "You don't need to keep apologising, Tiny." He remarks, mouth full of food.

A mixture of relief and playful disgust fill me as he continues to laugh with his mouth full of mushed pastry. I shake my head, a soft smile lifting my cheeks. I bite into one of the enticing, flaky pastries. Sweet jam oozes into my mouth, chunks of berries filling the sugary nectar that bursts from the layered cocoon. An unexpected hum of appreciation rumbles beside me as Damirius has already finished his breakfast. I look up, to find him lapping at the corners of his mouth where pools of sweet, sugary jam reside. I can't help but laugh at the sight, which seems to make him laugh in return.

"Where did you get these from?" he asks, his eyes ogling the paper bag in my hands. I toss him another. He eats happily.
I grin, his enthusiastic devouring of baked goods somewhat entertaining. "A baker gave them to me as a thanks for telling some kids off for stealing his food."
"He couldn't do it himself?"
"No one wants to tell off a group of teenagers – especially when one is half-orc," I chuckle at the memory.

The faces of the children - once they were caught red handed - was hilarious. I was almost certain one of them was going to faint from how pale they had become. Thankfully, all that was needed was a stern talking to. They quickly skittered away after that, and didn't seem to cause any more hassle from then on.

"Ahh – get the scarred, scary, tiny elf to do it. Makes sense," he grins, nudging me with his elbow.
"Of course, who else?" I shrug, my grin growing alongside his. I nudge him back. My chest feels

light, an almost whimsical happiness surging through me. It feels nice.

I watch the birds and bugs that fly past, revelling in the quiet between us now. It soothes the festering nervousness that resides within me from the earlier events. Our shoulders stay resting against the others, the gentle breeze running through my tangled hair. Methodically, my fingers entangle themselves in my hair, carefully separating the knots. Years of fixing tangles alone makes it an almost automatic response; no thought is needed as I can figure it out by touch alone. I turn my face upward, closing my eyes as I soak in the warm ebbs of sunlight above. The stings of earlier wounds are now only a dull ache. I'll soon forget about them.

"So," Damirius starts. He hesitates. "Uh…" I wait patiently. I expected he would want to know more. It's only natural. Plus, he was at the receiving end of that horrific display. It's only fair I provide some form of comfort about any fears he has about it, regardless of how harsh the comments are.
"Does…" He inhales, then exhales sharply. "Does *that*… happen often?"

I open an eye, watching him curiously. He stays close to me, his eyes not leaving mine. "You mean my magic going haywire?"
He nods, a small frown forming. By the look on his face, it looks as though Damirius is more worried about me than himself. But, I dismiss the thought. No one would worry for the beast that could easily kill them.

I look away, pulling at a stubborn knot in my hair. I can hear my hair rip. "Not much now," I finally admit, "I normally have a tight grip on it." I keep my eyes focused on my boots. I continue trying to untangle the knot. It gets tighter. Gritting my teeth, I yank hard. Then, larger hands appear over mine and begin deftly unknotting hair.

"So it doesn't hurt you much any more?" He continues to question as he smooths my hair out. "It's just when you have nightmares?"
Confusion surges through me, this entire interaction foreign to me. He leans over me, his face looming above mine as he focuses on the hair by my left ear. Despite his tall, clumsy frame, he is unexpectedly gentle with his touch. I barely feel his fingers disentwine my hair, aside from the loose

strands falling onto my shoulder as they get pried away from each other.

I stare up at him, my eyes not being able to leave him. I catch myself captivated by the simple act of tidying the tangles of my hair. I clear my throat, trying to look away when he turns to look at me. He smiles warmly, and I feel a heat rise somewhere in my chest. I cough, trying to expel the sudden warmth. His smile wavers as he watches me. "Does anything else cause your grip to loosen?"

"Why?" I question, my suspicion growing. Clearly he's trying to smooth talk me; the fiddling of my hair is to give me a false sense of security. It's obvious. I push his hands away.
He holds them up in mercy, "I only want to help," he claims. "If we're working together, I need to know if something triggers it." He pauses, watching me intensely. I scowl at him. I hate being under scrutiny like this. "Any help is better than no help, right?"

His smile softens, a meek expression compared to his usual beams and wide toothy grins. I hesitate, deliberating on his words. My head lowers, palms pushing against my temples as I close my eyes.

Multiple racing thoughts zoom through my mind at once. I look up, catching his eyes as he watches me patiently. Curse him. Curse his patience. And curse this entire interaction.

"Um...," I start, unsure what will follow as my thoughts continue to race. "My emotions. If I feel something really strongly, I can't control it." The words fall out, desperate to be heard before I can stop the verbal vomit that ensues. "I suppose it's because my concentration isn't on it as much?" A pause as I stare at him. He continues to listen, nothing in his demeanour pushes me to continue but I find I can't stop. "I'm not entirely sure. A lot of the time it's almost like the magic takes over so I just try to... squash it down, I suppose," I finish.

Heat trickles around my cheeks; heart pounding in my chest. Silence lingers between us again; an awkward, stifling feeling sticking to it this time. The quiet feels deafening. It begins to ring in my ears.
"So, good and bad? Or just bad?"
"Huh?"
He chuckles a little. A soft, heartfelt laugh that tickles below his breath. "Is it just bad emotions that trigger it?" He clarifies, a whisper of his smile just touching his mouth. "Or does making you

laugh result in a thunderstorm too?" His smile widens, trying to ease the conversation. I shake my head, the unease and uncertainty of this exchange calming slightly.

"Honestly, I'm not sure," I shrug. He casts me a curious glance, which I ignore.

"Well," he concludes, "Suppose I'll just have to find out."

"I'm not an experiment, horn head." I quip, silently shocked at my own quick wit.

The look of shocked bemusement on his face makes me grin, which only seems to cause his eyes to widen more. Laughter bubbles out of my chest and fills the barren road, followed quickly by the loud booming laughter of my new friend. The tumultuous start to our morning rapidly disappears behind the rolling hills as we continue down the long, winding path.

The sun hangs low in the afternoon sky, the gentle warmth tickling my skin as I lie flat on the now barren wagon floor. The clouds graze against the sky, their collective glide slow along the endless light blue sky. The wagon slows to a halt.

"Sorry 'bout the stop, folks," Mack calls back to us. "Bu' me an' Hazel are needing a break."

"It's no hassle, Mack," I reply. I stretch my hands out above me. My fingers spread open, almost encompassing the sun in my palms. "It's probably a good idea to get up and move, anyway."

I pull myself up to sit at the edge of the wagon. Looking around, the landscape looks the same as it did three hours ago. I sigh, defeated. The ride wouldn't be so dreary if the scenery at least changed a little.
I hop off with ease. Damirius follows suit, with no ease at all His foot catches the lip of the wagon, and nearly topples onto the weathered path. I whip around, ready to catch him, but stop when I see him haphazardly hop to try to regain his balance. I snort a laugh.

He glowers at me, but I turn my back to begin my stretches. My joints pop and crack, releasing their tension. I revel in the relief it provides, but I notice Damirius' gawking expression from the corner of my eye.
"Sounds painful." He states plainly, but the horror in his eyes is easy to spot.
I grin, bending backwards and laughing as he winces at my spine popping. I unfurl myself, my loose joints almost turning my body to jelly.

I continue to bend and contort myself, watching as Damirius pulls many ridiculous poses in front of me. I swallow my smiles, not wanting to encourage any more antics.

In a bid to get it to stop, I try to show him some proper techniques. However, this results in far more ludicrous poses; the final one ending in his buttocks pushing up to the air as he tries to twist his head backwards as if to kiss it. Inevitably, he collapses in the dirt, rubbing his neck. Giggles erupt from me, evolving into a hysterical laughter. I drop beside him on the floor, the pair of us laughing harmoniously until the sound of familiar boots announces the arrival of my favourite farmer.

8

Damirius

I look up at Mack, his bulbous head blocking out the majority of the blazing sun behind him. The tiny man shovels a handful of bright, crimson berries into his overbitten maw before feeding some to his mountainous companion. Juice trickles out of his gappy gums and down the protrusion of his chin. Hazel munches happily from his palm. Then, a smack of realisation hits me.

"Where did you get those?" I ask, perplexed. "There's basically nothing here!" I wave my arms over the barren landscape to emphasise my point. As far as I can see, the unwelcoming expanse of empty fields yields no nutrition. The empty shrubs that surround us confirm my suspicions.

"There's a few bushes further ahead," Mack responds, jutting his chin vaguely west off the road. "Hidden under a large oak. Jus' gotta know where t'look." The old man smiles wryly. "Few pretty flowers there, too," he remarks wistfully, his beady eyes looking at Nylani. He shares a smile with her before suddenly, she darts in the direction Mack had pointed.

Dust picks up behind her as she speeds away from the dirt road and into the adjacent fields. I look at Mack, who simply smiles and gestures towards the fields. Bewildered, I finally trail after her. The western region of the valley appears more alive than the rest; more trees scatter the grassland, the shade creating luscious groves littered with mushrooms and moss. The earth beneath my thin boots feels softer, the air lighter. The air cools as I travel through the continuous shade of a cluster of trees, following the swaying braid ahead of me.

Finally, I manage to catch up to her when she stops abruptly around a bunch of huddled bushes. She dips deep into the bushes, momentarily disappearing from my sight. I find her again as I get closer, her body hunched over a small bed of flowers. She almost becomes hidden under the mass of leaves from the bushes, the light grey of her shirt being the only thing that reveals her. She's eerily still. If she heard me behind her, she made no movement to indicate it. I step closer, peering over her shoulder.

Flowers, somewhat resembling chrysanthemums, lay ahead of Nylani. The petals around the edge are a deep midnight blue, with speckles of yellow and white scattering around in a random pattern, like stars in the night sky. The petals that huddle in the middle however, are brilliant white and curl into a curved point, giving the impression of a crescent moon. I'd never seen a flower like it. A moment passes between us. Nylani continues to marvel at them, but I've become bored. Although they are gorgeous, I just simply don't find any appeal in hiding under some trees to stare at something that doesn't even know of your existence.

"Gorgeous, aren't they?" Nylani finally whispers. Her eyes stay fixated on the flowers; her left hand slowly rises to stroke the petals of the one closest to her. There's tension in her wrist as her fingers extend. Every movement looks incredibly difficult. Her tendons look taut; like a puppet fighting against their strings. My eyes scan over her, analysing each point of tension and fierce concentration; her temples pulsing, her jaw is locking, eyes intensely focused. I'm at a loss at

how much strain she must go through just to be so gentle. How frustrating that must feel. With a rigidity I never knew existed in humanities' structure, I watch as she extends her finger and carefully runs a nail along one of the curled petals. She releases a small breath. Her jaw locks in concentration again.
"I've never seen anything like it," I finally mumble. Though I know I'm no longer talking about flowers.

She continues to spend a few moments looking at each individual flower, seemingly inspecting each one intensely. I'm no longer bored, as I appear to find entertainment in watching her interact with delicate things. Suddenly, with a speed I forgot she had, she pulls one out of the ground, and cradles it protectively in her arms. Immediately, she's off again, wandering back to the wagon.

She's unusually protective of it, holding it close to her chest as we continue our trek back to the wagon. I cast a questioning look to Mack, who simply shrugs and smiles. A sigh leaves me. Maybe I'm the weird one here. Are flowers really so important around here? Or maybe it's a cultural thing? I try to recall if Mama was ever so obsessive with flowers, but I come up short. However, a memory of Mama sulking at the pansies Papa bought home does appear in my mind's eye. They wilted within the week of their arrival. I chuckle to myself. She never managed to keep the poor things alive longer than a few days.

My eyes focus back into the present, only to find Nylani with her arm deep in her haversack. The other arm stays outstretched as far as she possibly can in an attempt to keep the flower as far away from her bag as possible. I suffocate the laughter that threatens to rise at the odd display. Eventually, she retrieves a small, battered, leather bound book from the depths of her seemingly endless bag.

Holding the weathered book seems to create a noticeable softness in her; wide, round eyes seem to grow larger. The stony greyness that normally resides in them hint towards silver within the sun's gaze. A soothing silence fills the air around us for the moment as she slides the moon-adjacent flower between two pages then presses the book closed.

The entire movement feels almost like a slow ballet. The long, fluid movements of her arm and fingers gracefully stroke the pages of her aged tome; the silent adoration she bestows the flower as she places it into an empty page; and the hum of pure, blissful happiness that radiates from the person that I had presumed was too far removed from such naivete. She swaddles the book's strap around the cover, smooshing the pages closer together as it closes. She hugs it closely to her chest before placing it back in her haversack with utmost care. Her dance concludes. And I feel myself finally pull away from the entrancing display.

I cough, shifting myself away from her as I face the sky. I try to push the lingering feeling of watching her be so vulnerable away. Was it endearment? Fascination? I can't tell.

"Thank you, Mack. We're ready to set off once you are." She says to Mack, her voice pulling me out of my head. Slowly, the wagon resumes its laborious crawl through the Whispering Valley. Creaks and groans of the wagon's wheels settle into the background noise of the critters that surround us.

"Didja like thems flowers? Thought they were a new find fer ya."
"They were lovely Mack. Thank you."

"They are, ain't they? I ain't never seen nothing like them before."
"They're normally only native to Ula'Rae."
"Makes ya' wonder what they're doin' over here, huh?"

A pause occurs between the conversation. The silence finally settles as Hazel continues to tug the wagon down the long, winding road. Mack keeps looking over his shoulder, a hint of concern shadowing his squashed face. Our eyes meet for a moment before Mack's eyes settle back on Nylani. The old man begins to speak, but stops himself and closes his mouth again.

"Do ya ever miss it?" The tiny elder finally blurts out, "Ya' home, I mean." I look at Nylani, keeping silent as I watch. She smiles kindly up to Mack, but I notice the smile doesn't seem to reach her eyes. Her jaw clenches. I go to comfort her again, but I pull myself away.

"Well, I suppose everyone misses their old home when they move, right?" Her voice sounds calm, but it's hollow. It's almost like she's reciting facts, rather than giving her own personal thoughts. The barricade that began to crumble is now slowly returning. I grimace.

Mack hacks a dry laugh out. "Tha's one way ter see it, I suppose. At least ya' can always return. It ain't too far."
Nylani agrees with a quiet hum. "Maybe one day I will."

She sounds dismissive. Who wouldn't want to go home? She continues to talk, but her voice sounds so far away. The tension I noticed earlier has returned; this time, settling in her shoulders, neck and chest. Her strings contort her to portray a visual of calm relaxation, but the taut stiffness alludes to her stress. I push the thought away. This is not my mess to meddle in. I roll my shoulders and slump against the wall of the wagon. I look to the open expanse behind us, the muffled chatter quieting the silence that threatens to smother us.

The sound of rustling catches my attention. I look back into the wagon, watching as she removes her haversack and curls into the corner. Somehow, she seems smaller than usual. Her head sinks, chin resting on her knees. I go to reach out to her again, but I pause. My hand has passed the threshold, but lingers in mid air. Her eyes raise to look at my open palm. She smiles. A sad smile. And it still doesn't reach her eyes.

"It's okay," she whispers. "I'm not having another episode."
"It's not that I'm worried about," I say softly. "I'm worried about you."

She seems confused. Her head tilts to the side as she looks at me, curiosity marring her face. "Why?"
"It's obvious that thinking of home hurts." I note, trying to keep my voice as soft as possible. I lower my head, hoping to convey my sympathies despite the factual observation.

My head turns away, though I still see her in the corner of my eye. Her eyes are wide. "I won't pry. But I do want you to know that I want to help, however I can." I emphasise my statement, trying to show my compassion towards the naturally untrusting woman. Gods knows she needs someone - even if it was the 'whore of Kohrmiir'. Her eyes relax. I stay silent, pretending I don't notice. I lean back against the wall again; I've done all I can do. What happens next is up to the coiled, silent elf opposite me.

The dreaded silence falls between us again, though I make no effort to disrupt it. It would be a wasted venture. We stay in silence for a long time. The only sounds that meet my ears are those of the consequential noises a wagon in the middle of nowhere would create. It's maddening, but I struggle to find anything of substance to break the silence.

"Could you..." The barely audible squeak of Nylani rips the silence apart. I turn my head to look at her. Her wide eyes peer up at me, a tangible worry sitting on the surface of her face. "Would you tell me about yours?" A pause. "Your home?" She presses, her whisper floating through the late afternoon sky. A flush warms my cheeks; the unexpected request paralyses my thoughts for a moment.

"Uh, yeah. Sure." I manage to mumble out.
Home. A tiny cottage smothered in extensions in the middle of the countryside; as many chickens as there were children. Well, as much as I could remember. I hadn't been home for some time. The thought pangs my chest. Bittersweet moments of Mama and Papa swim in the river of my memories; Papa waltzing with Mama in their shabby

kitchenette, his head resting against her heart; Mama bringing another misfit home in her arms claiming 'the hens were broody again!'; the smell of warm pumpkin pie filling the tiny cottage on the cold nights. I chuckle to myself, a wave of nostalgia hitting my eyes and trickling down my cheeks. The ache of homesickness has never been so pungent before, yet it felt so calming. If I miss it, that just means it was worth missing, right?

I turn to Nylani, startled by the wide, expectant eyes that gaze up at me. The enchanting grey eyes plead into my core, as if nothing else mattered. I clear my throat, desperate to remove the lump that has suddenly appeared. Heat rises up my neck and tickles the tops of my cheeks. I hate it.

"It was... well, is... a really uh... Humble kind of place." I start, fumbling my words. Despite every embellishment I've ever told of my life before, this was sacred. Mama and Papa could never be exaggerated. They deserved that much. No. They deserved a whole lot more. I clear my throat.

"My home is in the far west of Doxdel, near the border to Corrof. Tiny little cottage in the middle of nowhere." I begin, trying to hide the smile that threatens to grow as I watch her hang onto every word. How cute. "Mama, as you know, is half-elf. Papa is full dwarven. Dwarves are normally revered for 'staying with their own kind' but Papa liked to joke that it was nice to finally be with a woman that couldn't grow a better beard than him." I laugh at a memory; Papa becoming irritated when Rulwin - a dwarven brother - grew his full beard at twelve. I hear Nylani's quiet giggles and I'm pulled back to the present.

"I say I have nine siblings, but realistically it's more within the twenty to thirty range. The nine are more like permanent siblings, I suppose." I pause for a minute, the flashing memories of siblings long past running by. "The others either went to find their birth families or removed themselves from our family for one reason or another."

I look up to the now dimming sky, acutely aware of the eyes that follow me. "The house is surrounded by Mama's farm. We have cows, a few goats and so, so many chickens." I chuckle, "Mama used to say the hens were at fault for all her kids. 'They were being broody again' was her favourite excuse when she showed Papa their new child. He never

minded though." I smile, a reignited warmth filling my chest.
"It sounds beautiful, Damirius." Nylani remarks, her voice heavy with sincerity.
"It really is, Tiny."

Time glazes by slowly, the sky becoming speckled with the oranges and deep purples of the early evening. We rest in relative silence, watching the world continue around us. Birds chirp and chatter to one another in the distance, their tunes echoing across the empty farmlands. Mack hums a gentle, harmonious melody as Hazel's hooves beat against the ground.

I fill the time with stories of my various escapades – with relative embellishment, of course - and details of the long trek to Kohrmiir. Initially, I was a simple man wanting a simple life to find work. But, as someone that was never accepted by the residents, there was a limited amount of work I was allowed to do. With time, and a lot of wrong moves on my behalf, I found that the most intolerant tended to be the most curious bedwise, and one thing led to another.

"Why didn't you leave Kohrmiir?" Nylani eventually

asks after listening to my elaborate story. Genuine curiosity lilts her voice, her head cocking slightly to the side.

"I never had a chance. Until now." I keep my eyes trained on the path behind us, forcing all my emotions down. Anger, hurt, and even despair threaten to bubble up and overflow, though I know there's no need for them now. What's done is done, and at least I'm finally away from there.

A weight press against my bicep. Looking down, I see the top of Nylani's head against my shoulder, her body leaning into me. Her small, battle scarred hand pats my forearm gently.

"I'm sorry." She finally musters. "I never knew."

"It's alright, Tiny." My quiet, hushed voice replies. "I didn't want anyone to."

We continue to lean into each other as we watch the palette of the sky mix and muddle into the evening. Wisps of dark clouds stay smear against the gradient of the horizon, and a light freckling of stars become apparent in the darkened sky. The hum of waking night bugs trembles the still air. I take a deep breath in, the early evening air refreshingly cool in my lungs. Nylani shifts beside me, her weight pressing against my side more. A gentle breeze rushes by me, sending a soft tremble up my spine.

"It's nice, you know." she offhandedly comments, her voice soft. "It's been a long time since anyone's just…" She pauses. "Talked to me. Without expecting anything."
Just as softly, I respond. "Yeah. Me too."

A sudden wave of faces slam into my memory; a slurry of angry, greedy people. Hands grab my arms, my back, my thighs; eyes glare hungrily at me; forceful movements that make me stumble. I shake my head vigorously, pushing the thoughts away. I don't want the reminder. Not now. Not ever. I take a shaky, deep breath. The cold air rushes to chill my chest. Another breath. And another. I can feel her face turn to look at me. I keep my eyes trained ahead. Slowly, my breathing levels out again. I flop back, the cool floor of the wagon smacking into my spine. The moons rise upwards, filling my vision as I stare up at the sky.

9

Nylani

A few hours pass, and we sit in relative silence with each other. Damirius stays lying down staring at the sky, whilst I curl up in a corner and watch the night life of the valley. Fireflies flitter around us, their little lights speckling the early evening. Mack flickers the oil lamp on. The buzzing of moths begins to fill the silence, the occasional tapping on the glass case interrupting the hum of their wings.

"We're nearly there, jitterbugs!" Mack suddenly announces, "Just bout's a couple minutes 'til we're at the Harbour."
"Okay, thank you, Mack!" I call back. I turn to look at Damirius. He continues stargazing, his honey-yellow eyes glistening like the stars above.

The uncertainty of the task ahead has me worried; all I've got is a cryptic letter, and even then that produces more questions than answers. I shift into an upward seating position, my focus on the nonchalant man beside me. He seems to sense me, his eyes turning to look at me.

"The first thing we're going to need to do is find somewhere to sleep; an inn or something." I don't like how indecisive I sound. "I think we're going to be staying here for at least a few days."
He seems to be able to sense my faltering certainty as he rises up to sit across from me, arms and legs crossed. His eyes are sterner, like he's analysing me. I hate it.

"Well," he finally huffs, unfolding his arms, "am I actually going to know what's going on yet?" The question silences me. He continues. "It's great that you know where we are, what's happened and what we're doing once we get there, but I know absolutely nothing." I'm stunned for a moment, the realisation that I haven't shared anything at all hitting me square in the windpipe. My jaw slacks. I look up at him, readying an apology, just as I notice the hint of a shit-eating grin on his face.

I swallow my apology down. "Right."
Ass. I feel an aggressive wave of heat tickle my ears and burn my cheeks. I spot him out of the corner of my eye, grinning as he watches me rummage my bag for my map. I unfurl the weathered and beaten map and spread it out on the floor of the wagon. Though much older than me, the printed image of the Ularian Empire has stayed pristine on the aged parchment.

"The place we're going to is called Hush Harbour," I explain. My finger points to the southernmost section, to a small cluster of mountainous plains that encircles a large lake as I continue. "It's basically a ghost town or something, at this point. No one goes in; no one comes out. However, I've been given some information that there's something in the lake. One of the locals managed to find a way to send a distress signal, but we're going to have to ask around to get a better idea of what to expect."

Damirius' eyes widen, mouth agape. "So... that's it? We're fighting something that we know next to nothing about?"
"Pretty much." I like it about as much as he does, but it feels like something is calling me here. But

that something doesn't feel right. I crane my neck to get a look ahead of us; the large mountainous hills creeping ever closer. Hairs on the back of my neck begin to rise.

I shake, the chill of dread tumbling down my spine. I force my weariness down as I roll my shoulders and attempt to regain my stoic composure. A gloominess impedes the air around me, the night air turning drastically colder with each step our wagon makes. Damirius' face appears beside mine, glancing around nervously. Seems as though it's not just me that noticed the change. My eyes focus ahead, trying to notice if anything could be manipulating the atmosphere. Nothing so far.

"Lovely vacation spot," the tiefling drawls loudly, a goofy grin plastered to his face. I groan, my eyes nearly rolling behind my brain. I appreciate wanting to lighten the mood, but there's a time and place. Though, the whisper of a smile still tries to wriggle itself free. It gets smothered.

An apprehensive grumble calls for my attention at the front. "Miss Nylani, ma'am... I think yer got yer work cut out fer yer this time..." Mack remarks. The air is now bitterly cold. A wind picks up, whipping around me and chilling me instantly. Slowly, the wagon finally comes to a shuddering halt. Hazel snorts and paws at the dirt path anxiously. The poor mare's eyes are wide as she fights against her reigns. Mack manages to wrangle her to stay still, but it's clear she's not happy about it. Cautiously, I slide out from the wagon and wander to the front, eager not to spook her any further. I run my hand along her rump, pausing when she startles at first. I sidle up by her head, stroking her mane to soothe her. She settles against my hand, her muzzle snuggles into my palm. I turn my head to look ahead, now that Hazel has calmed.

At the bottom of the large slope before us rests Hush Harbour. Or, rather, the remnants of it. The large, crescent shaped harbour is flooded; water covers the buildings, large pond-sized puddles soak into the cracked cobblestone walkways. And from the view up here, I can't see a soul in sight. Shock ripples through me.

My limbs tremble, making it hard to step forward. I try to lift a leg, but the weight nearly topples me. I stare at my feet, terrified. I try to lift my leg again, but my foot seems stuck to the dirt. My eyes raise back to look at the dilapidated harbour, the sight of the crumbling buildings burned into my skull. A tiny hand rests atop mine, startling me out of my panic. "If yer can't save this town, ma'darlin', it ain't on you, okay?" Mack says, his voice hushed. The tremor is clear in his voice. I look up at him. His tiny, beady eyes look at me in earnest. His grip tightens slightly on my hand, his other hand strokes the top of my head. I gulp.

"I've got this, Mack. Don't you worry." I struggle to keep my voice level. My hand holds his a little tighter.
He shakes his head. "It ain't them I'm worried abou'. This is a big task fer lil' ol' you." He states, voice soft and concerned at the same time.
"There's no shame in admittin' somethin' is too big to do alone. Yer only one person, ma'darlin'."

The confirmation of my fear hits me hard in the chest. This is a monumental task. I take another deep, shuddering breath.
"I want to at least try, Mack. They deserve that."
 I shove the rising tidal wave of fear that threatens to slam into me deep into the pit of my stomach. Not now. Not here.
The old man nods solemnly, "I understan'." He pauses, his beady eyes watching me closely. He

strokes my hair, and a tear grows in my eye. I tilt my head back a little, hoping it will stay inside my eyelid, at least.

"I gots to go, ma'darlin'. Be safe."
"Always," I let out as a whisper. The sombre air around us thickens as I watch Mack steer Hazel away, trekking back down the path we had just arrived from.

My head turns back to the town, soaking in the dreary sight before me. The glacial wind chips away at me, desperate to be acknowledged against my normally fervent skin. I shiver, though it's not from the cold. Something menacing lingers here. I can feel it. A knot of uncertainty twists in my stomach, the tense sensation adding to my growing unease. The familiar, towering tiefling stands beside me, his presence almost soothing against this unsightly town.

"You don't have to do it alone, Tiny." He emphasises, his eyes focused on the desolate wasteland ahead. I keep my head down. How can you tell a stranger - an acquaintance, at best - that just having them with you makes this feel so much easier? Or are we friends now? I shake the idea away. There's no time to debate over personal affairs when a town desperately needs help.

Slowly, I tread the descent down to the battered entryway of Hushed Harbour. Even the gateway to the Hushed Harbour evokes the danger that lurks behind its walls. Where what I can only imagine were once huge, thick wooden gates now stands a broken, barren doorway. The archway is in splinters, brick and wood broken and burst into the mud in front of us.

Shattered, waterlogged doors hang onto their last hinges; algae drip off it, the hardwood rotting in the areas that have sunk into the ground. Gingerly, I step through the archway, trying to absorb the sight of the town.

The path I walk along was, presumably, once a straight, cobblestone road. But now, it's a desolated ravine of dirt, mud and rocks that lead directly to the massive lake that resides at the back of the village. The buildings around me look to have been crushed. Roofs flattened, supporting beams reduced to dust, and fences pushed deep into the ground.

Some structures remained – a corner section to a house there; a single, unbroken but leaning wall to another home over there. More secure structures are few and far between, and are feebly hidden away in the darker crevices of the town, near the hillside.

The lack of sound raises the hairs on the back of my neck; the silence ringing in my ears. My sudden, deep breath startles me. I hadn't realised I was holding it for so long. I continue my search through the deep, swampish dirt. What I'm searching for, I don't know. A sign of life, maybe. Or a hint to what monstrosity could commit this level of destruction. That would be preferable. At least then I would know where to aim my fists. Then, something catches my eye.

Something mud-soaked. And pink. My hands lift it up before I have a chance to even understand what it is. But once it's in my hands, I know. A teddy. A soft, soaked, hideously pink stuffed bear.

"Whatcha got there, Tiny?"
I turn to Damirius, my wavering will to hold my tears back faltering. His eyes survey me before they look at my hands. I can see his realisation and

horror manifest and work through his body in rapid succession. He looks at me, dumbfounded.
"Nylani," he whispers, "What do we do?"

Defeat fills his voice. Tears threaten to fall down my cheeks. I look down at the dripping, dirtied toy. Plush pink fur hides beneath the brown dirt that smothers its face and rounded tummy. Water fills my eyes, fogging my vision, but the image of the ruined toy stays clear in my mind. My fingers sink further into the grimy plush, the mud seeping under my nails.

The teddy sags pathetically between my hands, water cascading out of its puny body. I blink my tears away, focusing on the toy in my hands. Hand-sewn button eyes. Stitches around its left arm. Initials sewn into its right foot. Finally, a tear falls down my cheek.

But, as the first tear falls, a new emotion replaces the sorrow that sat in my chest. Rage ripples through me, the heat igniting my dampened mood. I scream in anger, my nails ripping into the fabric of the toy. Heavy, soaked stuffing stumbles out of the tear I created in its back, dropping loudly into the mud below. I snap, throwing the toy into the ground to meet its soiled innards. A roaring curse explodes out of me, ricocheting around the ruins that encapsulate me in this pitiful town.

A blazing hatred runs over me, sparking my electric to snap at the ground. With each burning impact, the mud instantaneously becomes fried and cracked. Rubble gets projected from the floor as more whips expel from me, their static crackling filling the suffocatingly silent air. I'm not sure what I'm doing, or where I'm going, but I don't care. Anywhere is better than being near that lost, lonely bear.

Damirius' thunderous, charging footsteps race after me, but I pretend not to hear. If I ignore him, he'll go away. Like everything does. Explosive symphonies of crashing lightning follow me as I charge through the decaying harbour. The floor trembles beneath me, and I pray that whatever creature ruined this town is trembling, too.

I prowl the relic of Hush Harbour, eagerly awaiting some sign of movement. When suddenly, I get hoisted into the air by a pair of large, lilac arms. I scream, my magic going wild as his arms coil tighter around my waist. My body thrashes violently, hoping to swing him to the floor, but he stays upright and unwavering.

My frustration builds, bursting out in a fit of incoherent yelling and wild magic slapping the air around us. His head rests against my shoulder, his horn pressing against my cheek. He feels cold against me, my skin growing increasingly hotter. His body shakes against mine, his legs wobble under the strain of my protest.

I swing my legs wildly in a desperate attempt to freedom, but it's to no avail. I yell, my throat and lungs shredding under the strain. A crackle of electricity sparks out, snapping at the already massacred floor. Rubble flies up, smacking against the pair of us.

"Hey, hey, hey!" I hear him shout. Another snap of electricity flashes, popping in the air before dissipating. His arms tighten. I yell again.

"Calm down!", he grunts, his head buried into my shoulder. I try to move my shoulder away. He holds me close. I kick backwards. My heel stomps against his shin. He grunts, angry air hissing between his teeth. I'm too angry to laugh at the victory. I lunge myself to the right, hoping the force will pull me free. His grip is too strong; he sways violently alongside me. I grumble, desperately clawing at his hands to pull them away. No amount of scratching or pulling seems to loosen his grip. I howl in frustration. Using my last resort, I flop back, using the momentum to send the pair of us tumbling to the ground.

Determined, I writhe like a rabid animal until finally, Damirius is forced to let me go. I start to skitter away, my fingers clawing through the thick dirt desperately. My arms move too fast for my legs, my waist getting dragged along the dirt. Just as I start to pull myself up, a large hand grabs my leg. My legs get pulled underneath me and I'm dragged back through the dirt.

I'm flipped onto my back, forced to face the sweating, exhausted face of the relentless purple man. I swing my leg upwards, silently smug as it connects with his stomach and he groans in pain. I go to swing again, but he forces his legs atop mine, pushing them into the dirt.

"You don't get it!" I scream, my rage starting to waiver. I'm getting too tired to stay angry.

"Then help me understand!" he bellows back, shocking me. I stare up at him, somehow at a loss for words. Cuts welt his lilac cheek, deep crimson blood trickling down towards his chin. Guilt slams into me, and finally, I begin to cry.

Tears stream down my face as I whimper beneath him. I feel him lower himself down, his weight pressing against me. An arm slides underneath me and pulls me into a tight hug.

"I should've come sooner," I finally weep. My face gets buried in his shoulder as his arm tightens around me. Mud slicked fingers cling onto his shirt as I continue to cry. "Maybe then…" I choke out, my sobs catching in my throat. "Maybe then it wouldn't have gotten to this point."

My body shakes as another mournful wail reverberates within me. His hand grabs my hair, holding my head to him. His body crashes completely into mine as he lets his other arm fall, wrapping it around my torso and pulling me close to him.

His breath tingles against my skin, his calm, consistent rhythm almost soothing. My tears stop falling, my breathing ragged. I force a deep breath, my throat sore from the yelling before. The cold air stings, but the bitter iciness numbs the raging heat. I feel myself slump; too tired to fight any more. My eyes slowly rise, reluctantly taking in the sight of the demolished town that surrounds us. A community. A home. Gone. All because I didn't get here in time.

"When did you receive the letter?" Damirius asks, his voice barely more than a whisper.
I look up at him. His yellow eyes were somehow soothing, like soft caramel. I find myself almost trapped in them; a welcome distraction from the overwhelming destruction that surrounds us.

My shoulders sag, sinking further into the soft earth that cushions me. A shaky breath leaves me, rattling steam into the cold air. He watches me, patiently, an inviting smile slowly lifting his lips. He continues to watch me, and I'm suddenly reminded that he's waiting for a response. I take another deep breath.

"About..." I think for a moment, the last few days merging into a blur. "Four days ago, I think."

He pauses; presumably to reflect over the past couple of days, too. "So, roughly about a day before we met in the tavern?"
"Yeah. I had just finished up a job when we met."
"Right." He stops, thinking. "So, how could you have gotten here any quicker?"

I go to respond, but my voice evaporates. My mind rapidly flashes for some form of a reason but I keep coming up short. Every excuse I can think of is quickly replaced with a reason.

"I – I could've..." I finally blurt out. He pulls himself up, looking down at me. His eyes watch me, a glimmer of gentle amusement behind his patience. My voice waivers and thins, fading away as I stay hard pressed for an excuse.

"There was no way you could have gotten here any faster." Damirius finally announces, his calm voice firm with conviction. "How is any of this all your fault?"

A pause fills the stagnant air. He pulls me upward, dragging me onto his lap as he sits down. The restriction seems comforting; the constant pressure around me makes me feel safe. I lean into him, his heart pumps beside my own as I hug him tightly. The steady rhythm of his chest is soothing. I take a deep, heavy inhale as his arms squeeze my waist and back. For now, I allow myself this moment of reprieve.

"From what it looks like," he continues, quietly in my ear, "this town has been like this for a while. Honestly, you could've been here months earlier and I feel it would've been the same."

I grumble. I hate that he's right; this entire situation was way out of my control. Doesn't make it any easier to accept, though. I stay in his arms a while longer, soaking in all the comfort I can get. The cool wind breezes around us as the early evening crawls to late night. I finally lift my head and glance around the graveyard of stonemasonry.

With calmer eyes I can finally inspect each section of the war torn harbour. Slowly, I'm lifted back to my feet. Damirius rises, placing me beside him and finally releasing me from his arms. His warmth no longer surrounds me, and I feel alone once again. For some reason, my body craves his presence. I shake my head, desperately trying to push the desire away. No. I can't be dependent. Not again.

I look around, digesting the image of all the crumbled buildings. My legs hesitantly step forward; one heavy step ahead of the other. Slowly, the buildings crawl closer to me as I continue my slow trudge through the mud. Then, something in the corner of my eye catches my attention.

An area nearby has been compounded into the earth; a shallow crater of a neighbourhood, crushed remnants of homes within it. My body changes course, immediately turning and walking briskly towards the sunken earth.

As I get closer, I see debris covered in water life; algae, bulrushes, and even the remains of lifeless aquatic beings coat the relics of these homes. Curiosity captures me, and I continue to venture through the waterlogged remnants of this squashed street. Water drenches my boots and bleeds into my thick, woollen socks as I continue my investigation.

Most of the houses' structures had been reduced to dust or clusters of brickwork. The powder of previous residency sticks to the water, creating a grey sludge that clings to anything that passes through the thickened water. I find myself standing beside a portion of a wall, propped up against a pile of rubble. Something sticks out underneath the large slab of cement; something wooden. With my curiosity piqued, I shift the wall away from its trapped, wooden prisoner. Slowly, and with as much grace as a large, crumbling wall can give, I lay it within the water.

A splintered, squashed dining table is revealed from the wall's removal. Its legs are splayed outwards, as if the top had been slammed into them. A dark mould climbs across the table, claiming it as its own. Water has seeped into the crevices of the wood, pushing splinters up and in various directions; amplifying the size of the cracks that mark the table top.

"How long has this been going on for?" I ask, to no one in particular. A chill runs down my spine. From the cold air, or from the eerie atmosphere, I can't tell. I shake the feeling away. Trudging through the deep mud, I continue my investigation. Squashed chairs, shattered plates, and broken tiles fill the floor of what once was a kitchen.

Unceremonious splashes announce Damirius' arrival behind me. I turn to look at him, watching as he crashes through my crime scene. Then, he stops and begins to search within a pile of rubble near the edge of the crater. Around him, metal beams are bent out of shape, almost enclosing him in the tiny area.

I cautiously step forward, careful of where to lay my feet. Splinters of a staircase decorate the surface of the water like threatening glitter, warning me of the danger that lurks within the quayside. I spot a section of a bed frame and move it to the edge of the pit; the middle now easier to traverse through.

We continue our search silently, lifting small mementos and placing them on the dried dirt outside of the murky lagoon.

"That's odd," Damirius suddenly mumbles. "There are no bodies here."
I pause, finally noticing it myself. "Let's just hope they're hiding." I finally reply, grimly. "I don't think I want to imagine the alternative."
The thought makes the rest of my search all the harder to complete.

The sun sets; the air cooling evermore, making my legs creak like old doors with each bend and flex. Our bodies shiver, thick mud cakes our arms and legs as we finally exit the shallow hole. We stand at the edge, looking into the murky waters. With all the debris set aside, I can see how the crater dips in the middle. All of the furniture seems squished, as though something pushed down onto it, instead of throwing it aside.

"Whatever it was, it came straight from above," I lament aloud.
"It must be huge to create such an impact like that." Damirius remarks, a whisper of horrified awe clear in his tone.

Another gust of piercing cold air rushes past us, and we shiver again. The mud has started to solidify on my clothes, and I'm starting to feel heavy. I start to pick and peel the larger pieces away. We glance at each other, silently agreeing to find somewhere to retire for the night.

We huddle together, hoping to keep the wind from whipping around us, as we begin to trudge away from our sodden excavation site. Moments pass in relative silence until suddenly, Damirius huffs in quiet excitement.

"I think we may have found somewhere to sleep, Tiny," he smirks. His hands cup my shoulders, and rotate me to the right of us. I spot a collection of buildings that are huddled together in the far distance. From the distance, the accumulation of residences look to be just another one of the many piles of rubble that cover the village.

The brashly built shelter rests in the crook of the huge hills that encompass the southern side of the harbour. Flickers of dim lights and thin smoke emit from a few of the buildings, revealing the people that reside inside.
I feel myself instantly relax. Finally, a sign of life. At least one non-antagonistic being is still alive here. A heavy exhale shambles out of me. The warmth of my breath creates a steady steam that evaporates around my face and fogs me momentarily.

"Well, let's go investigate... partner." He nudges me, grinning. Before I can react he already starts striding over to the buildings in question. I let out a scoff, trying to hide my amused smile. No one would believe we were fighting in the mud not too long ago. Well, aside from the dirt caked in my hair.

As we step closer to the buildings, I notice how the houses appear huddled, hiding in the crease of the hill that they reside upon; rooftops squished together, and wonky walls being shared between homes. If it weren't for the smattering of doors that were strewn about, the assortment of shambled buildings would look like a very long, very wonky bungalow.

The various roofs slump together but also sit at different heights from one another. Doors are slanted; some simply shoved into appropriately sized holes in ramshackle walls. The integrated buildings consist of what I believe to be an inn, and roughly four attached miniature houses. The bricks and stones that make the walls are covered in algae, and any windows have been hastily boarded up. Though, I can still see small flickering beads of light seep through the gaps of the rotting boards.

I incline my head towards the inn; a ramshackle hovel with a second floor and a flat roof. Damirius looks towards it as well and nods his head. I knock on the door, half expecting my knuckle to break through the wood with how feeble it looked. A creaking whinge above my head catches my attention. As I look up, I spot a crumbling wooden sign that shudders against the persistent wind.

The worn, sun bleached sign reads 'Babbling Brook' in chipped, blue paint. It hangs loosely from its thin rope. The right side dips lower than the left. Suddenly, the faint glimmer of candlelight from inside is snuffed out. Slow, deliberate footsteps make their way towards the door.

The door creaks open slowly, a face appearing behind it. The door has barely opened an inch and all I can see is a singular, powder blue, bulbous eye. It squints as it scans the pair of us in a suspicious silence.

"Uhh... Hi there, I'm Damirius. This is my friend, Nylani. We were just wanting to ask a few questions, please."
"Well, get on with it, then," the elderly woman snaps; her voice crackling somewhat akin to the crumbling wood that surrounds her.

I pull the yellowed, crumpled envelope out of my haversack, shoving it towards the hag's exposed eye. Her prickly demeanour is beginning to irritate me. Her large, bulging eye inspects the envelope, though she doesn't make any attempt to take it from me. Impatient, I take the ragged sheet of parchment out of the withering envelope, and I unfold it. I shove the letter in the woman's face. The bulbous eye widens slightly before it squints in suspicion again. My gaze hardens. She stares at me.

"I received a letter from an E. Burimir," I explain, "Would that be you, ma'am?"
The creaking of floorboards suggests the woman is repositioning herself. She seems uncomfortable. Good. At least now she might readjust her attitude. The section of face that is exposed contorts into a scowl.
The woman grumbles, "No. Never heard of 'er before."

I sigh, feeling my shoulders tense. Why does she have to be so difficult? A steady breath releases from me as I raise the letter up to the woman's eye again.

"It's clear to me that you recognise it, ma'am." My voice is tense, but I bite back my anger. The woman's eye glares at me. I take another deep breath. "Either you wrote it, or you know the person who did. If Mrs Burimir is not you, can you at least tell us where she is?"

The mysterious woman grumbles, like a snarling dog, before she leans in closer to the door. Her bulging eye almost passes the threshold, the tiny pupil darting wildly between Damirius and I.

"I don't know who this Burimir lady is, or what that letter is so if you ain't gonna pay for a room, get lost!" She suddenly barks. The door suddenly swings open, exposing the hobbled, weathering woman for just a second as she prepares for an almighty slam.

But, before it can collide with the door frame, my foot juts in the gap. The door swings shut and my boot absorbs the impact. A throbbing, angry pulse crushes against my foot. I let out a quiet hiss, fighting the urge to cradle my offended toes.

"Fine, don't cooperate." I finally snap. The woman stares at me, bewildered. I swallow my anger, though the lingering tension stays in my voice. "But we've nowhere to stay and we need to sleep." I pull a gold coin out of my pocket, and wave it in front of the elder's eyes, "I can pay upfront. Would one gold be enough for the pair of us for a night or two?"

Finally, the door tentatively open. A haggard old gnomish woman that reaches no farther than my shoulder appears from behind the door; her back hunched in a protective, standoffish posture. Her wild, strikingly white hair would have been in natural ringlets but they've been shoved into an unkempt bun atop her head. A few stray strands poke in every which way possible around her squashed, wrinkled face. Her bulbous, blue eyes are wedged behind a large, hooked nose that almost hides her thin lips. She scratches her chin, adorned with a smattering of white whiskers. "Fine. Yer can come in."

I walk inside, careful to not put pressure on my throbbing foot. The interior appears almost barren; aside from two tables and a random selection of chairs, there's nothing here. And even calling those furniture feels inappropriate – some chairs are nothing more than a small stack of deflated pillows roped together, and the tables barely seem able to stand.

I turn my attention to the floor, and I notice the rotten, moulding floorboards. A frayed, splitting rug covers the majority of the small lobby; presumably to hide the fractured wood beneath. I push the gold coin into the woman's bony, expectant hand before ascending the creaking stairs on the left of the room.

"First door on the right!" The grumbling, gnome woman calls after me. I don't reply. I've had enough of her for now. Slowly, I pull myself up the precarious steps. My foot wails every time I place it on the next step. Damirius suddenly appears at my side, holding me up as we make our way to our room. Secretly, I'm glad he's here. But I won't admit that to him.

Finally, we arrive at the doorway. A key sits in the lock of the doorknob, waiting for a patron, I guess. Slowly, I turn it open and pocket the key. Damirius closes the door behind us. It's a desolate room, and much like the foyer downstairs, only has simple yet tattered furniture inside.

A rickety double bed sits in the middle of the back wall, with only a yellow tinted blanket resting atop it. I hobble inside, resting on the bed. The screams of the harsh springs beneath do not bring me any comfort.

"Lovely," Damirius comments, amused, "Well, looks like we gotta share, Tiny."
"Obviously, there's not much choice." I instinctively remark. My voice softens, "It seems like they just grabbed what they could. Like they were building this place overnight."

I continue to inspect the room from the bedside, hoping to get some clues of this obscure environment. Anything to piece a coherent story together is welcome at this point.
Damirius' smile fades. "True… We need to figure out what's going on."
"There were a few hints to something in the letter… Though, it's very vague."

I look at the letter, reading the words for the hundredth time, before I pass it towards him. I turn at the edge of the bed, continuing my inspection. Damirius' voice penetrates the quiet, reading the letter aloud,

"WHOEVER CAN HELP,

*PLEASE. COME. SOMETHING EVIL IS HERE. IN THE LAKE.
SO MANY DEAD. IT TAKES THEM BACK THERE.
HELP. PLEASE.
HELP.
E. BURIMIR'*

He pauses for a moment, "How did you know she owned the inn, though?"

"There was a wax seal on the envelope," I answer, eyes focused on the lower portion of the wall and the connections to the floor. Water has soaked the interior. "It had the initials of the inn's name. Put two and two together when I saw the sign outside."

I can't help the swell of pride that bubbles inside when I spot Damirius' impressed grin out of the corner of my eye. The bubbling happiness quickly evaporates as I continue to look at the rest of the room. Damp marks, dripping wallpaper, and the stench of mildew seems to cover each section of the room. I scowl. "What I would like to know," I say aloud, "Is how every square inch of this town is completely soaked."

10

Damirius

I turn to face Nylani, an exaggerated rise to my eyebrow. "Maybe... the weather?"
A smirk plays on my lips; enjoying the exasperated groan and rolling of eyes as she huffs away from me. I know this isn't the ideal time, but it's the only thing keeping this gnawing, unsettling feeling in my stomach away.

"You know what I mean, you dunderhead," she says, though not unkindly. I chuckle to myself. I've been called worse. Finally, I shrug the bag off my shoulder. It squelches against the damp floorboard. I shudder. Gross.

I look up, seeing her watching me expectantly. I tilt my head in a mocking question.
"What?" I act confused. "It was just a suggestion, Tiny," I finally release my grin, enjoying the one-sided banter.

She huffs, arms folding over her chest as she grumbles something about making better ones. My laughter fights to be released, but I swallow it down. She looks like a toddler; face scrunched in a temper, with eyebrows furrowed so far down they could touch the bridge of her nose. It was adorable, really.

A moment passes between us, and her expression softens again. She unfolds her arms and sits forward, stroking her cheek. "I mean," she starts, her voice slow and deliberate, "Well, whatever this thing is, it's gotta be in the lake."

"Right...?" My voice trails off, wanting her to continue. I want to see where this train of thought is going.
"But it shouldn't be able to drench the entire town by itself, right? I mean, even the entrance was waterlogged!"
"Well, judging by the hole we saw, it's definitely a huge beast," I reply.

My mind begins to whir, trying to connect fragments of ideas together. "Maybe it causes huge waves when it hits or leaves the water?"

"That's a possibility...," she agrees, "Or maybe it could manipulate the water?"
"Hm," I muse, "Elemental manipulation isn't that uncommon."

I think back to my own abilities; most tieflings are gifted with some kind of elemental magic. Mine is water manipulation. Mother always berated me for not using them enough - or making it stronger - but there never really was much need for it. Still, it's a good party trick, at least.

"We need to explore more. Get a better lay of the land, and hopefully some more clues on what this thing even is." Nylani finally concludes. I nod my head in agreement. There's not much we can do by going in blind.

I turn my head to the window, watching the dark sky become almost void-like with how little stars appear through the slats of wood. With the adrenaline from the day finally running its course through me, sleep pulls against my eyelids. I find myself yearning for rest.

"I suggest some sleep first, though," I yawn, "You know... For a pair of fresh eyes, right?"

"Good idea." I can almost hear the smirk in her voice. I choose to ignore it as I finally kick off my shoes and dive into the bed. Wet clothes be damned - sleep was one of my favourite things, even if it meant sharing a creaking, damp bed.

I toss and turn on the bed, careful to not knock the grumpy elf at the end of it. Loud protests come from the squeaking bed frame as I adjust myself. Eventually, I curl into a ball against the wall, accepting that this will be as comfortable as I can get.

The sound of soaked leather peeling away from skin fills the stagnant night air. Then the thud of a boot hitting the floor. I can feel her shift on the bed behind me; her movements are slow, almost hesitant. Carefully, I crane my head to the side - just enough to be able to spot her in my periphery.

Silently thanking whichever deities are watching this awkward moment, I watch her as she readies herself for sleep. She works silently, her face almost vacant. Her cloak is stripped away and folded in an instant. She places it atop her bag. She unties the first few fastenings of her tunic, but then pauses.

I quickly shift, hoping it looks as though I was just moving in my sleep. I keep my back to her, curling up as much as I can so that she can understand that I'm trying to give her space. This bed is too damned small.

My knees are nearly touching my chin. I feel the bed dip; the mattress sinks further down as she climbs in behind me. The bed creaks as she shifts a little. At least it's not only me that's uncomfortable in this awful bed. Finally, she settles for the evening; her weight sinks into the mattress, and her breathing finally finds a steady pace. My head grows heavy, and I finally feel myself drift away.

I startle awake in my childhood home; the warm breeze of summer laps at my skin. The smell of the familiar farmscape eases me. Home. I take a deep breath of the rustic, earthy terrain. The sound of a thousand footsteps running amok surrounds me. *Oh, I've missed that sound.*

The squeals and hollering of my siblings fills the open air of the farm. The pigs join in and snort as loud as they can. They must be chasing Betsy and her piglets again. I'm not sure who enjoys it more -

the kids, or the pigs. I chuckle to myself. It's good to be home.

"Miri?" a familiar voice calls, "Is that you, dear?"
"Mama!" I yell back.
I turn on the spot, trying to find the owner of the soft, comforting voice. Then, I see my darling Mother. Her silhouette stands by the open kitchen windows, steaming pie in hands. I can't stop myself; my feet charge towards her. As I close the distance, I see her greying hair that rests in a low bun. My charge slows.

She's aged a lot since I've last been home. Her smile crinkles her eyes. Her pale, paper-thin skin has more wrinkles than before. My heart sinks in my chest; the excitement of seeing Mother quickly diminishes. The euphoria of being home becomes tainted with the realisation that I spent too much time away. Guilt fills my stomach.

I continue towards the cottage. Though, the trek seems to take forever. Regardless of how many steps I take, the distance doesn't seem to change at all. Actually, no. If anything, the distance is getting farther. Mother's face is no longer clear any more. Soon, only her bright yellow pinafore stands out against the shrinking image of my childhood home.

"Come on, darling!" Mother calls out to me, "Before your food goes cold!" Her voice sounds miles away. Her normally chipper, perky voice echoes and fades across the expanding landscape. The cottage stretches out before me; the pathway becoming a strained, taut line in an empty expanse around me. "I'm trying, Mama!" I yell, my throat straining. "You're too far!"

Silence follows. I doubt she can hear me anymore. The path seems never ending, now. I can barely see the microscopic image of my home. It looks dwarfed by the endless stretch of empty countryside that encompasses it. Begrudgingly, I continue to walk for what feels like hours. No matter how many steps I take, the cottage stays fixed far in the horizon. My muscles ache; each step reawakens the pain. Finally, I stop.

The cottage taunts me ahead. Exasperated, I crumple to the floor. My head turns, looking behind me, and the sight of an endless path greets me. The path stretches to nothing more than a fine line in an empty void. My stomach drops.

Something suddenly slams into my back. My face nearly collides into the dirt, but I brace my hands into it instead. I push myself up and twist, trying to locate my attacker. I glance down, and see the face of my baby sister, Arwyn. Her round, pale human face shines up at me, her wide, gappy-toothed smile beaming. Her hair has grown into copper braids. The last time I saw her, her hair just about touched her shoulders. Her hair was wild then; her curls made it look like her head was alight.

"Big bro!" She squeals, "You came back!"
"I told you I would," I tease.
The sinking feeling continues to sit in my gut, but I try to ignore it. Her piercing blue eyes stare up at me. For some reason, this unsettles me more. Her eyes seem vacant. Her smile isn't touching her eyes.
"So how much money did you make this time, big bro?" She asks, snapping me out of my thoughts.
"Huh?"

I had heard what she had said. I just wish I didn't; Mama always made sure to never let the young ones know. She didn't want the younger ones to stress about money. She had made that mistake with me.

"Well, that's all you're good for, right?" Arwyn continues, her grin deepening. The corners of her mouth almost touch her ears. It's unsettling. "That's why Mama keeps you around."

My voice disappears. My chest aches, as if she had sucker punched it. I force a breath. "Arwyn..." I start. My voice shakes. I clear my throat. "Arwyn, that's not polite." Thankfully, my voice sounds stern. I lick at my dried lips.

"Neither are your clientele, you whore," Arwyn sneers. Her voice reverberates around me. I can feel my bones rattle. "All those people you bring to bed, and no one treats you nicely." She continues, contempt clear in her tone. A lower, more insidious voice joins her shrill mockery. "Maybe it's because they know how much of a lowlife you really are. You're nothing more than the cow crap that cakes the bottom of your shoes."

I quickly step back from Arwyn, who cackles maniacally. The corners of her mouth have stretched to almost touch her eyes. But her eyes stay wide, staring deep into my soul.

"Who are you?" I choke out. Another pang hits my

chest. I cough, the air rapidly leaving my lungs. The image of Arwyn bellows a demonic, guttural laugh. The overlapping voices cackle in unison. The sound drills into my head.

Slowly, she paces towards me. The maniacal laughter erupts from her menacingly still, sneering face. Immediately, I back away. She continues her approach. I almost don't feel the floor below me as I retreat as fast as I can. I need a way out. My head whips around, and I'm met with nothing. No cottage. No farmland. No dirt path. We stand in an expanded nothingness. My pounding heart plummets to my stomach.

"I'm you." Arwyn's mouth is no longer moving. The voice continues to swirl around me. The duet of voices becomes a symphony of many voices, and a singular voice all at once. The sheer expanse of its reverberation shakes my core. "I'm what you really think. How you really feel."

I shake my head, and the entity laughs harder. The mocking, jeering laugh shakes the horrifyingly large expanse of space around me. If anything was visible, I would presume it's spinning. Nausea hits me like a hurricane. I clutch my stomach, silently praying that the vertigo will go. My eyes stay trained on Arwyn. Or the monster in the shape of Arwyn. I can't tell.

Whatever it is, it tilts its head as it looks at me. The malicious smile stays plastered on its face. I can feel myself shaking, but I try to hold it together. The last thing I need is for this thing to realise I'm terrified. Our eyes lock as I force myself to stand up again. My stomach feels like it's somersaulting, but I ignore it.

It looks up at me, still grinning, as the skin on Arwyn's face bubbles and melts. Like candle wax, it droops and sags down her face. My body goes to hurl, but nothing comes out. I choke, gasping for air, but no reprieve comes. A clawed hand grabs my face and forces my head upwards. Filling my vision, the bubbling face of my darling baby sister becomes a mirror image of my own. Pale skin blotches with hues of purple and pink until the white canvas turns mauve. The temples extend and stretch into the shape of my horns. Gaps in its gums fill and point into my fangs. And the mouth smirks at me.

"You can fool yourself, all you want, little Damirius." The impeding, thunderous voice continues, "But I know what you really are."

The smug, menacing imitation of myself glowers at me. The impossibly large smile suddenly flips into a snarling frown. Its head rears back before using the momentum to slam into my skull. I brace myself, closing my eyes as I prepare for an intense collision against my forehead and nose. But no pain comes. My eyes slowly open, and I witness the torso and legs of the imposter pass through me. Then, in an instant, my world turns black, and I fall, tumbling, into a void that hovers below.

11

Nylani

The morning comes quicker than I anticipated. Thin glares of light hit my eyelids, disturbing my sleep and coaxing my eyes to open. Despite me tossing and turning, trying to return to the realm of slumber, I can't seem to fall back to sleep. Eventually, I admit defeat. I stretch. My shoulder pops; I blame the mattress. I could feel the springs digging into me throughout the night. Still, it's better than sleeping on the waterlogged floor boards. The thought alone makes me grimace.

Finally, I relent, accepting that I have to get up. I try to sit up in the cramped bed, only to fall back onto the stiff mattress. An unexpected weight anchors me down. A muscular, mauve-tinted weight. Damirius' arm rests along my stomach. He squeezes softly as I try squirming to my freedom. Regardless of how much I move, he stays asleep. "Hey," I groan. I shake his arm. No response. "Oi! Get off me, you big oaf."

Nothing. I huff in annoyance. Frustration threatens to bubble into violence. Begrudgingly, I shove the temptation to smack him down. Teammates don't hit each other. I have to remind myself of that. An exasperated sigh expels outwards. Just as I begin to accept my fate, he shifts against me. Hopefully, he'll move himself. I catch my breath, watching him attentively. His torso twists and stretches, before his weight collapses onto my chest.

His nose presses against my temple; his arm wrapping around me like a cobra ensnaring its prey. I can feel the warmth of a leg in between my calves. Bewilderment keeps me still. From the limited view I have under the lanky dolt, all I can see is his neck, a shoulder, and the dilapidated ceiling behind him. A few faded bruises hint under the skin of his neck. Gross.

I try to push him upwards with my free hand, but to no avail. He simply hugs me tighter. The hand pinned by his stomach has begun to lose feeling. I try to shift from underneath him and I find myself more stuck than before. His shoulder sinks into my neck. I gasp for air and, thankfully, he has enough sense still in him to move. Albeit, just enough for me to breathe again. Warm breath tickles the tips of my ears, and I can feel myself burning up. Damn him. Damn him and his warm, heavy body to the depths of whatever godsforsaken lands there are. His face smothers itself into my hair; his heavy breathing flutters stray hair across my face. The sensation somewhat soothes me; the steady rise and fall of his chest somehow calming. I sink into the bed, accepting he won't wake, but hoping he will soon. Then my windpipe gets crushed by his shoulder again.

Right. That's it. My legs entrap the one he has jammed in between them, and I use my free hand to grab the shoulder pushing against my throat. I shove up and to the right, pushing his body over mine. Suddenly, we're both completely flipped; he lies on his back, with me above him. And he stays asleep.

"WHAT?!" I scream, incredulous. After all that, he continues to sleep?! How heavy a sleeper is he?!

Irritation overwhelms me. I want to hit him. He nearly choked me and he's not even conscious! How obtuse can one person be?! My fist slams into one of the flat pillows and it bursts from the force. The dense, compact filling flies out. Some of it splatters over Damirius' face. And his eyes snap open.

"Woah!" he exclaims. My jaw hangs open, in complete and utter disbelief. My fist clenches again, and it takes all my strength not to punch him. His eyes finally notice me above him. A sly smile stretches his lips.
"You know, I could get used to this view."
I finally hit him.

My palm collides with his right cheek; the smack loud enough to leave a resounding noise of satisfaction in my ears. I climb off the bed, pulling my somewhat dried boots onto my feet. I suppose I'll have to get used to everything being relatively damp whilst we're here. Unfortunately.

"What was that for?!," Damirius' indignant voice whines from behind me. I turn to look at him. He's finally sat up, his hand soothing his offended cheek. His face is a perfect picture of aggrieved surprise. His wide, puppy dog eyes are enough to make me laugh, but I keep it together. He deserved it.

"You're a heavy sleeper," I respond, as nonchalantly as I can. "I was just making sure you were awake." He whines as I turn my back to him again. I have to stifle the grin that threatens to expose me. I duck my head down, feigning tying my boots. If he knows I'm laughing I'll never hear the end of it.

"That doesn't explain why you decided my chest was the perfect seat, doll," he coos. My amusement is quickly replaced by disgust. The bed creaks as he shuffles to the edge. I resurface from pretending to tie my shoes, to find his face mere inches from mine. My stomach flips, the startling image of his honey-gold eyes filling my vision making me a little unsteady.

"If you want a trial run all you have to do is ask." The lower, suggestive tone to his voice almost makes me gag. Ugh. His pointed teeth glisten, his smirk stretching impossibly wide. He leans closer to me. I swallow the bile that threatens to surface. I keep my face neutral. If he knows he's gotten to me, then I lose. And I won't lose.

"You know, I think I preferred you asleep," I muse. My hand shoves against his face and forcibly pushes him backwards. His back collides with the mattress, and his skull with the wall. Although the wind gets knocked out of him, a wheezing laugh still manages to emanate from the insufferable man.

"I definitely don't, Tiny."
I ignore the flirtatious jab. "Get up. We've got a monster to find."
Damirius nods, albeit disgruntled, "Fine. Let's get to it, then."

With a secure lock of the door, and with me double checking that it cannot be opened, we descend the stairs. As we reach the bottom, I hear a quiet muttering.

My ears strain, trying to figure out where the voice is coming from. I crouch. Slowly, I scoot forward. After a moment, I hear the voice again. It sounds like it's coming from the back - probably the kitchen. The hairs on the back of my neck stand up. Something isn't right. I turn to Damirius. He's crouched behind me, though he looks very confused. My finger rises to my lips. He nods in understanding, though he still looks perplexed. I turn away. I'll explain later to him. I'm just glad he's following instructions.

Slowly, I continue creeping along the miniscule foyer. The doors to the kitchen seem so far away, yet it'll only take a few steps to get there. It's eerily quiet now. Despite the walls being paper-thin, I can't hear anything. Only the sound of my own heart pounding in my ears reverberates in my skull.

I stay low; the dense musk of the damp floor pungent from this height. My eyes nearly water from the intensity. I scuttle across the broken floorboards, intensely aware of the sound of my footsteps. Finally, I reach the loosely held up double doors to the back. Snappy whispering comes from behind the doors. Tentatively, I push a door open. It only makes a few millimetres before it creaks. The squeal of the door moving rattles my bones. I stay frozen; hoping that whatever entity lies beyond doesn't notice.

"Who's there?!" A voice snaps. I stay frozen, barely breathing. My eyes strain through the miniscule gap between door and frame, hoping to catch a glimpse of whoever was talking.
Heavy footfalls shuffle around the kitchen. A

clanging of metallic utensils fill the air; the sharp twangs almost painful in the tense silence. Then I see her. The familiar hunched back and bulging eyes fill the gap of the doorway. But, her eyes are a startling milky white. No pupils are visible, and the entirety of her eyes seem clouded over. Obvious tear tracks cover her face. It looks like she's been crying for hours. I remain still. It doesn't seem as though she can see me. I'm grateful for that, though the pang of guilt is still very prominent. Her face turns away from the door, and she stumbles farther into the kitchen.

"Stupid Egret," she suddenly snarls. Her voice is remarkably quiet, but sounds horrifyingly loud in the stifling tranquillity. "Mother is ashamed. Stupid, mean Egret."

A sudden smack of wood against skin bursts into the air. My blood runs cold. Another smack ricochets through the building. My limbs lock into place as fear tenses my body. Though I can hear her yelling between the aggressive hits against herself, I can't discern what she's saying any more. My ears are trained on the violent hits against skin.

"You are nothing more than a pitiful bully, Egret

Burimir!" a voice yells. The sudden shout startles me, and I nearly tumble backwards. The voice sounds almost like a contorted combination of the woman's own voice and a gravelly, guttural counterpart. A strange familiarity comes from the deeper voice, but I shake the thought away. No. I refuse to believe it's him.

A rapid firing of sharp smacks ring in the air. I have to curl into myself to stop my magic flying out. My arms shake from the tensity I hold myself together with. My stomach flips before it plummets. The sound of her crying almost makes me vomit.

An object clatters onto the floor, the sharp sound splitting through the sobs. The hairs on the back of my neck are stuck up like pinpricks. Silence suffocates the inn, aside from the gentle, shaken sobs that leak out of the innkeeper.

My breath catches, almost choking me as I lean closer against the door. I daren't make any noise for fear of alerting the elder. Or whatever plagues her mind. I refuse to think about the voice any more. I can see Ms Burimir's back. She's hunched over, hands over her head. Her quiet sobs echo through the empty kitchen.

"Please. Get out of my head. Please."
She shakes and crumples in a corner, disappearing from my sight. I can't seem to move away. Gasping sobs break between her near whimpers.

"I was young. I-I was stupid then," she blabbers. Her quiet pleading grows into a desperate beg. Another terrified whimper escapes from Ms Burimir. The shaking weeps fill the stagnant, tense air. My chest feels heavy. I keep silent; my body trembles.

"Please, stop," she pleads. "Just... Just go away." Her whimpers turn into full sobs. My stomach sinks further, the motion almost making me hurl. I strain to listen past Ms Burimir's sobbing, hoping to catch the voice of the person she's conversing with. However, I can't hear anyone – or anything - responding to Egret's pleas.

"Stop it!" Ms Burimir suddenly screams. The screech echoes in the empty air; it rings in my ears, my already shaking hands now trembling. I strain again, listening for a reply, but there's no response. Shuffling comes from within the kitchen; Egret must be moving. My eyes stay focused on the floor.

I spot a pair of well-worn, spotted slippers scraping along the crackled tile floor. Then, I notice a wooden spoon not far from the slippered feet. This must be the 'tool' Egret was using before.

Slowly, my body leans forward, ready to sneak in to retrieve it. A desire to keep it away from Egret fills me. My hand gradually inches forward, my fingertips almost able to grasp the handle.
Then, in one fell swoop, Egret leans down and her face is near inches from mine. She retrieves the spoon. My breath is quickly removed from my lungs. It takes a tremendous effort to not cough and pull some air back.

My eyes stay trained on her horrifying, milky eyes. Slowly, I retreat. With a snap, Egret's face turns towards me. I can feel myself quake. Her eyes are red raw from crying. Tears effortlessly glide out of her bulging eyes. Bruises smatter her forehead and cheeks. I want to cry. I want to scream.

Instead, I let out a shaky breath. It's not clear how well Ms Burimir can see, but since I haven't been pounced upon, I'll presume it's not well. I can't help but stare at Ms Burimir as she persistently pivots her head this way and that, as if she's trying to follow a noise that I simply cannot hear. My feet gingerly take a step backwards, then stop.

My ears almost hurt from straining so much, trying to pick up any noise my footsteps make. Suddenly, Ms Burimir's face contorts into a frown; her brows creasing and her jowls drooping. A tear rolls down her cheek as her eyes remain open, unblinking. Ms Burimir pauses, her face pointed to the ceiling as she listens intently to nothing. Her lip quivering as she continues to weep silently. More tears stream down her withered, wrinkled face.

Old hands shake as the wooden spoon raises above her bulbous head. The bony fingers tighten their grip against the thin handle. The ferocity of her grip causes her knuckles to whiten. The crying continues, though quieter than before; a defeated whimper of a hapless victim. Suddenly, the older woman's face snaps to face me. A harrowing sneer pulls at her sorrowful face. The corners of her mouth pull at the sagging cheeks; an impossibly large, menacing smile. Her mouth moves, but the voice enters my mind instead.
"Hello, darling." The voice was the same deep tone that joined Ms Burimir's earlier. The same voice I had pleaded to not recognise. The same voice that

finally found me. "It's nice to see you again." A strike hits Ms Burimir's temple, and she howls in pain.

I rapidly retreat from the door, uncaring of how much noise I make. Damirius catches me. The repeated slaps and screams that reverberate behind me are haunting. My chest is ready to explode.

I grab Damirius' arm and run, quietly thankful to not feel any resistance. We exit the inn rapidly, my feet barely touching the ground as I bolt from the doorway. From the slap of wood on skin. From blind, milky white eyes. From the cries.

We approach the outskirts of the lake, my pace finally slowing. I can breathe again; my chest heaves as I take large gulps of air in. My body shakes violently, like a leaf in a hurricane, but I force my limbs to still. He's not physically here, I think to myself. I hope.

12

Damirius

I stumble behind Nylani, my outstretched arm pulling me along at a rapid pace. The chill morning air slams against my face, burning my eyes and nose. The hair on my arms and neck prickle. My feet stumble clumsily behind me as I get dragged along. Nylani doesn't seem to notice, as she continues charging forward.

I don't know what she saw, but from the glance I got of her face, it was nothing good. Finally, we stop. By the looks of it, we're near the lake. She whips around to face me, her eyes wide. From the dim light of the morning, I can barely make out her face. But her eyes seem to be bulging from her head. I nearly try to reach for her, but I stop myself.

"Something's in her head," she suddenly blurts out. Her speech is quick. Panic seeps into her tone. "Talking to her, I think. It was torturing her." Her breathing is ragged, her chest heaving. I step closer to her, ignoring her babbling. Instead, I place my hands on her shoulders, catching her attention. She flinches at first, but seemingly settles herself.

"Deep breath in," I softly remind her. She looks at me, bewildered. Deep curls stick to her sweat-plastered face. Big, doe-like eyes stare up at me. I can feel her shaking under my hands. I don't mention it to her. Finally, she takes a lung full of air in.

"Good," I count to ten in my head. "Now let it out." She complies. It doesn't fix everything, but it gets her to stop shaking as bad. She repeats it, her composure steeling each time she does it.
"She was terrified."

"I can imagine," I respond, calmly. As heartless as it makes me sound, I can't help but feel a little relieved. If the person can mess with people's minds, they could probably interfere with people's dreams. And someone was definitely interfering with my dreams.

I look at Nylani, who stares at the lake. She stares so intensely that I'm surprised the water hasn't bubbled over and produced steam.

"Alright," I finally say. My voice seems to startle her out of her thoughts. "Well… It's not much to go on. But, it's information nonetheless." I muse, watching her closely. "Did you happen to hear the voice?"

If it was the same deep voice I heard, it would definitely narrow it down to one suspect. I couldn't imagine having to deal with two assholes.
"No." It was almost instant. She blurted it with such ferocity I don't dare to argue it. But her body shifts, closing herself away from me. She continues to look towards the lake. Whatever she saw - or heard - must have shaken her horribly.

"We need to get more," she decides. Her voice continues to shake, but there's a determination behind it that I can't dismiss. "We need to find something. Anything." I simply nod; we have nothing else to do but to get more information.

We start our search with the nearby mass of homes and structures that reside alongside the inn. It takes a while to inch Nylani in the direction of the inn, and when we arrive at the mass of crumpled brickwork, it's near impossible to find anything. Moss and vines blanket the dilapidated relics of homes, making it hard to distinguish where houses end and begin. Until, eventually, a rickety house on the far right catches my eye.

A faint yellow glow resides within it. The house's entire structure has an intense lean as it uses the hill to keep itself upright. It's sloped alongside the incline of a hill, and squashes around some other houses. It looks almost as though the other houses are propping the home upright; though, I won't be surprised if that's actually the case. The flat roof seems caved in. A gentle concave shape at the top completes the malleable design of the entire house. I step closer, soaking in the entirety of the miniscule hovel.

Individual planks of wood are sunken into the moist dirt to create a quick-fix wall. The haphazardness of the assembly creates a derelict fencing, rather than a stable wall for someone to shelter behind. I nudge Nylani gently, getting her attention. My chin juts out, pointing in the general direction of the house.

"Seems like we may have a witness or two," I quietly notify her. I watch her intensely, trying to figure out how she's feeling. She's trembling. I go to reach for her, but stop myself. A sinister, malicious jeer invades my head for a split second. The flash of my own distorted face grinning at me startles me.

"Looks like we do," she agrees, her voice distracting me from whatever is invading my mind. Carefully, we venture towards the ruinous remnants of homes. My knuckles hit against a plank of wood I presume to be the door. A moment of silence passes. Then, it slowly inches open to reveal a young human couple.

The pair look dishevelled; both have dark circles under their eyes. Their faces are pasty and hollow, as if they hadn't eaten in weeks. Their pasty skin stretches over the sharp points of their jaws and cheeks. Hints of blue colour their lips, and they shake under the biting wind.

Bony arms cross over their torsos, holding onto their biceps as they hunch over themselves. The smaller of the two - a woman - stares at Nylani with a hungry wonder. It makes me nervous. I stand closer to Nylani, almost blocking her from the woman's view. Cracked lips open and exhale a shuddering breath. When the woman finally speaks, her voice is croaky. It's barely a whisper.

"You're here... To get rid of that... Thing. Aren't you?" the woman stammers, her entire body shaking. "Tha... That giant rock thing in the lake. Please tell me you are."

Nylani's eyes widen; new information. And so quickly, too. Nylani steps closer to the woman, her arms opening slightly. The woman shuffles closer to Nylani, encapsulating herself in a worn, thin, shawl.
"We are," Nylani reassures her, her voice soft yet enquiring. "What can you tell me about this thing?"

The woman flinches, clasping her ear like something is ringing in it. "It... it - uh - *whispers*, to us," she fumbles, trying to hurry her speech. "It... It destroyed most of the harbour. Takes people away."

There's a pause. Tears gently roll down her face as her hollow, brown eyes dart between Nylani's and my own. She aggressively rubs at her left ear, "It- It's whispering at me now. It's angry." Her voice wavers, the woman's tears falling easily now. "Angry that I'm telling you, I think."

The woman cries, her tiny frame wobbling under her. Long hair sticks to her face as she weeps. Instinctively, I cup the woman's arm. Trying to be soothing and gentle, I hold her loosely. Slowly, she regains her composure. Deep, deliberate breaths rattle the woman's frail figure. If she inhales any harder, I worry her ribs will crack.
"What is the voice telling you?" I ask, softly.

"That... That I'm worthless. Ugly." Dry sobs fill the air. The woman's chest heaves as she gasps for air between her cries. "Reminds me of all the things I did wrong."

The sickening memories of last night resurface; it sounds too familiar to my nightmare. But... how do I ask without scaring her any more? I can't afford to feed this woman any more fear. If I do, I fear she may collapse. I ruminate on the thought for a moment.

"Is it...?" I start, trying to find the right words. "Is it in dreams that he talks to you? Or while you're awake?"
There. If I act as though I don't know, hopefully that won't scare her. Though, I can see Nylani

staring at me through the corner of my eye. I gulp, relaxing my face enough to look neutral.

The gaunt looking woman shudders a breath. "It - uh - It starts in your dreams. At least, that's how me and Grant started." She motions to the man beside her. "We started getting nightmares. Then it changed to happenin' all the time. Seein' horrible things. Hearin' horrible things." She shudders, and I have to stop myself from joining her. Great. At least I know what to look forward to.

Nylani steps forward. Her face is a mixture of fury and concern. And I'm not sure which emotion is going to win. As if answering my silent thoughts, she forces her shoulders to relax and lets her anger melt away. She crouches in front of the woman, her eyes softening.

"Just one more question, and then we'll let you rest, ma'am," Nylani soothes. The woman visibly relaxes, her shoulders and head sagging slightly. She nods to Nylani, and I step back a little. The cramped home doesn't give us much room, but I want to give as much as I can.

"The voice," Nylani starts, "Does it come to you

mentally, or is it from the big rock creature? Do you know?"

The woman thinks for a moment. "There's only one voice," she finally says. "But it gets stronger when the rock monster is out of the water." She stops, thinking hard. "I don't know why, but I thought the voice came from the monster. But now I'm not sure."

Nylani smiles. Though, I can feel the sadness seep through. "It could be because everything happened at once. You just couldn't see the connection," she muses. The woman nods in agreement. "Now it's all out in the open and you've had a moment to think it all out, it's beginning to make sense. Right?" Her voice is impossibly soft.

A deep melancholy has washed over Nylani; her eyes are downcast, her back hunches, even her perpetual stony stare has softened to a saddened frown.

"Yeah," the woman replies. "I suppose it is making sense now." For the first time since we arrived, the woman finally smiles. It's a weak, tiny thing, but I can't help feeling a huge wave of relief.

I turn to look at Nylani, startled to find she's already looking at me. Her eyes bore into mine; a flash of worry ghosts over her brows. I hold my stare. A sudden flash of Arwyn's melting face jumps in front of my eyes.

Nausea stirs my stomach. My chest flutters, and I can't breathe. In the back of my mind, I can hear the spiteful vitriol trying to worm its way to the front.
Disgusting.
Insignificant.
Whore.
I visibly shake my head, as if that will make the voice go away. Nylani continues to stare at me. My eyes drop to the floor. Shame rushes through me. The voice gets louder. More abrasive. More bold.
Worthless.
Spineless.
Disgraceful.

Dull nails rest atop my skin, shocking me out of my combative mind. The nubs of nails are far too short to do any damage, though the sudden contact was unexpected. My head turns to the woman who holds me, her eyes wide in terror. I clasp a hand over her trembling ones.

"It's... It's t-tellin' me I'm next," the emaciated woman whimpers. Heavy sobs shake her body. Her partner, Grant, swoops to her side and tries to soothe her. His bony hands rub circles on her pointed shoulders. I shuffle back, trying to give them some space. I glance at Nylani.

She's also moved back, watching the woman sob helplessly into her partner's chest. There's a taunt tension in her jaw. However, her eyes were wide. Terrified. It was hard to not sink into the terror that was palpable in this home.

I look back at the woman. Her once brown eyes were now marred by a milky white glaze. It takes everything in me to not yell. Her eyes are pupiless. They look at nothing, but she continues to stare with such intensity. A steady stream of tears continuously fall from her eyes. My stomach drops. I want to scream. I want to yell. Hells, I don't even know if I would be able to.

"I do not know if you can hear me," Nylani says, her voice low and tense. "But I promise to destroy this thing. You will have your home back. I will make sure of it," she vows with ferocity. I can feel the heat of her anger simmer from her. The few inches between us does little to lessen the blaze.

The lady nods her head furiously. Her unblinking eyes stay blind, but manage to direct themselves to Nylani's face. Her bottom lip wobbles as she squeaks out, "Please... Please get it out of my head."

A sob escapes her as she finally collapses into her partner, weeping silently and clutching her head. Her lithe fingers wrap into her hair and cling to her scalp. Her body shakes - from either fear or the biting cold wind that begins to pick up. Both are as bad as the other.

My eyes move over to Grant, watching as he wraps his tiny lover in a protective embrace. He's also crying. A pang of pity hits my chest. They've gone through too much, it seems. And they continue to go through more. The gauntness of his face shows his exhaustion and stress; most likely a constant flow of them both. It doesn't seem as though the people here have known peace for a while now.

Tears seem almost a permanent fixture to his face. The streaks on his cheeks break up the residue and dirt that covers him from head to toe. The pair look virtually the same; tired, sorrowful, and lost. Slowly, his dark eyes rise to look at me.

"Please," he whispers. His voice is broken, cracking with disuse. "She's all I have left." My heart hurts. A billion questions fill my head; where was their family? Their friends? Did they have children? I refuse to ask.

"We will do what we can," I reply. My voice wavers a little. I clear my throat. He doesn't need to feel my fear. He has enough of his own.

I look back at Nylani again. Her jaw is set and tense. Her eyes lock onto mine. Those bright, light grey eyes hold a fire in them that almost scorches me. I nod curtly; she responds in kind. I leave the home, and step into the barren, broken streets of the harbour.

The morning chill seeps into my bones. The wind cuts through me like a knife in butter. The damp air clings to my hair, curling it, and my breath mists around my face. Shaking hands cusp around my mouth; praying the heat of my breath will warm my numb fingers.

13

Nylani

"Nylani ... Everything okay?" Damirius probes, once I leave the couple's residence. His head tilts down towards me, almost as if gloating his height. I wave a dismissive hand.

"No one should feel unsafe," I simply remark. "Especially from some weird-ass lake monster that gets in their head."
I don't want to indulge him in my knowledge of the owner of the voice. It would bring up too many questions. Too many memories. He doesn't need to know all of that.

The sinister atmosphere makes the hair on the back of my neck prickle upwards. My shoulders peak towards my ears, trying to shake away the feeling that I'm being watched. My chest tightens. This is too familiar. I hate it.

I hug myself tightly. I force my lungs to open; breathe in, hold it, breathe out. I repeat the cycle.

Slowly, my panic subsides. He's not here. He won't take me again.

"We need to look for more clues," I finally decide. Anything to keep my mind busy will be pleasant. "We need to get an idea of what this thing looks like. Or even just how big it is."
"Makes sense," Damirius agrees, "Best bet is to just go to the lake, right?"

Reluctantly, I agree. My feet immediately take off to the lake. Damirius trails behind me. A small twinge of dismay settles uneasily in my chest. My hand itches to reach out. To hold onto his ridiculous shirt. To grasp his hand like a lifeline. My head violently shakes the thought out. No. We have a harbour to help. What good would holding his hand like a child do?

My eyes scan around the lake, hoping to catch any hint as to what this 'giant rock thing' could be. Mud squelches under my boots as we traverse the grassland that surrounds the bank of the lake. I continue to inspect the ground.

Between the rubble and rummaging through the debris, there's nothing here that I haven't already seen. Large dips in the dirt, broken shambles of homes, and reminders that the homes once had life in them. My eyes quickly move away from the personal items. I don't think I can manage another outburst like yesterday. My body aches from the previous rampage.

My feet move carefully through the destruction around me, before noticing another crater. I pause. Water rests within this indent. Dust from broken brickwork coagulates within it. But that isn't what catches my attention. My eyes raise, inspecting the ground beyond me.

"Oh. Oh no," I mumble. My hand motions for Damirius to join me. My eyes stay fixated on the floor, as if expecting the craters to come alive. A part of me considers it a possibility. From what I can see, a trail of deep, circular indents travel through a passageway of where homes once were. My head turns to the left.

Similar tracks create another pathway there, as well. My head turns again. Another. And another. And another. Tracks of the colossal beasts' path surrounds us. The cavity we inspected the day previous is part of a track. Each pit I can see is encumbered with rubble, water and slick mud. My stomach drops. My voice is less than a whisper, "These are definitely footprints."

"That's… uh, That's definitely a problem," Damirius' voice joins me, on my right. His movements slow as he finally reaches me. Water clings to his clothes. Suddenly, my mind begins to accelerate.

My eyes rapidly scan the hole that encompasses us. I begin to feverishly clean. Habit makes me organise the rubble. Between the pair of us, we hope between the current crater and its nearby companions. Soon, the tracks of the behemoth start to appear as we clear the clutter. With the debris removed, it's easier to follow the footsteps. I pause. Stepping backwards, my eyes start adapting and join the newest footprints to one of the tracks.

"Seems as though it mostly walks in straight lines," I contemplate aloud. My eyes continue following the trails. They almost look like roads from the sheer size of them.
"Could it be because of its size?" Damirius chimes in. "I guess it's really heavy, so maybe it takes a lot of effort to move?"

"Seems like it," I agree. The vague thought of its magnitude is enough to make me shiver.

"It seems like it could be a golem," I say, turning to look at Damirius. I pause. He stares at me, blankly. "It's a giant being made of rock and stone," I explain. He nods like he understands. I hope he does. "Normally, they're exceptionally large and just like to hit things. Tend to stay in forestry and overgrown terrain."
I stop. My mind goes into overdrive; rapid facts of golems slamming into the forefront of my brain. Why here? Why is he using one? Nothing makes sense. My brows furrow together in concentration.

"Though... I've never known one to have the ability to communicate through telepathy. Or even taunt someone, for that matter," I say slowly, trying to concoct something other than the idea of that old bastard being here.
The idea itself is washy. I hope Damirius latches onto it. I scratch the back of my neck. My magic begins to whir within me. I can feel the heat rising; stress is building. I look towards the towering tiefling.
"Why is this one so special?" I ask aloud, more for myself than to him.

He hums, deep in thought. His silence worries me more than I'd like to admit. It means he has some ideas, but doesn't want to share. Fuck. My heart sinks, slowly. Agonisingly slow.

I had hoped if he latched onto the half-baked idea of a sentient golem that we could try to explain everything else away. Now I'm left with the horrible truth. He's here, somewhere. Somehow. And he knows I'm alive.

I can feel myself trembling. I grab my arms, trying to get them to stop. We stand in silence for a moment longer; the lake as still as our conversation. A slow chill creeps up my spine. I shudder. The wind begins to pick up. I wrap my cloak around me, but to no avail. Eventually, the frigidity seeps into my bones, my teeth chatter.

The dull ache is unpleasant but bearable. I clench my teeth together to stop them chattering. A painful iciness begins to crawl up each individual notch of my spine. A pang of sudden shooting harsh bitterness hits my shoulders and neck. I roll my shoulders, hoping to move the pain out.

"Ah!" Damirius suddenly cries, almost making me jump out of my skin. Immediately, my head whips around to him. His hands dart to his back, and he doubles over.
"Shit, that hurts!"

I rapidly run to his side. Panic rises in my chest as I fall to my knees. My hands rub his back, hoping and praying that it can soothe him. "What happened?!"
"Not sure," he grumbles, "Felt cold, though." I continue to rub some warmth back into the tiefling's body. He leans into my touch. I take that as a sign that it's doing something, at least.

My eyes close, trying to sense my magic. The torrential, disorderly surges run through me like a rapid loop; there's no beginning, nor any end to the pulses. Ebbs and flows shape the white-hot energy that runs and intertwines with my very being. But now, I want to push it towards my hands. I'm uncertain how to even do it; manipulating my magic never goes well. It's too random. Too wild. Each push or pull makes it snap.

I plead mentally, trying to coax it to my fingertips. Just enough pressure to make my hands warmer.

Slowly, my eyes open. And I see the white glow that surrounds my hands. Surprise keeps me silent. Curiosity keeps me going.

Inching along, my hands glide to the lower part of his back. The heat of my hands begins to steam the dampness away from his clothes. A hum of presumed relief comes from Damirius. I can feel a smile grow on my face.

My shoulders sag; a sense of ease overcomes me. My hands run along his bony spine. The pronounced spine and ribs are hard to ignore, but I force myself to ignore it. Alleviating the chill in Damirius' body is my focus right now. A moment passes as I continue to warm him up. My hands brush over his skin as unobtrusively as I can; the sensation of flesh under my grip has always unnerved me. But I muscle through it. I need to. He needs heat right now, and this is the best way I can give it as quickly as possible.

Then, something moves in the corner of my eye. Slowly, my head turns to face the movement. The water of the lake beside us starts to shift. My eyes focus intently on the movement. It's only a slight shift - unremarkable, if it weren't for the unnatural stillness of the loch. A tiny, insignificant ripple is all that documents the movement. I have to mentally instruct my hand to move; my magic has retreated from my hands. Friction is my only solace for heat now.

Suddenly, the middle of the loch plummets like a sudden sinkhole. Then, oddly, it rises again. This movement repeats, each dip and climb growing in intensity. The water rushes back and forth, like an invisible force is pushing and pulling it. My eyes can't seem to look away, though dread fills my stomach.

"Hey, why'd you stop?" Damirius whines, his voice almost piercing. His blazing yellow eyes pout at me. They were blinding in this bleak atmosphere. "That felt really nice." I didn't realise I had stopped. "Look at the lake," I mumble. I fear if I talk any louder the lake will hear me. It seems mad enough as is.

Damirius lifts his head slowly. I can feel his breath catch under my hand. I quickly move it away. The water suddenly dips in the middle of the lake, before it thrusts upwards again; the persistent motion causes overlapping, violent ripples of waves.

Then, a shimmering, brilliant blue glow pours out from the middle of the lake. The skittering fragments flicker across the top of the water, making it hard to determine where exactly the source lies. Bubbles scatter the lake as a harsh shift from under our feet rumbles the ground. Something is definitely moving. Another shift sends a new cluster of bubbles up to the surface, and nearly topples me off my feet.

The earth below rumbles angrily. The quake jostles some loose wreckage around us. Segments of homes crumble into the gargantuan footsteps that cover the town. Water sprays up from the plunging sections, smothering another layer of liquid onto the sodden bank. Another rumble, another shake. The tumultuous roar of crashing rubble surrounds me. But my eyes can't leave the lake ahead of me.

Water sloshes and crashes into the bank; the lake has become a turbulent, terrifying swell. The depths thrust themselves back, creating a mountainous peak before slamming down and colliding into the lakefront. Rapidly, the water rushes backwards. A cavity the size of a house swallows the water, until the water sits eerily still once more. Silence replaces the rushing of water and thundering of falling homes. A single pillar of blinding, blue light points upwards to the sky; almost as a warning of the danger that will come.

Damirius grabs my arm and I'm jolted from my feet. It takes me a moment before I can twist myself to join him in bolting away from the ominous blue light. His grip remains firm on my forearm, and for some reason I find myself thankful. His long legs take him further; each step he takes is roughly three of my own.

At the speed we're going, my feet are barely touching the ground anyway. Each time my foot and the ground connect, it's used as a launch to a new leap Damirius carries me through. I use my free hand to cling to his arm. Adrenaline soars through me, my heart pounds in my chest. An incoherent stream of curses and profanities spill out of my mouth; the drivel barely catches my own ears before being whisked away in the blustering wind.

A familiar chill snakes up my spine. I know it's not from the growing winds. My brain forces me to ignore it, and instead focuses on the rapidly approaching inn.

In an instant, I'm flying through the door against my own will. Damirius tumbles in after me. Our chests heave. We're both shaking. My back presses against cold, damp wood. Somehow I find it comforting. The pillar of light has burnt itself into my skull. Each time my eyes close, I can see it. Shit. Shit, shit, and fuck.

The adrenaline starts to ebb away, and I take in the familiar dilapidated interior of the inn. I glance at Damirius. He spares a knowing glance to me. We sit in silence, my ears trying to detect any sound of our deranged innkeeper. Nothing. We share a nod before we dart to our room.

Fumbling blindly, my hands grab the simple metal key I stored in my pocket. It slots into the doorknob, and I swing the door open. We dive into the safety of our room. Damirius slams the door closed. Immediately, my body collapses onto the floor. My back presses against the creaking floorboards. Somehow, the sensation of cold dampness is soothing. Damirius pants quietly beside me. The urge to hold his hand arises again. To soothe him. To soothe myself. I force my hand to sit in my lap instead. We lay in silence. My chest heaves as my lungs struggle to grasp a deep gulp of air.

"What in the fuck was that?!" Damirius suddenly squawks. I stare at him. Horror fills me. My legs feel numb. My heart pounds in my ears.
"I..." I start. My voice catches in my throat. "I think... I think the monster's awake."

I finally admit aloud. He's here. He's actually here. He's found me. I want to cry, but my body won't let me. I can't cry. Not here. Not now. My face scrunches up, and I rub knuckles against tears that won't fall. My fingers entangle themselves in my hair and I grab my skull like I'm trying to keep my brain inside. I suppose, in some weird way, I am. My brain feels like it's running a million miles an hour, and not a single thought makes sense.

My head is pounding. My eyes can't seem to focus on any point past my nose. I give up, closing my eyes. The now familiar sensation of my teammate's arms surrounds me, and I get pulled to his chest. I allow myself to rest my head against his shoulder. One of his hands touches my temple. I relax.

"You said that golems are somewhat simple, right?" Damirius abruptly asks, shattering the silence. My eyes lift to look at him. I don't say anything, hoping that it will prompt him to continue. "Well, what if someone had imbued the magic into it? Sort of like…" He pauses, seemingly trying to find the right words. "Like a standing guard, or sentry?"

The words hit me like a battering ram. It makes sense, I know it does. But a part of me wishes it didn't. It was the only logical explanation - for anything here, really. A section of my soul was yearning for any other reason; anything to explain his voice appearing in my head, the familiar hum of his magic, or even why a godsdamned fucking golem is tormenting people in their own minds. But there's only one real answer. And I hate it.

"But… Why against innocent people?" I ask. It wasn't meant to be asked out loud. My brain is running too fast and I can't seem to contain my thoughts any more. "The town is so out of the way and small compared to somewhere like Dororra. Why here?" Once the question leaves my lips, I feel

the answer sit deep in the pit of my stomach. It knocks the air out of me, leaving me choking and gasping. My heart lodges itself in my throat.
It was a trap.

The unwelcome chill returns, grazing up to the nape of my neck. I shudder. I try shaking it away, but I know it's futile. The clinging cold encircles the bottom of my neck, like a glacial hand that gently crushes my oesophagus. Like a glacial hand I remember too well. A pale white hand at my throat snaps into my mind; it's gone as quickly as it came. The sensation stays. I shudder again, but not from the cold. It's never from the cold.

Slowly, it inches up to the back of my head; the clawing, gnawing fingers pierce my scalp. I don't flinch. It doesn't matter if I did, anyway. That never stops him. More icy handprints smother my head. The weight makes my head droop. I know they're not actually there, but the feeling of him pushing against my temples feels too real to dismiss. It's almost like he's trying to burrow his fingers into my skin.

Boring fingers press against my skull, my cheeks, my ears, until all of a sudden the pressure alleviates. But a hefty weight lingers at the back of my skull. My head feels heavy. My eyelids droop. I feel sluggish, but I have to persevere.

My companion is holding his own head. His horns protrude between his fingers. His body is shaking. I can't stop my body from moving. My mind is swimming, but I know he needs comfort. Before I can comprehend what I'm doing, I'm already kneeling in front of him and holding him close. He sinks into me, and we tremble together.

"It's in your head, isn't it?" I ask. I'm not searching for an answer; I already know.
"Yeah..." He breathes, his head pushes into my shoulder. My hand rubs his back. He seems to relax under my touch.
"Feels like..." he starts. His eyes scrunch up, like he's concentrating. "Like it's in the back of my head, you know?" I mumble some kind of noncommittal understanding; he doesn't need to know he's in my head, too.
"It's like a song you can't get out of your head," he continues. "It's driving me crazy, Tiny."

His head burrows further into my shoulder. His arms wrap around me, tightly, hands clinging onto the back of my shirt. If he holds any tighter I think my shirt will rip. The weight in the back of my head begins to crawl across to the front of my skull. The pain is almost dizzying. My eyes flutter, my focus dissolving.

My face scrunches, trying to force my eyes to focus. Damirius needs me now; I can't be weak. I manage to lift him up, and pull him onto his feet. Slowly, we fumble to the bed. His head seems almost stuck to my shoulder. It makes it hard to move. I have to push him away and shove him onto the bed.

"You know," he mumbles, "If I knew this is how you'd treat me, I'm going to be a damsel in distress more often." He lets out a weak chuckle. I just shake my head and push his legs onto the bed. But the smile creeps along my lips anyway.

14

Damirius

The sun finally sets, though I can only tell because my eyelids have grown darker. After what feels like hours, Nylani finally clambers into bed. She's eerily quiet. From what it sounded like, she was just sitting at the foot of the bed until she decided to climb in.

My hand unclenches from my head and I fumble around blindly, searching for the ragged blanket. My finger hooks onto a moth-bitten hole and I pull it over us; it's better than nothing. Especially against the steadily growing chill I can feel. But it's not enough. My body curls into itself. I can feel myself shivering. It feels like my bones have frostbite. Shaking feels like it's cracking the ice of my bones. A deep, harrowing ache has settled in me. My head pounds. I'm lying still but it feels like the room is spinning.

The bed dips behind me. The blanket slides over me, almost touching my chin. I can hear her gentle breaths; she must think I'm asleep. I can almost feel her gaze bore into me, but I don't turn around. I'm so tired. My muscles cry in agony. Everything hurts. My brain is slamming into my skull. My rib cage rattles against my heart. My bones feel like glass; each minute movement causes a break. Then, I feel her hand on my shoulder.

The heat from her palm subsides the pain for a moment. My body melts and I feel at ease for the first time in hours. I hear her suck in a breath, and I stay as still as my shaking body will allow. If I start, I'll just scare her away. She's already scared enough as it is; I've seen it in her eyes. This thing has terrified her. I don't want her to be scared of me, too.

The silence drags. It feels as though an eternity has passed. "Would..." She begins. She stops. She takes another deep breath. "Can I hug you?" she whispers, her voice quaking.
"If... If you want." My voice is shaking. If I had the energy, I'd be embarrassed. But I don't. So I'm not. I don't even have the energy to face her.

"I think it'll help," she says quietly. "I am quite warm." Her hand moves to the back of my neck.

Her knuckles graze it gently, a small wave of warmth flushes over my skin. The momentary relief is blissful, and I find myself yearning for more. I nod my head as much as I can, which isn't much. It seems to be enough, though, as I feel uncertain arms wrap around me. One drapes over my shoulder and the thin blanket. Her arm lays across my chest.

Buds of warmth soak into me immediately and I feel myself relax. The other arm wriggles between my torso and the mattress. It rests against my own arm, her fingernails gently stroke the top of my hand. My skin feels covered in a blanket of warmth. My muscles ease, and I feel the ache leave my body. My body begins to uncurl. My back straightens, my legs extend, and I feel comfortable for the first time in hours.

I readjust myself slightly, keeping a conscientious note of giving my personal radiator some space. But, I feel her body shift closer. Her chest pushes against my mid back, her head between my shoulder blades. Heat radiates from my cheeks. I'm grateful she can't see my face right now. The side of her face presses against me, a blooming burst of that beautiful warmth seeping into my spine. Her legs lie alongside my own, her feet rest against my calves. Small trickles of heat spread to my feet, stopping them from freezing. My head begins to swim, the blissful relief of warmth sending me to slumber. My eyelids droop. Exhaustion finally hits me. The arms wrap around me a little tighter as I let sleep take me.

Dawn welcomes me as I startle awake. My heart pounds in my ears. I blink, and the terrifying snarl of Arwyn's face lingers behind my eyelids. It was the same nightmare as the night before, but it felt more vivid. More real. If that was possible. My body shakes. The same biting chill as last night seems to be lingering within me. I force my eyes closed, the image of Arwyn's distorted face fading as I focus on my breath. My chest heaves for a moment, but it's not long before I'm calm.

Nylani's arms stay wrapped around my chest. Her arms have me locked in a tight hug, her hands cling onto each other like her life depends on it. I chuckle quietly. For someone so awkward about physical touch, she gives great hugs.

Slowly - awkwardly - I twist in her arms. My body turns so I can face her. Her head falls into my

chest. My heart nearly explodes as she snuggles further into my chest while she sleeps. Then, a familiar voice speaks directly into my ears.
You're not worth her time, it spits.
Pitiful, orphan boy.

The voice grinds in my ears, like rocks scraping along each other; the low, baritone notes reverberate against my skull. It was almost painful. The voice hisses at me, like a viper intimidating a mouse.

"But I'm not an orphan," I muster, "I have a family."
The venomous voice silences for a moment, but I can feel the increasing chill invade my temples. Seems as though I've made them mad.
A family you can't trust, apparently. It counters, *Don't want them to know you're nothing more than a whore, hm?*

A bemused smirk fills my lips. Whoever this voice is, they're not very good at hitting below the belt. "I'm not sure telling children I sell my dick for money is a good idea, do you?"
I regret the retort as a stab of pain slams into my

forehead. My head spins for a moment. Well, that certainly pissed them off.

The voice has become nothing more than shrieks of vile insults that ring in my ears. The deep rumble of the voice almost bursts my eardrums under the pressure of their yelling. The constant battering of verbal abuse makes it hard to think of little else.

Eventually, the voice ceases. The yelling, venomous words quieten, and I can finally hear myself think. The ache lingers, my head thrumming in pain. But it's an improvement, at least. A persistent humming drills against my head, like an angry bee stuck in my ear canal. I rub my temple, hoping to alleviate the pain. It doesn't.

"You know," I grumble. My temper rises, the sound grows with my irritability, "You're not very original with your insults. It's all things I've heard before."
Ah. So that's why she's with you.
The voice is clearer now. No anger lingers in the tone. I can almost see the smug grin on a pair of undistinguishable lips.
"What? Because I can take a verbal beating?"

The irritating humming turns into a high pitch alarm; a long, monotonous squeal that could slice my eardrum in two. I clutch my head with both of my hands. I swear the bodiless voice laughs, but I can barely hear it over the screeching pitch.
No. She pities you.

The squealing tone disappears as the voice speaks. It's a deep baritone of an older male. His laughter fills my head; a malicious, deep chuckle that punches my chest.

"She doesn't pity me," I manage to choke out. Though, I don't sound confident in my statement. "So, she didn't let you join her because you practically begged her?" The voice asks, much clearer than it had been before. Sarcasm drips from his question. Uncertainty makes my stomach turn. I go to respond, but my voice has left me.
"Even now, she only keeps you warm because she pities you."

My eyes fall to the sleeping elf that has nestled herself on my chest. The heat that radiates off of her feels scalding now. Warmth singes my skin. I try to move away, but her hands are still locked together. Her comforting embrace is now my prison.

"You will never be on her level, Damirius. She will always look down on you. Just like everyone else does."
I gulp a deep breath. I try to find my voice, but it stays hidden. My head shakes instead. A deep, guttural laugh ricochets around me.
"Oh, dear Damirius. You didn't actually think she cared, did you?" Without my response, the voice continues. "Everything she has done is because she pities you. Nothing more." His voice is terrifyingly calm; as if he's just reciting facts. And then I feel his presence leave.

Warm tears touch my chin. I wipe them away quickly. My hands are shaking. The icy thorns that were clawing at my mind are gone now, but my head still hurts. Thousands of thoughts rush through my mind. I can't stop the tears that continue to fall. My trembling hands roughly push them away.
I feel stupid. For crying. For believing this was different. For thinking any of this was a good idea. How the fuck am I going to help in a fight?

The blue glow from the lake fades slightly against the brightening sky. A new day has begun. Not that I want to go back to sleep, anyway. The sinister smile that stretched Arwyn's face stays prevalent in my mind's eye. Pitch black eyes instead of her usual vivid green. And the deep, disdainful voice that now seems to haunt me instead of her chipper, melodic hollering.

His apathetic remark feels justified as my eyes graze over the sleeping elf that lies across me. Muscular, scarred arms lay limply in my lap. Arms that could definitely hold their own in a fight. My own arms are long. Slender. Muscular - yes - but not to the extent of Nylani's. Mother always said I had a 'dancer's body'. Whatever that means. But I know for definite that dancers did not invade battle fields.

I sigh. Her arm moves with my chest. If I didn't feel like shit right now this would have been cherished. Instead, I slide myself out of her grasp. My leg stretches over her tiny frame. I'm careful not to disturb her; it seems like she rarely gets a good nights sleep. My foot touches the floor and the board creaks. I stay still for a moment. My eyes stay trained on her. She stays asleep.

I sway my body over Nylani, holding my breath. My body slowly leans over her. My hand rests in a tiny section of mattress beside her head. Taking immense care to not even brush against her, I slowly roll myself over to the floor. The boards groan under my weight. Once I'm fully on the floor, I slide my boots on. They squelch as my foot goes inside. I grimace. A gentle grumble escapes from the bed. I turn. She shifts, her body curling up. Slowly, I stand. My hand grabs the flimsy blanket and I slide it over her.

The pulsating blue light fills the room. Everything is tinted in a deep, cerulean filter. My body creeps towards the window, and I squint through the rotten boards. My vision is limited, but I see blue light blanket the buildings. In the crook of the hills, on the waterlogged floor, and amongst the ruins; everything was a shade of blinding sapphire. Then, the cyan saturation fades away. Before my eyes can adjust to the natural hues, the same blue light fills the harbour once again. Back and forth, the light ebbs and flows from the centre of the lake. It's almost like the light is breathing. In. Out. In. Out.

A small mound has broken the surface and sits in the middle of the lake. It looks like the light retracts and expands from the mound. Aside from the light, the mound's pretty unremarkable; if I didn't know any better, I would have thought it was simply a rock. But I know better. My eyes stay trained on it. The constant shifting of blue light is distracting, but I force myself to focus. A slow ripple of bubbles surrounds the base of the mound. Only a few at first. But then more bubbles accumulate. The water begins to rock. And the rock rises half a metre higher.

The mound is now a small hill. It widens at the base and continues to push past the surface. I can see a hole in the side of the mound. It's half submerged in water, and looks deep enough to be a cavern. That same pulsing blue light seeps in and out of the water. Then, a piercing blue orb floats to the top of the hole. And stares directly at me. The light is blinding, but all I can feel is the haunting chill that runs down my spine.

I step back a few paces. My eyes stay on the growing hill. More bubbles rapidly churn from below the water's surface, and the hill continues to grow. A deafening creak punctures the air as the beast continues to rise. Inch by inch the hole lifts from the water. And another joins it. It's not long before I realise that it wasn't just a hole I was looking at - I was staring at one of its eyes.

A cold sweat washes over me, my heart thumping in my ears. My head shakes, forcing me to snap my eyes away. I dart towards the bed. I kneel before it, and gently shake Nylani. Slowly she opens her eyes, blinking sleepily. Then her eyes snap open. Quickly, she sits up. Her eyes widen at the blue filter that smothers our room.

"What's going on?" she asks. But her tone suggests she already knows. I gulp. My nerves are shot, but I need to control them.
"Golem." I blurt out. My chest heaves as I try to calm myself. "Think it's finally coming out of the lake."
"Alright," she says. "Let me look."

She rolls out of the bed soundlessly. She walks to the window, a calm determination settling over her. Her face peers close between the boards. Her eyes analyse the scenario outside. Then her eyes widen. She stares, soundlessly, at the loch ahead of us.

"Nylani?" I call out to her. She doesn't respond. She seems almost frozen in time. Cautiously, I rise from the floor.

"Nylani," I say, my voice shaking as much as my hands. "Come on, Tiny, now's not the time for jokes."

My hand grabs her shoulder as I get closer. She doesn't respond to my touch. I shake her shoulder. Still, nothing. I step around to look at her face. Her eyes are milky white.

15

Nylani

"--Lani? Nylani!"
His voice sounds so far away. Like a voice above water whilst I drown below. My head feels so heavy. I feel so tired. Ice cold hands wrap around my head and throat. Those glowing blue eyes stare right at me. I want to look away but my body won't let me. I try to shift my arm but it won't budge. My feet are planted into the ground. I'm paralyzed. The familiar chill presses against my lungs and I hear the familiar, deep voice ringing in my head.

"Hello, darling," he coos. My stomach turns at his voice. "I've missed you terribly." His voice drips with affection, but I can hear the menacing tone underneath. I want to respond, but I physically can't. Probably because he knows I'd tell him to fuck off. He chuckles, and my blood runs cold. I hope he can't hear my thoughts.

"I see you bought someone with you, sweetheart," he continues. The golems' eyes turn to Damirius. I can feel myself shake. "You know I don't like to share." His voice is sinister. I can feel a phantom hand press against my lower back. Claws dig into me. Claws that I know aren't there. His voice is in my ear, like his head is looming over my shoulder, "Remember that."

Finally, the weight on my chest alleviates. I can finally breathe again. My body relaxes. My limbs feel like jelly. I can hear Damirius talking, but I can't make out what he's saying. I turn to him. My head feels sluggish, like my brain is swimming through pudding. Everything is slow. Everything is muffled. Everything, but the constant pangs of throbbing pain at the base of my skull. He's still there. I know he is. I doubt he will let me go.

"Nylani!" I finally hear Damirius. "Nylani, are you okay?"
"I'm alright," I lie. He doesn't need to worry about me.

An impertinent bitterness creeps around my neck, and cradles the back of it. It's like a hand, holding my head in place.

I dip down and yank my boots on, trying to escape Damirius' watchful gaze. My body is shaking. I need to get myself under control. I force a breath. And another. The hand clenches around me, grabbing at a few stray hairs. Determination boils inside of me. I let it fuel me. He needs to go. My eyes wander back at the window, watching the blue haze intensify as the beast rises. My brows furrow, jaw clenching, as I glare at the creature. Glare at him.

"We're taking that thing down now," I grumble. Determination turns to anger, and I let it bubble in my chest. Acrid, seething fumes of malice seep through my teeth. Enough. I refuse to be his hunting dog any more.

I can feel my temper growing. Manifesting in the sparking flashes of white-hot magic that snaps at nothing. I'm already out of the inn, the biting air whipping my hair around me.
"Now, now, pet," that familiar drawl echoes in my head. "Let's not get ahead of ourselves."

Bitter iciness creeps around my throat again; a hand cusping below my jaw. I've stopped in my tracks, his interruption making me pause. I grumble, and rub my neck furiously.

I continue my charge. Scatters of electrical whips smack the earthy ground around me. A glacial force smacks my stomach, and I gasp. But I continue to march towards the lake. I can feel his anger; sharp iciness prickles my scalp. My feet continue their pursuit to the lake, my anger rising to meet his. Then, another slam hits my stomach and I fall to my knees, gasping. I clutch my stomach, choking for air.
"Enough," he hisses in my ear. "You know this won't go well for you, pet."
"Fuck... You," I choke out.

Condescending laughter echoes in my head. I push myself up, then steady myself as my head pounds from his cackling. Each pound against my skull makes my anger rise. It bubbles; fiery rage fills my chest. My magic courses through me at a speed I can hardly register. My arms are jittery. Sparks are flying continuously and slam into the ground as I walk. Steam rises from my body, combating the malicious chill that has settled around me. My feet stop at the edge of the lake.

I stare at the golem, and it stares back.
"Looks like I'll have to snuff this rebellious streak out," he ruminates aloud. My stomach drops at the sinister tone in his voice.
"Don't worry, darling," he continues. "I'll make sure the golem doesn't break your pretty face... too much."

A resounding, low groan reverberates the ground. The beast begins to rise; water, algae, and duckweed slide off the rocky terrain of its bouldering body. The goliath easily reaches the same height as the hills around us. Once it reaches its full height, it's hard to even see the head.

Each limb seems to be a collection of various boulders held together with magic. Globules of blue light work as its joints, and hold the limbs to the main body. The torso is the size of a miniature island. A hollowed cavern sits in the middle where the pulsing blue light seems to emit from.
Sparks engulf my arms; too enraged to be scared. I can hear my magic humming. The rush that whizzes through my bloodstream starts to become

erratic. Brilliant white flashes of magic whip out and lash against the surface of the lake. I breathe in shakily, but my eyes stare at the golem. And it stares at me.

The heat within becomes overwhelming. Sweat trickles down my back. A crackling of tiny sparks pop in the air. Suddenly, my vision explodes in a white flash as large arcane bolts shoot from multiple points of my body. The force of it makes me stumble backwards. I regain my footing as another surge of magic streaks through the air and collides into the golem's body.

Steam billows into the air, burning my arms as the heat leaves my skin. I watch the golem, trying to see if any part of it looks hurt. Nothing. Fury swallows me, and all I can hear is the deafening squeal of electric carve through the air and scrape across the solid skin of the golem. My rampage intensifies, and my magic becomes unruly. Blood trickles down my arm; once, twice, a third time. My arms sting from the slices, but it doesn't matter. Just as long as I can get this bastard to leave.

A deep, powerful punch hits my gut, and I collapse to my knees. My lungs heave, but I can't seem to

breathe. My legs are trembling. My arms pulse under their wounds. My eyes drag over the golem that stands, unmoving, ahead of me, and I notice there's barely an indent on its mountainous hide. Icy tendrils spread from the area of impact on my stomach, and grow into a freezing handprint. A second handprint blooms around my throat. The ice digs into me like nails. Nails I'm sure he'd love to sink into my skin. The grip around my throat squeezes a little tighter.
"Last chance, darling," his voice hisses in my ear. An angry venom drips from his lips; hatred fills his words. My body trembles at the sound of it, but I force my rage to continue.

An almighty roar escapes me as my overwhelmingly scorching magic builds and releases from my chest. It launches with a speed I can't recognise. My feet sink into the mud to stop me from toppling at the sheer force. The singular beam of concentrated energy slams into the golems stomach and breaks a section of rock away. My left arm flies forward, and a bolt of unrelenting electricity jolts from my fingertips. It extends outwards and releases as I snap my arm back, propelling the line of festering volts towards the beast's face.

With a crack, it whips the beast across the cheek. One of its cavernous eye sockets begins to splinter; the glowing orb that resides in it starts to fade. Whip after whip of concentrated lightning erupts from me in a way I had never experienced before. Rocks tumble and crash into the water as my magic carves away at the golem. My brain is registering his angry reprimand in my ear, but all I can hear is my own scream. I can't hear him if I scream.

Then, everything goes silent. I'm screaming - I know I'm still screaming - but I can't hear any noise. I can't hear my own voice, the crackle of my magic, or the slam of rocks hitting the water. My body twitches. Multiple icy, piercing handprints start to smother me. Grabbing, pulling and pushing my body to twist and turn. My body braces itself, sinking my feet deep into the dirt. Then, a piercing, icy stab hits my spine. My legs crumple beneath me, and my face slams into the dirt.

"You will obey!" His voice fills my head; the only thing I can hear. His yelling echoes through my head, pounding the inside of my skull. "How dare you defy me, child!"

Hot tears fill my eyes, but they won't fall. My body shakes. Ice spreads up my back and between my shoulder blades. His enraged, contorted face fills my vision; those burning blue eyes can burn harsher than the sun itself. My lip quivers. I'm scared.

I force a breath. My mind focuses on expanding and compressing my lungs. He continues to berate me, but I can't hear him any more. I shift my focus onto my limbs. My hand pushes into the thick, oozing mud and I push myself up. The sharp pain of the spreading ice tenses my spine but I push through the pain.

His voice snaps in my ear drums, making me wince, but I keep my eyes on the golem. It stands perfectly still, its ominously glowing eyes concentrated on me. My stomach screams in agony as another slam of icy force hits it. I curl towards my stomach, hugging it tight. I know I'm screaming but I can't hear it over his yelling. My throat is straining, and I'm finding it hard to breathe. Then, my vision goes white, and an explosion of white-hot magic erupts from me.

The force pushes me up enough to see a furious bolt slam straight into the chest of the golem. But it also flies me backwards, and I'm forced to watch as the sky rushes past me. My vision is quickly filled with the image of the ground rushing to my face, but a pair of arms suddenly appear and wrap around me. Familiar, lavender arms.

"Nylani!," I hear Damirius cry. "Nylani, I'm here."

16

Damirius

Her eyes snap up, locking on to mine. Her anger is palpable; it's clear in her eyes. Eyes that were terrifying. Once, they were a soothing, calming grey, but now they're piercing white. There's almost no colour in her eyes aside from the endless void of her pupils. It takes everything in me to not shrink away from her intense stare.

An intense heat radiates from her. Pulse after pulse expands into the air around us. Sweat slides down my brow and the back of my neck. Breathing feels too arduous a task in this air. But I can't leave her. She needs me. She's shaking like a leaf, despite the fury that sits on her face. Slowly, I rise to my feet, pulling her up with me. She uses my arms for support, and I ignore the hissing of my skin.

Her palms are like miniature suns, scorching my forearms as she stands. But nothing compares to the scowl that she directs to the golem before us. Hesitantly, I step away from her once she's steady.

She moves closer to the lake, and I allow myself to step back into colder, breathable air.

"Step. Back."

It takes me a moment to realise the orders were growled to me. I glance her way to find her terrifyingly bright eyes staring right at me, expectantly. I stumble backwards, my eyes too scared to leave hers.

Immediately, a burning white light consumes Nylani. It's so bright I have to close my eyes and turn away. Worry spurs my feet forward, but sparks fly and scatter into the empty air around us. I force my body to still. Squinting, I look at the beacon of light in front of me. The outline of Nylani's body is barely visible against the harsh light that has engulfed her. I watch silently, my breath stuck in my throat. A deep rumble fills the air as she storms to the edge of the lake's bank. The water has finally stilled. The golem is still. My eyes strain to look up at its face. Its eyes are focused on Nylani. A deep unease causes the hairs on my neck to rise. Something feels wrong.

Silently, I step towards the bank, carefully

sidestepping the staring match. My focus shifts to the water, the still surface reflecting my terrified face back at me. Uncertainty sinks my stomach. But I have to try. Some help is better than none... Right?

I crouch, my hands inches away from the waters edge. My fingers extend, the familiar buzz of magic coasting around my fingertips. The cool pulse spreads across my palms. My fingers curl upwards, trying to coerce the water up. A few droplets rise, freckling the air. They don't seem intent on merging together.

"Come on," I hiss under my breath, "Work with me here!" My temples throb under the strain of my focus. Slowly, steadily, the droplets glide together to form a singular globule of water. One hand stays stationary, holding the orb of water afloat, as the other pulls a small stream of water up. The single thread connects to the floating ball, piercing the surface and changing the orb into a pillar. The pillar widens and grows; the initial, awkward movement now pushing a consistent current. Once the water begins its continuous wave, the strain lifts away from me.

My only focus now is to hold the shape. It will grow on its own. Relief relaxes my shoulders as I watch the pillar stretch and widen. It's almost eye level with me, and as thick as my forearm. Then a thunderous crack snaps my attention away. My head whips over my shoulder, watching stray bolts of lightning split and crack against the slick mud. Nylani's arms brace in front of her face, her heels digging into the rubble and dirt.

A cursory glance upwards shows the golem still, unmoving. But Nylani seems angrier than before. Electricity surrounds her as she yells. I can't make out what she's saying, though, I don't think I want to know. She pounds a fist into the dirt; bolts of manic energy surge up and out. The electricity that engulfs her arm darts into the dirt and scatters across the surface of the lake. Vines of skittering volts intertwine around the golem's legs, violent cracks marking their trail. But then a sudden, bright snap shocks my hand and I yelp in pain. My hand flies back, the pillar of water slamming into the bank. I cradle the injured hand to my chest. Another roar erupts from Nylani, and I'm drawn back to the fight.

Another wave of electricity shoots from her, though this time it shoots in a singular line towards the stationary golem. The beam moves at such speed that it almost splits the water apart as it charges forward. It collides with the beast's stomach with a deafening boom, and chunks of rock splinter away. The crashing of rocks slamming into the water is the only sound that penetrates the air; Nylani has fallen silent.

My head turns to find her crumpled on the floor, clutching her head. Instinctively, my body lurches forward. The overwhelming urge to wrap my arms around her pounds through my chest. To soothe her. Protect her. But then, a shrill, piercing squeal pierces my ears. I fall to my knees, clutching my head.

Dirt meets my face as the perpetual screeching pounds on the inside of my skull. My world turns white as the only thing I can comprehend is the ceaseless ear splitting pitch. My head feels like it will rupture. My fingers are clawing through my skull. My throat strains. Though, if it's from screaming, or not being able to breathe, I can't tell. Suddenly, my world goes silent. And my face presses into the soft, marshy earth.

The ground rumbles, violently shaking me. I force my head to turn. The early morning light is blinding against my weary eyes. It takes a moment for the lacklustre light to not be painful any more. Another rumble, and I'm jolted around viciously. My temple smacks against the damp ground. The golem finally begins to move.

Its thick, trunk-like legs slowly rise and crash into the lake. Slowly I push myself up, fighting against the unstable ground. Instantly, I spot Nylani, curled up on the ground not too far from me. My legs sway beneath me as I stumble forward to her. An unnerving blue light floods the area ahead of me and I stiffen in fear. Cautiously, my head turns to look at the source of light. And I'm met with a terrifying glare from the slow approaching golem. The intense concentration the beast had is unnerving, to say the least. The piercing blue, unworldly eyes barely register me as they glance over the lakeside before pinpointing on the immobilised elf. My breath catches in my throat.

Everything seems to slow; it feels as though I have to push my legs through tar. My calves burn from the exertion. My feet pound against the ground, though Nylani doesn't seem to be any closer. The familiar high pitched squeal ruptures my ear drums and my footing falters. My head tumbles under my feet before I collapse on my back. The persistent scream in my mind rings my ears. My palms push into my ears, praying that the pain will subside. It doesn't. Iron nails scrape the inside of my skull, and my body writhes in pain. Then, in an instant, the sensation dies.

My breathing is ragged as I haul myself up again. My vision finally settles, and I'm immediately drenched in a brilliant blue light. The light begins to pulse; a rhythmic beat that's almost hypnotic. The light washes over the harbour with each pulse, dousing everything in a gorgeous azure tint. It gives the illusion of being thrown under sea, before retracting and yanking us all back ashore again. Each wave disorients me for a moment until my eyes can adjust. Then the light changes and I'm left orienting myself again.

It takes me a few minutes to get completely used to the changes, and the godsawful goliath has inched itself a few feet across the lake. I rise to my feet, uncertain if to leap towards the lake or the crumpled heap of my friend. The uncertainty leaves me idle. And that's when I see the source of the unending fluctuation of light. A large cavernous hole sits near the top of the golem's torso, tucked haphazardly just below its gargantuan chin. Inside the cavern resides a large aquamarine gem, surrounded by curved slats of rock. Each slab rotates around the large chunk of crystal, like a spinning shield. Magic continues to seep through the gaps, holding each mountainous boulder of the golem aloft and basking us in its ethereal glow.

A loud, booming crack jolts me out of my focus. My head whips behind me, towards Nylani, her crumpled body inching to the bank of the loch. Small zaps rapidly spark off her; needle-thin strands of magic crackle and pop from her skin. My feet move at their own accord, dragging me to her side. A hand rests on her back, ignoring the searing pain that comes from her sweltering hot skin. She doesn't respond to my touch. I crouch beside her.

"Tiny?" I say, my voice hushed. I can feel sweat building across my face. Her body radiates enough heat to rival the sun. My hand feels like it will blister. "Tiny, look at me." She doesn't move. Desperation courses through me. Both hands clasp her shoulders. I can feel the skin of my palms singing against the heat. "Come on, Nylani." My voice shakes. "Look at me. Please."

A moment passes. Then, her head slowly begins to rise. Her lips are set in a thin line. Her angry stare bores into me. The stone grey eyes I had wanted were still a terrifying, incorporeal white. The irises were only noticeable by the sliver of silver that ran around the edge. Otherwise, they would have been lost against the white of her eyes. Her pupils, however, were void of any light at all.

Anger seethes from every part of her; the way her jaw sets, how her muscles tense, and each calculated movement she made as she stands. Her eyes focus on me, the intensity unnerving.
"I'm. Looking."

The air around us begins to shift. Her magic whirs loudly. The air is thick and suffocating. The electricity hums and cracks the air as she stares down at me. Our eyes refuse to leave the others. Tension festers as I finally rise. Only her eyes follow my ascent. The volatile magic grows deafeningly loud, streaks of white hot threads whipping around her body. Another thud announces the golem's footfall beside us, and

Nylani's head turns towards it, ignoring me completely.

The thin strands of electric magic intensify; the speed that they circle their master is unfathomable. It's almost impossible to see the individual ribbons of magic until they snap off and attack the sky. A stray whip of electricity catches my forearm, though I try to suppress my cry of pain. The last place I want to be is at the end of her ire. My feet dance across the lakeside, dodging more white-hot whips that pursue me. My good arm nurses the other, my thumb pressing into the wound to slow the bleeding. It stings. But I won't complain. At least, not now. Those unsettling alabaster eyes stay fixated on the monster. She sinks down, her arms poised as electricity sparks from her hands and shoulders.

"There's a gem in its chest!" I blurt out. Her head turns towards me and I lose my voice for a second. The ghostly white eyes stare, expectantly. "Damage the gem." My voice wavers. "It could stop the golem completely." A tense pause. She continues to stare. I want to look away, but I can't. I pray silently that whichever deity is watching us right now will get her to listen. Her eyes remain unblinking, studying my face. My body freezes, my breath refusing to leave my chest. Finally, a miniscule nod is granted my way. My lungs almost collapse from the strain. Methodically, her head turns back towards the beast approaching us. It stops as soon as she looks at it.

A piercing scream fills the air, and I jolt backwards. Bright, white-hot electricity fills my vision, obscuring the colossal golem from view. The current of volts expands into a large sphere around Nylani, before suddenly shooting out into a thin line. The bolt of electricity arcs across the lake, and whips against the golem's rocky chest.

A deafening crack echoes across the mountainous planes as stone flies into the air. The rubble scatters and flips haphazardly across the sky before it slaps the surface of the lake. Water sprays upwards, hitting against the large, cliffside legs of the beast. An ear splitting creak reverberates through the hillside as a chunk of rock slides off its chest. The large hunk of earth crashes into the water, a tidal wave announcing its return to the lake's depths.

Smaller rocks pitter in after it, the small plops of their fall filling the tense silence around us. I can hear Nylani's laboured breathing beside me. My heart pounds in my ears. Another flail of electrifying energy zaps from Nylani's arm. It makes an impact within a split second. A loud groan erupts from the golem as a deep carve splits its side. Its body starts to tilt to the right.

Without thinking, my body sprints to the edge, plunging my hands deep into the cold water as I desperately try to will it to climb again.

17

Nylani

The beast's impassive stare points directly at me. Its owner screams in my head. He has been for gods know how long, now. Profanities, threats, and promises of what he will do when he gets his horrible, cold hands on me. The same tripe he always says. Only now, I know it means nothing.

My focus is on where to hit next. The gem. My magic goes haywire, excitement surging the magic's already volatile nature. It snaps at everything it can reach - even me. My body screams, but I refuse to acknowledge it. Blood trickles down my arms, my legs, and even my face. But I don't care. I won't care. Not until this bastard is capsized.

The golem moves again. The creaking of heavy boulders grinding against each other rumbles around me. The insistent squealing gets broken by snaps of rogue rocks breaking away from the pressure. With each thunderous step, the ground beneath me shakes. I tense my legs, digging my heels further into the dirt. My body hunches, while my eyes study the best place to strike. The colossal creature inches closer and closer, its shadow completely engulfing me as it approaches. Its left arm rises, ready to strike. In an instant, I'm smothered by electric bolts.

They cocoon around me, the electrical whirring filling my ears. Wild snaps and slashes hit against something hard, but I can't see past the blazing streaks of magic. A deafening, angry bellow resounds against the continuous sharp cracks. Heat rises around me, my neck dripping with sweat. The impossibly fast tethers of magic begin to lash out, thrashing at whatever they can. Bits of earth fly into the air as the ethereal whips slice against the ground. The lake splashes its water at me when a few pound into the water's surface. A rapid succession of bolts directly charge into the golem's chest, chipping away at the cavernous hole by its face.

The beast falters. It sways, the torso slipping backwards before it rights itself. The momentum of its boulder-like arm pushes it forward, the hand's descent rapidly approaching me. I hold my breath. My magic surges as anticipation shoots my nerves.

Small sparks of erratic magic pop and skitter across my palms. Its impatience is palpable. The colossal hand swings down, open palm shifting into a closed fist, aiming to crush me beneath it. My body jumps aside, the enormous fist scraping my boots. The rocky knuckles catch my calf. The familiar sticky sensation of blood soaking my trouser leg appears quickly.

My knees slam into the ground as a bolt of electricity arcs from my arm, and through the monster's wrist. A burst of power races through me, the intensity almost knocking me flat on my ass. My right hand grabs my arm, forcing it to stay pointed at my target. My weight sinks further into the soft ground. My left arm screams, like it's being lit aflame, as wave after wave of angry flashes continue to fly from my skin and slash into the golem's wrist.

Rocks spray into the air as the beast stumbles back. The weight of its hand no longer anchors it forward. The fist crashes into the lake below, and its arm flails as it tries to readjust. Before the arm can swing backwards completely, my body darts forward. I leap and crash onto the massacred wrist of the golem, my right hand clawing onto its rough exterior. The blue aura of magic that encompasses the barren wrist flickers and dies beneath me.

Instantly, the rocks that surround me begin to loosen and drop, crashing into the water. My foot slips and kicks a larger segment away. Quickly, I scramble upwards, kicking more rocks loose as I climb. My left arm screams at the effort, slick blood coating my skin and leaving a trail as I race up the forearm. My body slams into the jagged skin as it tries to shake me off. My face scrapes along the uneven surface, and it takes everything in me to not holler in pain. I won't let him get satisfaction from my pain. Not any more.

I sink into the golem's arm, pinning my knees into it as I hold on with all the might I can muster. My muscles tense and quiver as a blast of explosive volts charge from me and drill into the rocks around me. Immediately, the rocks and stone beneath me tumble down. My hands struggle to find purchase as everything begins to fall. My feet kick off the boulder nestled between them and I leap towards its bicep.

Slippery hands slap against the rocky exterior and I panic. Instinctively, my arms coil around the arm, my legs mimicking the motion. My head collides with a jagged outcropping, and my vision spins for a second. I shake the vertigo away. Panting, I crawl my way up its arm, my bleeding arm throbbing with each movement. I finally reach the apex of its shoulder, and I'm able to see the cavity in its chest.

The continuous, pulsing light doesn't seem to be able to reach up here. The brute's stance sways, and I'm set off balance. My chest slams into its shoulder and I deflate, wheezing for air. My lungs heave, desperate to refill, as my throat struggles to open again. Shaking hands vehemently search for a surface to cling onto. My chest pushes a cough out, forcing my throat to open and inhale. I splutter, my spit flinging into the air and out of existence, as I can finally breathe again. My legs manage to stabilise on the uneasy flooring as I haul myself up. The wind whips against my face; my eyes squint at the assault.

A shadow passes over me. My head tilts up and I'm greeted to the sight of the secondary humongous hand reaching over to grab me. The shoulder tilts and I struggle to keep myself upright. I crouch, digging my nails into the crevices of rock. My body tenses, my legs ready to push. It's a mad idea; but a mad idea is better than none. My heart hammers in my chest. The hand swings down and I leap. As my body rockets upwards, I curl myself into a tight ball. The skin of my back scraping against rough terrain lets me know my plan was successful. Somewhat.

My back slams into something hard and my arms fly out. My feet fling past my head and I flip out of control. My shoulder collides with the golem, and I instantly snap my arm around the stony terrain. My fingers bruise as I hold onto the jagged edges as tightly as I can, pulling my legs up and close to me. The heels of my boots dig into a small crevice. My head whips back and forth, trying to get an understanding of where I am. I spot the broken arm across from me, flailing around uselessly. I look up. A pulse of blue light fills my vision. I must be near its elbow.

Slowly, I shimmy my way across the forearm. My legs throb as I constrict them around the limb, my thighs squeezing to hold my position. I haul my torso upwards, and I can spot the gem ahead. The magic within me sparks, awake and alert, as I keep the gem within my field of view. I wince as my magic flays against my already battered arm. Just a few more hits. A few more, and then this will all be over.

My arm shakes violently as I lift it, aiming towards the chest. Pressure builds up in my arm as I try to suppress the outbursts. My veins throb. My hand tenses. My bicep squeezes against the rock. Then, I finally release. In quick succession, the magic slams into the centre of its chest.

Boom after echoing boom thunders around me as multiple bolts of electricity charge against the spinning centrepiece of the golem. A fragment of stone ricochets off the golem's chest, before it slams against its shoulder and disappears behind it. The gem burns a brilliant bright blue; the broken shield barely encapsulates the light any more.

Relief washes over me as I stare at the cavernous hole, watching the spinning slats of rock shake and falter. Weightlessness encompasses me. And it's only when I see grass below me that I realise I'm flying through the cool, damp, harbour air.

Whistling wind whips past me as I soar through the air. My torso twists and pulls in impossible directions, my spine nearly popping, before I slam into the dirt. My head screams as my face scrapes along the ground. My legs fly behind me, making my body flip. Friction pulls at my skin as I continue to skid against the floor on my back. Finally, I stop. The sky is spinning. I close my eyes tight, hoping to surpass the motion sickness. However, within seconds, my wounds scream for attention. My bruised, bleeding body begs for a moment's reprieve. But I can't. Not now.

I struggle back onto my feet. My legs cry out in protest, but I persist. I always do. My body's trembling, arms shaking as I force them to my eye line. Small threads of chaotic, wild magic begin to entwine through my fingers like ribbons. Even they seem to be tired. That's new. But with a push, they begin to overlap each other, like rapidly growing roots. A stronger, thicker thread of magic wraps around my arms.

The familiar crackling fills the air as the magic strengthens itself; the innate urge to submerge in rage powering the ties to this unexplainable power. My eyes flicker up to the golem, unsurprised to see it staring at me.

"Last chance, child," the stiff, commanding voice growls in my ear. I suppress the instinct to shudder, hoping that the feeling of his breath is just my imagination.
"Fuck. You." I grumble under my breath. But I know he heard me. The silence was telling.

My hands grab the tangible rope of wild magic, ignoring the stinging of my palms. The magic crackles angrily under my touch, but the familiar snapping of my skin is easy to tune out. The magic is pulled taut with both hands, pointing straight to the golems chest. Relentless charges of energy pulse through the cord in my hands, vibrating with anticipation. My arms tense, forcing the shaking of my hands to steady. I release.

Like an arrow, it rockets forwards and collides with the large, spinning mechanism within the cavity. A loud, angry whir squeals into the empty air; an impossibly powerful object butting heads against an undeniably strong contender. Even the golem looks shocked - if rock could convey emotion, at least. Time seems to freeze, as if the Gods themselves wait with bated breath. The thunderous clanging rumbles the sky, and threatens to topple me over. The impact pushes the golem backwards, toppling slightly, but it corrects itself fairly quickly. With an alarming speed, it leans towards me. It gets so close that I can see that one of the slates in its chest cavity bends at an awkward angle. It presses against the gem, preventing the other slates to continue their perpetual spinning. Then, the ground flies above my head again.

A crushing, solid weight sinks deep into my right side. My ribs creak under the pressure before the sickening sound of breaking bones fills my ears. The air chops at me relentlessly as I fly through the air. My body is virtually useless; my legs limp beneath me, arms cradling my stomach as my head lolls. The flipping snapshots of ground and sky spin around me. I can barely breathe as the air in my lungs is ripped away from me, adding to the barrage of cold swipes that wrack my body.

Eventually, the crashing impact of the floor encompasses me again. Immediately I heave, the stale breath I managed to grasp instantly removing itself as I vomit. My body collapses, the screaming agony of my ribs potent with each slight movement. My eyes close, my concentration solely on finding a way to breathe without causing too much pain. There doesn't seem to be one. A faint chuckle appears in the farthest part of my mind. I want to stand and scream, but the idea alone is enough to spike a painful throb in my side. I wince, my hands cradling my ribs gingerly. Even the feather-light touches of my fingertips feel like needles piercing through my skin. Defeat fills me. I should get up and continue to fight. But what's the point? He'll always win. I could fight my entire life, and I will still end up in chains.

I close my eyes, waiting for the crushing weight of a stone hand wrapping around me. I'm ready to accept the hellish conditions that await me. But, it doesn't arrive.

Instead, rushing footsteps dart to me. The footsteps stop and a shadow lingers over me, darkening my eyelids. I'm too tired to panic. Too tired to open my eyes. A sudden waft of warm breath skims over my skin, and I jolt, unexpecting the sensation. My side wails and I gasp out in pain.

My eyes fly open and Damirius' face fills my view, just a few inches from my own. Fear lingers in his features, but they relax into a concerned worry as he studies me. Tears prick my eyes; whether it's from seeing that beautiful, infuriating face, or from the pain, I'm uncertain. Maybe it's both. Large, gentle hands cup my cheeks and tears suddenly fall. His mouth falters as he watches me, his eyes glistening with pain.

"It's okay, Tiny," he almost whispers. "I'm here." Slowly, he pulls me upwards and cradles me. Even with him being gentle, it hurts like hell. I try to squash the yelp that nearly bursts out of me. His head nestles beside mine, the rhythmic, warm breath that ghosts my shoulder a surprising comfort. My head sinks into the crook of his neck. An arm hesitantly wraps around me. I'd feel secure in his arms, if it weren't for the sharp stabs in my ribs.

"This is gonna hurt, Tiny, but we need to get you up." He whispers softly. The sorrow in his voice is clear. I whimper in response. His arm squeezes the tiniest bit of reassurance into me. With a hushed count to zero, his arms slowly lift as he stands up.

Scorching pain blossoms from my side, buckling me almost instantly. A holler of pain rips out of me as I fall into Damirius. He grabs hold of my arms, standing me upright as we clumsily rise to our feet together.

"I know, Nylani, I know," he says, his voice panicked but trying to soothe. "But we gotta get you up, darlin'. It's not safe here."
"It's not safe anywhere," I manage to grunt back. The pain makes me irritable. Though, he huffs a small laugh.
"True," he admits. "But behind some cover is marginally safer."

Gingerly, my hand braces against my side. The skin pulses angrily underneath my palm, my bones wailing with each movement I make. I grit my teeth as I force my lungs to inhale. My body sings a horrendous symphony of pain, but I'm still able to stand. A small victory.

Lavender hands tentatively encase a hand and support my back as I balance on my feet. Instinctively, I hold a bicep for balance as we slowly retreat from the lake's edge.

18

Damirius

"I got you, I got you," I keep repeating as we shuffle along the ruins of Hush Harbour. I'm half-carrying Nylani, her body too weak to support itself. She's basically lying in my arms at this point; her legs can barely move any more.

Finally, I can spot the remains of a cobblestone wall, just barely big enough to squat behind it. We manage to fumble our way behind the wall. It's not an amazing shield by any means - it barely reaches Nylani's hips. But it's upright, and that's all we need right now. Cautiously, my grip on her loosens, allowing her to slide against the wall to sit down. Hisses of pain leave her as she cradles her stomach. A pang of anguish hits my chest. I hate seeing her in pain.

Involuntarily, I look at the golem. It's staring right at us, but it's not moving. Apprehension grows between my shoulders and I feel myself tense. I don't like the sudden stillness. It feels like it's planning something. My attention goes back to the crumpled elf on the floor. I kneel in front of her. "Can you lift your shirt?" I ask softly, "We need to see how bad it is."

"No," she grunts, "What we *need* is to pound this stupid bundle of rocks into dust." She growls menacingly. Her stubbornness is almost irritating. "You can look at me after this thing is gone," she hisses.
"Nylani you can barely stand on your own," I try to reason. She just glares at me. I'd be pissed too, if my ribs just got pounded by a sentient cliffside. But we can't do anything about it if she's not willing to let me help. "Please... Let me just see what we're working with," I plea.

Silence stews between us. Her glare continues, her grey eyes almost burning into mine. The deep purple bruise that's forming around them makes her eyes look even brighter.
"I want to help," I continue. I'm barely whispering at this point. "But I can't if I don't know what's going on." There's a small pause. Then, she shifts rigidly. Her brows crease tightly, discomfort clear on her face. Her body presses into the wall, and

she groans loudly. Finally, she nods as she fumbles with the hem of her shirt.

"Alright…" she finally agrees. Her anger melts into a sullen defeat. "I'm sorry."
My head tilts in confusion. "For what?" I finally ask.
"… For not being a better partner," she eventually mumbles. Her head lowers, shame marring her features.
I shake my head, a small smile quirking my lip. "Neither one of us are good partners," I admit. "But, then again, we also didn't expect a golem that can talk in our heads." I half-laugh. To my surprise, Nylani's lips lift into a soft smile.
"True," she agrees. My smile grows as we chuckle at the absurdity of it all.

Finally, she lifts her shirt just enough to expose the right side of her torso. I crouch lower, dipping my head to get a closer look. An angry, red welt smothers the entirety of her side. The bottom of her ribcage is a deep purple, and looks sunken in. Each shallow breath seems to be a struggle. I lean in, the dent in her torso more apparent as I get closer. I sigh. She jolts and yelps in pain. The swollen, irritable marks pulse and throb. Quickly, I shuffle away from Nylani.

The vibrant red that swallows her wounds starts to settle into a deep burgundy. Bruising is already starting to show across the rest of her chest.
"It's, uh..." I stammer. "It's definitely broken." A dissatisfied grumble answers me. "You need to rest. Ribs are difficult to heal at the best of times, much less broken ones."

"Well, I can't rest!" She snaps. "You just said that we need to work together!" Her angry glare softens to something of sadness. "I can't let you fight that thing alone," she finally murmurs.
"You can barely stand, Nylani." I counter, my chest heavy.
"Then what do you propose we do?" She practically squeals. "Run?!"
"No! No, of course not." I instinctively argue back. The idea of running is appealing, though. Really appealing. But the gnawing nag of guilt would definitely eat away at me. And I doubt Nylani would flee, anyway. "We just need a plan," I find myself saying.

Suddenly, a thunderous footstep rumbles the ground. I'm immediately up, staring at the golem charging towards us. One booming stride follows another. And another. And another. The cumbersome weight of its body somehow doesn't affect its movements now; it charges forwards in a terrifying stampede. Water sprays from its feet as it crashes through the lake, and soaks our waterside battlefield. Fear spikes through me. I can't run. My legs are heavy.

The colossal monstrosity closes in and I'm certain I'm no longer breathing any more.
Instinctively, my arms lift and cover my head. I hope Nylani can forgive me for not fighting. There's just no way I could've stopped that monster at such a speed. A deafening crunch resounds from above me. My eyes close tight, preparing for impact. But there is none. The world is silent. Silent, except for a constant rippling of water.

Slowly, my eyes open. A shimmering light glistens around me, smattering the floor and Nylani's face. Her eyes are locked on something above me, behind my head. A wide smile plasters her face. I lift my head.

A solid, dense wall of water separates the golem from us. The golems head is twisted at an odd angle. That must have been where the loud crunch came from. My hands shake, but I keep them high;

fear of what could happen if they lower keep my arms upright.

A hoarse chuckle sounds from below, "You could've told me you can manipulate elements, ya jerk."
"Really?" I whine, exasperated, "We nearly got crushed and you're reprimanding me now?!" I groan, my head sagging. "It's not normally this strong," I explain.
She grins, weakly, "Well, it is. Looks like we have a fighting chance, after all."

My hands lower slightly, and the barrier mimics my movement. The golem pounds against the wall of water, and it feels like the fist collides with my arms. In a panic, my arms fly upwards again and the water shoots upwards. It smacks the golem backwards. It takes a moment to find its balance again. I huff heavily, my chest heaving as my heart pounds in my ears.

"Imagine it in your mind," Nylani says. Her voice is weakening, a raspy whisper that's barely audible over the sound of shifting water. My eyes flick down to look at her, my arms still aloft above my head. Confusion silences me.

"You wanted a wall, and you made it." She pants heavily, clutching her side with shaking hands. "Think. What do you want?"

My brows furrow, and I look at my hands. Slowly, I inch one hand to the side. The water sways to mimic my movement. The golem attempts to walk through the wall, but it has little success. Silent relief washes over me. But then my knees begin to buckle as the golem starts pushing its weight against the water, instead.

I grit my teeth as I force myself upright. The familiar icy prickles invade my mind again. My legs threaten to crumple beneath me, but I refuse to fall. My hands clench into fists; the water rumbles and bubbles in response. My temples pulse as a seething frostiness scrapes across my skull. My eyes twitch at the pain, my stance faltering slightly. The wall drops a foot lower, and the golem immediately tries to push it further down with its remaining hand. In a panic, my left hand shoots up to the sky, pulling a pillar of water upwards at breakneck speed. The impromptu post slams into the jaw of the beast, sending the miniature boulder of a head rocketing up to the sky.

My arms drop from exhaustion. Water splashes unceremoniously over the torso of the golem, and sprays over everyone. But I'm surprisingly unbothered about being drenched. Fighting against an animated mountain leaves you pretty aloof, apparently.

Algae slides over the rocky terrain of the golem's torso and arms, before plopping onto the lake's surface. The golem stays upright, despite its missing head. Even without the large boulder atop its shoulders, it's still terrifyingly huge. Trunk-like legs shamble forward, inching closer and closer to the small segment of wall that hides Nylani.
Panic drives me.

My arm swings forward again, despite my muscles screaming to stop. A column of concentrated water jettisons out from the lake and slams into the headless slab of stone. The impact forces the golem to step back; but it doesn't stop it from trying again. The golem continues its pursuit, and my arms fly to direct more aquatic missiles into it. Slowly, the golem stumbles back, submerging into the lake once again. As it retreats, I follow, leaving the crumbling wall behind me. Water continues to fly as my arms swing and punch the air.

The shattering cracks of rock splitting echo through the silent valley, followed by the heavy sloshing of water. Both hands rise to create another liquid wall just as the golem tries to swing its arm in my direction. I sink my feet into the ground, hoping that the force won't knock me over. The pressure rattles my bones, but somehow I stay firm on my feet.

Sweat pours down my neck. My breathing is ragged. Regardless, my arm swings up as I punch the air. A pillar of water blasts upwards and slams into the would-be stomach of the beast. My arms become a flurry in front of me. Relentless swings force wave after wave to hit the headless torso. Sections of the golem's arm break away. Rock and rubble tumble into the lake, disappearing from view. Its arm consists of little more than several boulders, held together by thin strips of faint, blue magic. But I'm growing tired. My arms cry for my mercy. My chest heaves. And my hands are unsteady.

The water shifts uncertainly as I try to raise another barrier. The slab of liquid rolls and tumbles unsteadily. Its ascent is slow; a struggling climb to the sky. Then, without warning, a large boulder cuts through the wall. The water splits. Instantly, I'm soaked. But all I can think about is the pain in my stomach. Air rushes out of my lungs. The pain chokes me, and my body flies backwards. Immense pressure crushes my pelvis. Somehow, during my short flight, the boulder shifts and plummets to the floor whilst I continue my aerial pursuit. Something collides with my back, and I'm forced to suck in air.

A piercing pain jabs the middle of my spine. The air I had just sucked in immediately screams back out. My body shakes, the pain wracking me. My legs want to rest. My arms whine in displeasure. My lungs struggle to work. A familiar, unwelcome reminder of the golem's master returns. A pulsing, bitter iciness spreads across my forehead. The sharp sensation is enough to rouse me from my premature defeat.

My eyes snap to the golem. It meanders towards me again. Slow. But threatening. Like a silent promise to end it all for good now. Gingerly, I hoist myself up. Whatever lodged itself in my back inches out of my skin. Metallic, warm liquid trickles from the wound. Nylani appears in the corner of my eye, trying to scramble to her feet. Our eyes lock. Her face is distorted - the right side is swollen and discoloured, while the left looks drained and haggard. Silently, I shake my head. She's in no fit shape to go against this thing. Her death can't be in my hands. It just can't. She goes to protest, but she sinks to the floor, clutching her ribs again. I'm quietly thankful she's unable to fight me. Gods know she would, if she could.

The golem continues its death march. The thuds of its colossal feet quake the ground as it inches closer. I step forward, my legs like lead beneath me. Tremendous effort goes into each step. And each excursion of movement drains me. My body is screaming; my stomach and back a wailing harmony around my torso. But, I continue. The golem raises the remnants of its arm again. Water flies from it as the string of rocks and magic rapidly descend. Instinctively, a new wall pushes up from the lake. The punch is deflected, but the pressure still hits me. I yell, my stomach protesting from the sudden movement.

Another sharp stab of ice pierces my skull. My teeth grit. The pain is almost unbearable. A shrill ringing fills my ears and my head pounds from the pain. The arm tries to swing at me again. I manage to duck out of the way, though it scrapes against my horns. The force knocks me onto the floor, the deafening squeal of rock against hard keratin replaces the intense ringing in my ears. Clumsily, sluggishly, I get to my feet again.

My head is spinning. My eyes close tight, hoping to push the vertigo away. Another hit slams into my stomach, and I'm pinned to the floor. I scream, but I choke on air, eyes watering. The weight pushes down, slowly crushing me into the soft, pliable mud beneath. My lungs can't expand. My hands can't move. I lay, shame and defeat filling me.

A sudden, deafening snap flies past me. A flash of light invades my foggy vision. The weight on my stomach immediately lifts. My eyes slowly come back into focus, just as the colossal titan stumbles backwards. My head whips around, and I spot Nylani sprawled on her stomach on the ground. Her left arm sparks, continuing to spit magic at the golem. More blasts drive the golem backwards, sloshing through the lake haphazardly. Ignoring the wailing of my stomach, I shuffle towards Nylani. My arms gently scoop her up. Our breathing is ragged and acidic bile coats my tongue.

"Thank you," is all I manage to wheeze out.

"Let's kick his stony ass," she mumbles. She grips my shoulders, hauling herself to her feet. It hurts, but I bite my tongue.

We turn to face the stumbling golem together. A hand rests on Nylani's back, just as one of her hands holds onto my bicep. Determination sets in; I feel stronger with Nylani by my side. My free hand shoots up.

A swirling, pointed pillar rises from the lake, spinning in place. My fingers push together, thinning the pillar. It becomes a fine, spinning needle that continues to climb and pull from the lake. My hand slams forward, sending the water like a javelin into the giant's chest. A piercing squeal thunders through the harbour. The bent rock that pins the gem pings out of place. It hurtles through the air before finally crashing into the loch. The force nearly knocks the torso off of its legs. However, it manages to hold on.

Though, the torso slants further to the right. Its bulbous stomach grates against the rocks that form the top of its leg, the squealing of rocks threatening to make my ears bleed. Somehow, there is still no hindrance to its movement. After a moment, the infuriatingly resilient beast starts its perpetual dawdle towards us.

Incredulous indignation replaces the dread and fear. My hand whips the air repeatedly, my arm now numb to the constant ache. Silently, I plead for the water to consume the titan whole; if not to win the fight, but to just subdue the damned thing for a minute.

The water lashes relentlessly, like a raging wave at sea. Debris gets ripped away from the golem. Rocks tumble and crash to the bottom of the lake. I'm wheezing, my chest is heavy, but I can't seem to stop. Lashes of aquatic whips carve into the stone skin. My movements are slowing, but so is the golem.

The hand on my bicep squeezes me gently. I glance down to see wide, grey eyes looking up at me. She nods, reassuring me. An unexpected surge rushes through me, and reignites the burning determination in my chest. With a steadying breath, my arm soars into the sky. A rippling pillar explodes out of the lake and takes the remainder of the golems left arm with it. The boulders split apart from each other as the magic twine binding them snaps. Without thinking, I pull Nylani closer as rocks scatter through the air and collide with the lake and ground alike.

My eyes stay transfixed, watching the broken pebbles of golem rain around us. Suddenly, the aches from the fight return, and I'm left gasping and wheezing. I double over, my stomach howling in pain as my lungs refuse to cooperate. A sudden clap on the back forces my lungs to behave and inhale. I look up, Nylani's face a few inches above me.

"Well done, big guy," her soft voice murmurs. A weak, yet sincere, grin pulls at her lips. And I find myself smiling right back.

19

Nylani

Slowly, we adjust to stand upright, leaning against each other. Relief washes over us, and I can't contain the weightless feeling it brings me. The golem, headless and now armless, doesn't have the same ominous feeling as before. If anything, it was almost... pitiful?

"Alright," Damirius mumbles to no one in particular, "Power of Friendship versus a giant, moving mountain. Let's see who wins." The chuckle that bubbles its way out of my chest was entirely unplanned. As was the pained groan that follows. My hands cradle my ribs gingerly as I gasp out in pain. In an instant, Damirius holds me close as he tries to help. And for a moment, I feel safe.

"Don't get comfortable, darling," the snide voice taunts. "Remember who you belong to."

My entire body fights the urge to shudder. But the lingering feeling of unease crawls across my skin, anyway. Goosepimples raise at the haunting sensation of his hands on me, his breath against my ear. I can't go back. I won't.

I grit my teeth, ignoring the flipping anxiety that churns my stomach. Frail sparks of energy scatter off of my arms. My body is too weak. Cautiously, I glance up at Damirius, only to find him already looking at me. His eyes are soft; watching me with gentle concern.

"Whatever you do," he gently whispers, "You don't have to do it alone."
Silently, I nod. Gingerly, my hand slides into his, and I push my weight against him as we hobble closer to the lake. Damirius carefully wraps his spare arm around me. His hand feels much stronger than my own, holding onto me whilst also bearing my weight on it with little difficulty.

My side twinges in pain and I hiss at the sudden throb. I nearly collapse into Damirius, but he keeps me upright. A platitude of small encouragements fall from his lips as he braces me. My body shakes; I can feel the familiar rushing static of my magic coursing through me. The magic is relentless, but my body is too tired to contain it. A shock splits out from my shoulder, snapping at the air.

"You should step back," I warn Damirius, my voice shaking. He shakes his head, a soft smile on his face.
"Nuh-uh, Tiny. We're a team, remember?"
"You– You're gonna get hurt," I try to argue, but he continues to shake his head.
"It's nothing compared to a cliff to the stomach. Now come here and let me help."

His arms snake around me as he keeps me upright, deliberately keeping clear of the throbbing ache in my ribs. The violent thrum of magic whirs through me, before it cracks through my arm, and smacks against the ground. I quietly gasp at how sharp the sting is; it's been years since the magic was potent enough to feel so fresh. I cradle my arm to my chest, the warm trickle of blood pooling between my fingers.

"Come now, my love," a menacing tone lingers over

his honeyed words. I can feel the bile rising in my throat. "You can barely stand." He tuts like a disapproving parent. I can see the glowing resentment in his eyes behind my eyelids. "Stop, before you really get hurt."

The ghost of a hand grabs at my neck, trying to force me into submission. But I know it's not there. I cling to the warmth of Damirius; the musty, sweetened dampness of his shirt a surprising comfort. He seems to realise something's bothering me - his arms squeeze me just a little tighter. "Deep breaths, Tiny," I hear him say, "You're okay."

My body sinks against his chest, and my magic goes into a frenzy. An intense flash jumps from my arm and leaps forwards, skittering across the lake's surface. The erupting electricity creates a billowing steam, my skin sizzling from the wound. I cry out and bury my head into Damirius' chest. His hands splay out across my back, pushing me further into him to keep me from falling. The bolt of magic zaps through the lake without issue.

Within a flash, it drills into the stomach of the golem and cracks the underside. A hefty chunk of the rotund yet hardened belly falls into the lake below with a resounding crash. All I can muster is a whimper to celebrate. A smattering of flickering bolts leap out of my skin; my body too exhausted to contain the magic any longer.

Solid arms lift me higher, my face no longer sliding down Damirius' chest. My side is set aflame as the shooting pain returns. I whimper, uncaring of how childish I sound. I'm cradled as my head is guided to his shoulder, delicate fingers moving my hair from my face. An arm pins my hips to his, lifting my feet away from the ground. The other hand lifts my arm, and points both of our hands in the direction of the slow approaching golem.

Rhythmic thumps announce the incessant progression of the formless lump. It inches closer and closer, the glowing core burning furiously. My mind is silent, but the hairs on the back of my neck stand upright. Another impulsive flash rockets out, lunging forward and slashing the lake. I groan, the exhaustion making my head swim. Damirius' hand keeps my arm aloft. His head rests atop mine.

"One more hit, Tiny," his voice softly rumbles in my ear, "We can do it."

"No," I petulantly whine. My eyelids droop; exhaustion hits me far harder than I had anticipated.
"That's not very 'Team Friendship' of you," he teases. His hearty chuckle bobs my head against his shoulder, forcing me to wake up.

"Just one more hit, Tiny," he repeats. His fingers interlock with mine. It's only now that I realise our hands are submerged in water. Shifting my head slightly, I get a closer look; an orb of gelatinous looking water encompasses our interlocked hands. The orb continues to swell through a small thread that joins the sphere to the lake. My fingers feel the continuous flow of running water pass by. It's almost relaxing. Pressure builds as the orb grows; the gentle trickle of water becomes a repetitive current that rushes around our fists.

"When I say so, put as much lightning as you can into the orb."
"What?!" My eyes widen. "No! No, that'll hurt you!"
"I know," he acknowledges dismissively. "But I'll be alright."
"I can't control it, Damirius." I plead, trying to turn my head to look at him. Honey eyes ooze into

mine. I can feel tears prick my eyes. "It'll attack you just as much as it will the golem."
"Can't be any more painful than being squished by a boulder."
I sigh, defeated. "Fine."

The globule of water continues to grow, and eventually submerges the entirety of our arms. The sensation is baffling; a rolling undercurrent weaves around and in between our arms, palms and fingers. Pushing us away and then pulling us together. Calming, yet threatening, all at the same time.

I close my eyes, sinking into the feeling of Damirius' magic flowing freely around me. My own erratic and excitable magic hums to the soothing fluctuation. The momentum begins to build. The surge of energy gains speed, coursing through me in a perpetual loop. A streak of rogue magic snaps away, but no pain follows its exit. Slowly my eyes open, and to my amazement, the sight of an electric bolt spinning through the bubble of water greets me. The water shines a brilliant white as the lightning zips around our arms. Amazement keeps me silent.

My jaw slacks as I watch my magic intertwine into the water's current. It zips and glides painlessly, lighting up the water like a beacon as it moves. Gradually, the thick sphere narrows to a point, morphing into a liquid javelin. Damirius moves our arms as one, pointing our hands directly at the golem's glowing chest.
"Let it fly, Tiny."

No more instruction was needed; a thousand cracking whips jump from my arm and plunge into the water. In an instant, the water rockets away from us and into the glowing cavern.

Electric swirls madly within the water, the column of water shines a brilliant white light; the intensity beating that of a mid-afternoon summer sun. The glowing arrow zaps through the air, the world darkening around the pillar of hot, intense electricity. It slams the golem's chest, scattering stray threads of lightning over the surface.

The water continues to push, pillowing and ploughing into the golems cavern, the intensity splitting the rockery apart. More of my magic pours out, pulling more ammunition for the crackling attack. The water cracks the rock, then fills the cracks and splits it further. Burning white collides with brilliant blue as the large crystal becomes airborne. The needle point of the pillar slices through the large, iridescent stone shattering it into tiny fragments that glitter in the morning sky.

The golems body instantly shatters at the crystal's destruction. Thousands of small rocks and pebbles plummet down. The torso and gargantuan legs have a less ceremonious fall, creating a large wave as each boulder crashes into the water. Then, the water stills.

No ripples, no rumbles, and no other movement can be heard. Silence blankets the lakeside. The dusting of the once grand gemstone begins to scatter. A faint shimmer settles onto the top of the lake, glistening in the first rays of light of the morning sun.

My body shakes against Damirius', as his does against mine. Suddenly, we buckle, his knees giving way. Our pillar of light and water dissipates, allowing the natural hues of the world to finally come back. The soft, earthy floor encompasses us, our limbs entangled as we collapse. Our breathing is ragged, our wheezing filling the silent air.

Bruised, bloody bodies merge into one as we sink into the dirt. My eyes finally close, succumbing to the exhaustion that pulls at my eyelids. Sleep takes me quickly. The burning aches become a distant memory that I refuse to acknowledge until I'm conscious once more.

20

Damirius

Clouds drift lazily across the sky, hues of white and blue fill my vision. The sun hangs in the middle of the sky, and glistens across the surface of the lake; the water a rippling gem. An unfamiliar warmth kisses my skin, though a lingering dampness clings to the air. The sounds of shuffling feet and distant voices are barely perceptible, but are enough to rouse my curiosity.

My entire body screams in protest as I slowly try to sit up; the weight of Nylani's body makes the endeavour near impossible. My head grows heavy and pulsates in pain. My stomach wails, an intense ache slams against my abdomen. Nausea passes over me like a tidal wave. Acidic bile rushes up my throat, threatening to spill over the grass. I cough, clearing the bile away, but the acidic burn lingers in my throat.

I sink back to the floor, my eyes closing as I focus my efforts to pull cold air into my lungs. The chill crispiness is soothing. A few silent moments pass as I appreciate the gentle light of the sun against my eyelids. But then, I hear the sound of footsteps behind me again. My neck cranes to look in the direction of the sound.

I see people. People exiting their ramshackle homes. People talking, laughing and busying themselves amongst the ruins. Banners rise from rusted, bent poles, and the waft of warm food finds its way to me. People are rushing to and fro, arms full and smiles wide. Their glee is almost infectious. Gentle pluckings of music slowly fill the air; the humble twangs of an inexperienced player the most illustrious tune I've heard in my life. The excitement of their renewed freedom is palpable, even from the sodden patch by the lakeside where mine and Nylani's bodies lie.

Her face is basically merged with my shoulder. Our arms and legs are a tangled mess. But I have no desire to move just yet. Everything hurts. My stomach refuses to quieten; the constant waves of aching desperation assault my body. I force the urge to cry out in pain down; this is a moment of celebration. I'm not ruining it. At least not yet. My eyes continue to watch the residents of Hush

Harbour. The liveliness seems almost foreign against the dreary backdrop of their home. Pale, weathered skin is glowing against the soft sunlight; gaunt bodies build stable structures; and tired eyes gleam.

A weight shifts against my arm. Nylani shifts subtly, but the pained groan that comes out of her indicates she's at least semi-conscious. She attempts to sit up. And she immediately falls back down. Hisses of pain fill my left ear, and I wrap my arms around her.

Her hands hold her ribs. She curls into me, and we stay on the floor like this for a while. Gasping, heaving, breaths are shared between us as the bruises, cuts and crushing pains finally ravage our bodies. I fall into her just as much as she falls into me. My head lies heavily against the top of hers. Our legs stay entangled. Neither of us seem to mind.

Curiosity pulls an eye open, and I glance down at our legs. Nylani's battered calves almost pin my legs to the ground. I suffocate my chuckle. She doesn't even seem to realise how tightly she's holding on to me. A dirtied, somewhat cream blanket catches my attention.

It rests over Nylani and myself; though with its multiple tears and holes, it seems more appropriate to say it rests around us. I pluck the blanket away, the threads almost disintegrating between my fingers. Upon closer inspection, I recognise it. It's the same blanket that was in our room in the inn. I can't suppress the smile that consumes my face.
"We-," Nylani's voice suddenly gasps in my ear. She pants heavily. "We did it."
"We did, Tiny." I agree, my smile unwavering. "We did."

A moment of silence washes over us. Feeble hands rub my back and I feel my heart melt. I'm sure it would turn into putty if she delved in and grabbed it. Her temple rests against my chest, her breath tickling my skin. I've not had someone hold me so tenderly before. No one that wasn't family, anyway.

I want to pull her closer - squeeze her in my arms - but I know it will hurt her. Instead, I keep my arms loosely wrapped around her. We stay entangled. And just breathe together as the world around us continues.

"Well done, Tiny," I finally whisper. "You saved them."

"No, *we* did," she emphasises. Her head tilts upwards to look at me. "Well done... Partner." A gentle smile flashes in my direction. I can't suppress my own.

We fall into each other, head on the other's shoulder, and relief-filled tears easily slip down our cheeks. Shaky breaths are shared in our secluded bubble; my shirt tightens under her grip, my arms constrict the top of her arms. I cough out a half-sob, half-laugh as the immense sense of peace floods over me. We did it. We're alive. We're safe.

Finally we separate, chuckling as we fight to untangle our legs. The numbness in our limbs makes it hard to move, and results in some amusing acrobatics in the dirt. I don't think the smiles have left our cheeks since we awoke. It almost hurts. But glee stops me from caring.

I prop myself up, ignoring the petulant whine of my stomach, and try to get a better view of the town. People continue to rush to and fro, blissfully unaware of our presence. Silently, I'm thankful for it. Food is laid out on a large serving table made of rocks and planks of wood; the scent of warm bread and tantalising soups make my mouth water.

Stomach-churning aches ripple through me, and I'm temporarily winded. A hand rushes to the pain, and I gasp at the tenderness of my skin. I don't want to look - don't want to ruin the peace - so I ignore the tenderness and gingerly rub my stomach in an attempt to soothe the ache. Watchful, grey eyes linger in the corner of my eye, but I act as though I don't see her. She doesn't need to worry about me.

My eyes focus on the streets of Hush Harbour. Somehow, the desaturated tones of waterlogged brickwork glisten in sunlight. Joyful tunes fill the vacant air around us. The novice twangs are accompanied by whistling pipes that create a melodic jig; an accordion finds its place somewhere in the harmony. I can't help the chuckle that huffs out under my breath. It reminds me of home - noisy, melodic, and most importantly, happy.

It's been so long since I've gone back. My eyes close as I slip silently between the melodies that echo through the hills and valleys. Memories of Mother and I singing melodies to my younger siblings swim through my mind's eye. Slowly, the memories shift; the children grow and begin to join the homely choir with their squeals and hollers of glee. Tender fingers wrap around my right hand, the gentle sensation pulling me back to the present. Reluctantly, my eyes open. I glance down, seeing Nylani's face near my knee. She lies on her back, sun pouring over her battle-worn body. Her tanned skin is a patchwork of deep purples and blues; blood soaks through her clothes and hair. "Thinking of home?" she asks softly.

Her breathing's shallow. Her free hand continues to brace against her ribcage, fingertips barely grazing over her shirt. I nod absentmindedly, my focus shifting to her side. The sound of familial laughter fades away as I continue staring at the broken elf in my lap. Blood and bruises cover her face, like a horrifying mask. Old scars look like they've reopened, but I'm not sure. I lean closer, but the proximity does nothing to help my vision. Another wave of pain rolls through my stomach as I bend to Nylani's face, but I force myself to ignore it.

"Can I check?" I ask, nodding my head to indicate her ribs.
She nods. Carefully, I slide my legs away from

under her head and rest on my knees by her stomach. She takes a moment to reposition herself, hissing as she does. Eventually, she manages to lie down and lift her shirt. Only her stomach and the lower rungs of her ribcage are visible, but it's all I need.

A visible indent pushes the lower two prongs of her rib inwards. Deep purple markings swallow her entire rib cage, and splatter across her stomach and hips. With each inhale, I can see the rogue ribs move against their kin. Even shallow breaths seem arduous. My own breath gets stuck in my throat.

"That bad, huh?" she jokes weakly. A sarcastic laugh wheezes out. It ends prematurely when her ribs poke against her skin.
"You could say that," I say. My eyebrows feel like they're trying to climb into my hair. I try to relax my face, but my muscles don't seem to listen to me any more. Instead, I manage to gently pluck the hem of Nylani's shirt and pull it down again. Just as I do so, a ravenous growl erupts from the stomach below my knuckles. Nylani's hands fly to her face in embarrassment, and I can't stop the snort of laughter that bubbles out of me.

21

Nylani

"You're hungry too, huh?" he chuckles. My cheeks flare under my fingers. Gentle hands pry mine away from my face. Tender, golden eyes smile at me, warmer than the sun itself. "Come on then," he continues, "Let's go get something to eat."

He rises first. He looks like a newborn lamb, his legs unsteady beneath him. A snicker quietly escapes at his third somewhat-stumble over his own ankle. The giggle is quickly snuffed out as the jostling strains my ribs and I grimace at the pain. Tender hands hold onto mine, and guide me to stand. Muscles scream and cry as I'm pulled into animation again. Pitiful whimpers tumble out of me, my feet struggling to support my weight. His hands move to the top of my ribs and my waist, trying to help keep me upright.

"I'd say it serves you right for laughing at me, Tiny," he quietly teases, "But I'm not that mean."

The soft jab brings a smile back to both our faces. I tut and roll my eyes, and his grin grows wider.

Our trek is slow. Aching, battered bodies can only move so far. Damirius keeps an arm around me, and my hand anchors to his bicep. I wish I could help him, too, but I think we both know I would collapse under my own weight alone. We hobble forwards together, and the enticing waft of warm bread graces my face.

My stomach whines again, mouth watering, as the aroma strengthens with each step we take. My feet catch cobblestone as we finally arrive on the outskirts of the streets. Simple, bright banners greet us as we descend the streets. People give hollers and cheers as they run past us; others try to help guide us to the centre of town.

Hands clamour to hold onto us, but my whimpers of pain deter them from touching any more. I'm quietly grateful for it. The noise and busyness is overwhelming. I swallow the bitter attitude; my face moulds into its familiar, calm, neutral mask. We finally reach the heart of the town, with a small crowd of people following us. Twinkling lights dangle above our heads, hung from the highest pieces of rubble that encircle the makeshift plaza.

The twangs of stringed instruments penetrate my ears; broken crockery full of warm pastries make my mouth water; and platters of piecemeal fill the impromptu tables. A large pot of soup rests at the tableside, steam billowing out and encircling everyone. Then, the music stops. Everyone pauses.

A sudden eruption of cheers, tears, and sobs explode my fatigued head. My brain strains under the sound. A cacophony of thanks, praises, and clapping assaults my ears. My nails sink into Damirius' arm - if I drew blood, neither of us noticed. His grip tightens on my hip. It's oddly comforting to know neither of us are feeling receptive to such a loud appraisal.

A sudden, sharp clap silences the crowd. The civilians step back, revealing the hunched form of Egret Burimir. Her bulbous, cold glare has transformed into a warm, twinkling smile. Heartfelt, joyous tears tumble through her wrinkled eyes and down to her jowls. As she approaches us, she motions for us to sit in nearby chairs.

"Please, please," she implores. We stumble into rickety chairs, and my body almost melts into the unstable woodwork. She sits in a chair opposite us, her soft demeanour a stark contrast from the woman we met a day… two days…?
"How long were we asleep for?" I blurt out.
"You've been out for nearly three days, sweetheart," Egret explains, her voice soft. "We didn't want to wake you. Seems like you needed it."
Damirius' eyes meet mine; the shocked expression mirroring my own.

The moment passes quickly, as she announces the beginning of their feast. Warm soup fills my belly and my body relaxes completely for the first time in a week. Our glasses were never left empty; weak ale was always immediately poured into them when they were deemed 'too low'. I stomach the ale, my normal repulsion for the drink evaporated against the need to quench my thirst. Over the course of the meal, Egret begins to divulge what had happened before we arrived.

"It was ravaging the town for the better part of a year," she explains, "Our homes would be attacked, and people would start disappearing. But it was only a few months ago that the whisperin' started; that was when we decided to cut contact with the rest of the world." A shaky breath leaves her as she recounts, "That beast made us relive our darkest moments and shame. I'm certain it was to keep us separate from each other."

I continue to listen to Egret's tale, my interest piquing as she describes how she had realised that only one person could be tormented at a time. The rest were left in a state of unease after their 'session', as she called them. It was only during one of her lucid moments that Egret had managed to scrawl a letter seeking help.
She was lucky to find a messenger bird the original inn used to house; she presumed they had all fled. Then she was left with just a faint hope that the bird managed to find Mack and he was able to find someone foolhardy enough to help. It was the only thing that kept her sane after her 'sessions' were extended, once the beast realised what she had done.

I'm in awe at the woman's unwavering resilience; she pulled through a harrowing ordeal, and continues as the matriarch of the harbour. Yet she thanks me for delivering the final blow.

"You're the hero here, Ms. Burimir," I remark, softly. The elder's lip wobbles, but she lifts her jowls into a miniscule smile.
"Thank you, dear... But we couldn't have done it without you two." Her hands clasp mine and Damirius', and she gives a small squeeze. Then, she turns and ushers two women over to us. The women carry a basin each, with a few cloths draped over their arms.

"It's not much," Egret admits bashfully, "But let us at least clean you up a little and heal some of the minor wounds."
Damirius almost jumps at the chance - if he could jump, that is. Carefully, the women work on removing the grime and blood from our faces. The woman attending to me - an older woman by the name of Francine - is extremely delicate.

A thumb and forefinger barely touch my chin to hold me still as she ghosts the damp cloth against my skin. Each flinch or wince of pain I try to hide is met with a gentle apology before she continues. Once my face is cleared, she dips a finger into a small glass container of ointment. With a delicate precision, she smears the ointment over where I presume minor cuts are. It tingles.

Once Francine finishes on my face, she turns her attention to my arms. I take this opportunity to glance at Damirius. His face seems much brighter; the murky deep purple has returned to his natural lilac shade. Small cuts adorn his face, most of which are lightly coated in a sheen of ointment. More severe slashes mark along his shoulders and neck, and a pang of shame slams into my chest. I lower my head and watch Francine lovingly care for my wartorn arms.

We became the stars of the festival, much to my dismay. People dance and twirl around us as musicians compose songs in our honour. It's all so overwhelming. My head pounds at the noise, but I try to keep my composure. The familiar feeling of Damirius' hand lightly touches my knuckles. My head turns to look at him, and I see his gorgeous, sunset eyes are full of worry. He tilts his head, asking a silent question. My fingers interlock with his in response.

The festivities die long after the moons rise, the music winding down as the people finally return into their rickety homes. Though, the atmosphere is different. People are dawdling. They're watching the stars and moons in the sky. Feet roam paths that haven't been touched in months. Hope lingers in the air, no longer stale with fear.

Finally, we haul ourselves back to the inn. The townsfolk are eager to help, but we decline each time. My body continues to ache, but the cries of my muscles become mere whimpers. The promise of sleep seems to soothe them for now.

The minor clean from earlier seems to have calmed the cuts, but I've now been made aware of deep gashes that have appeared across my arms and neck. My tunic is soaked in dried blood. My skin feels tight; I'm wary of the wounds reopening as we walk. But the persistent screaming of my ribs demands my attention. Everything else feels miniscule to their constant wailing.

Finally, we reach the stairs to our room. It feels like we're climbing a mountain as we ascend to bed. The battle and consequent celebration has stolen any energy I had left – if there was any at all. We collapse as carefully as we can onto the bed together. Our limbs barely miss each other. But we don't care. Within seconds, we're fast asleep, limbs entangled. And I have no intention of waking until my body is ready.

22

Damirius

Groggily, I rise from my slumber. A smattering of sunlight scatters across the hills that sit outside our window. The lake sparkles in the sun; a happier, more fruitful colour in its ripples. But it was neither the sun, nor the sound of birds chirping, that woke me up.

Rushed footsteps and yells echo through the Harbour. Nylani is already sitting upright; the noise must have alerted her, too. Her elongated ears twitch as she focuses on the ruckus below. It's quite cute; like a cat inspecting a new environment. She stalks towards the window, her eyes focused as she continues to listen.

Her hand instinctively cradles her side as she hobbles along the floor. Her face seems calm, but I can see her nostrils flare under the stress. It's easy to look for signs when you know what you're looking for. The sun seems stronger today - if that's possible. The sunlight pours over Nylani's face as she approaches the window. It highlights the deep valleys that split across her skin; old and new. Red and purple marks smother her face, and I feel my heart squeeze at the sight. Her eyes squint. Something's caught her eye.

I prop myself up on an elbow, watching Nylani as she leans closer into the window. She stands, motionless. Then a proud smile fills her swollen, split lips. Curiosity gets the better of me, and I slide out of bed.

Once I reach the window, I lean over the tiny elf, hand planted on the wall beside her head. I'm greeted to the sight of busy streets; the humans are scattered everywhere, running to and fro. Some bark orders, others are rushing with arms full of materials, and many of them are shifting debris. It's awe-inspiring to watch. The thrum of anticipation and excitement is palpable in the air. It practically buzzes across my skin as I watch the townsfolk go.

I glance down at Nylani, who I find is already looking at me. We both silently nod. Stumbling, we grab our bags and trundle out of the inn. The sun warms my cheeks as soon as I step outside. My muscles immediately relax. My eyes close and I soak in the heat. A gentle breeze wisps around me, waking my weary bones. Somehow, I feel more awake than I have done in days. And it seems the rest of the world feels the same.

The grass looks greener, the sky's more vibrant, and even the lake appears to have changed shade. It's almost as if I'm walking through an entirely new world.
Slowly, we make our way towards the centre, glancing at everything that crosses our path. There was a renewed sense of wonder within the harbour. Everything that was here before felt fresh - rejuvenated, even. Excited chittering and the commotion of people hums around me, whilst the distant sloshing of the sea whisks crisp sea-water air into the carefree quayside.

Suddenly, a flustered looking Egret rushes at us. Her arms wave above her head as she yells, "Wait! Stop, you two!"
Immediately, Nylani stops. I pause. Egret continues to approach us, hands on her hips like a scolding mother. It's quite endearing, actually. "There's more than enough people here to help. No working for you two."

Nylani responds first. "But... We're feeling much better." Her head whips to me, eyes pleading. My confusion must be visible, because her face drops. She looks defeated. "It feels wrong to not help." She finally concedes. Egret's face softens as her hands gently cup Nylani's cheeks. Grey eyes flutter at the touch. Then Nylani's brows tense. Egret doesn't seem to notice.

"You took a great, big battering, young lady," the older dwarvish woman says. Her voice is soft, but firm. Her instinctive behaviour makes me wonder if she is a mother. The idea hurts my heart.

"You mustn't do anything else, okay?" The harshness evaporates; a soft plea is all that remains. Nylani has fallen silent, her eyes downcast. Mole-dappled fingers gently stroke the ruined landscape of Nylani's cheeks. She pulls her head out of Egret's hand, her face unusually sour. The contorted, pained expression quickly fades and gets replaced by her default stoic self. But her eyes seem to be leagues away.

Egret's hand falls back to her hip. My hand craves to caress Nylani's back. But I don't. Something is telling me I should give her space. Egret catches my attention from the corner of my eye. I turn to face her, and she offers me a knowing, sad smile. I return it.

"Anyway," Egret hurriedly continues, "I actually came here to give you a gift."

Before we can object, a crinkled, yellowed envelope is pushed into Nylani's hand. Her eyebrows rise, but she doesn't show any other emotion. I edge a little closer to Nylani. Something doesn't feel right. Egret turns, pulling my attention away from the tense elf. The miniscule elder points towards a set of hills that rest to the north-east of the harbour.

"There, in the crook of those two hills, is a healing spring," she continues. "The woman there will heal your wounds, both new…" She trails off for a moment. Her eyes dart towards Nylani before she trains her eyes on me. "…and old." My eyes flit to Nylani. Her jaw is clenched tight. Whatever silent conversation the women are having is not a good one.

Egret clears her throat and my attention is drawn to her again. "The envelope you hold will tell her what you have done here. She'll treat you well." A wry smile appears beneath the wrinkles. "It shouldn't take you long to find the springs. Just follow the path up the hills."

I send a questioning look to Nylani, then point my eyes to the crumpled, flimsy envelope in her hands. My head tilts, and an eyebrow raises the silent question; do we venture forth? She responds with a nod, which I smile at. Time for our next adventure.

The walk to the barely standing entryway of Hushed Harbour was silent. Egret toddles ahead of us, hands clasped ahead of her. My eyes repeatedly wander to the elf beside me, but nothing penetrates the stoic mask she has lifted. Before long, we're under the near collapsing sign we started at. Suddenly, Egret's tiny hand clasps mine.

"I'm sorry," she mumbles, looking up at me apologetically.
"For what?" I ask.
"You two deserve much more for what you did here," the elder says. Regret twangs in her voice, "But this is all I can give as of now. And a promise that no matter when we shall see you next, Hush Harbour is a home for you."

Without much thought, I bend down and wrap my arms around the tiny woman. Her frail hands pat my back.
"There's no need for any reward, Mrs. Burimir." I whisper to her. "Don't fret about repaying us. The greatest reward is seeing your town alive and well."

Foreign tears dampen my shirt, and her hands tremble against my shoulders. I squeeze her a little tighter. The ghostly touch of a hand grazes against my arm – a confirmation that my partner agrees. My eyes lift to look at her. A weak smile pulls at elven lips.

Slowly, Egret pulls away, eyes watery but smiling. "Take the envelope and enjoy yourselves. You deserve that much, at least." Slowly, Egret returns through the rotten archway and into the Harbour. And we're alone, once again.

23

Nylani

"Well," Damirius proclaims, shattering the silence, "Let's get movin'." His head tilts towards the general direction of the hills before us. A cheeky grin cocks his lips, the protrusion of his fangs peering past his smile. A small smile presses my lips as my eyes roll. The lingering tension of Egret's probing looks finally melt away.

It's obvious she meant well, but the constant smothering attention makes my skin prickle. My mind forcibly pushes the thought of her insistent eyes away. Slowly, I trudge past Damirius, desperate to get away from bulbous, intrusive eyes. My feet can barely lift off the ground; the soles brush against gravel as the trek goes into a slight incline. The familiar, supportive arm wraps around my back. My hand naturally finds his free wrist, and I stabilise myself. Secretly, I'm relieved for the help.

Eventually, after an arduous trek, we arrive at the springs. The sun hangs low in the sky, resting between full, puffy clouds. Streams of golden light break through, and glisten upon the white marble exterior of the solitary reservoir. The singular structure looks almost holy; a grand, lustrous temple nestled in the intersection of two hilltops. The entryway is a large arch in an open doorway, the reception area in clear view from our position just outside the building.

The same white marble fills the interior of the building - in a very unnaturally organic way. Everything merges to the floor, as much as the floor merges to the furniture. It seems as though the marble was pulled from the surrounding hillsides, and shaped into the forms of a building. Like a statue chiselled out from a slab. Or a series of sculptures made from clay. It's hard to tell. Especially when everything joins together seamlessly.

Slowly, we walk inside. We head for the reception area, and I notice a seating area on the right-hand side. Spacious enough to seat a handful of customers, but it is empty. Everywhere is empty. An uneasiness settles into my stomach. Damirius seems to feel the same way. He settles us into some seats, but he keeps close to me. His arm stays around me. Despite looking soft, the chairs are rock solid. The same cream-coloured marble makes up the luscious looking benches - and all the superficial wrinkles of hard cushions. Approaching footsteps alert me, and I go to rise.

My ribs groan, and I humbly sit down again. My body slumps against Damirius. He holds me gently. Just then, a human woman in a simple, silk white robe comes into view. Her deep brown hair is slicked into a tight bun, and her dark almond eyes brighten as she sees us. A large, kind smile pushes against taupe skin. She stands out against the dazzlingly white building.

"Hello," the woman says. Her voice barely above a whisper, but it still echoes against the empty halls. "I am welcoming you to the Healing Springs of Cresthill. How can I be of helping?"
I stumble slightly, her dialect confusing me momentarily. It was easy enough to understand once the initial uncertainty leaves. I fish the letter out of my pocket.

"We were told by Mrs Egret Burimir of Hush Harbour to give this to you," I reply softly as I hand it to the woman. Her elongated fingers open the letter with ease. I'm almost certain the sound of ripping parchment was nonexistent. A tense silence fills the barren foyer as the petite woman stands and reads the letter in great detail. Deep, dark eyes lift to look at us. She studies our bodies, almost scanning us from head to toe. The hairs on the back of my neck practically jolt upright.

"Miss Burimir is saying lots about you two," she finally states matter-of-factly, as she lowers the letter to the desk beside her. "It is said you were the ones to be destroying of the golem in their lake?" She tilts her head in question innocently, like a misunderstanding pet.

I look at Damirius. He shrugs half-heartedly. Silently, we nod in acknowledgement to the strange woman. She smiles. Her lips stretch a little too far.

"Well, it is certainly looking like you did. Golems are definitely hard of hitting." She gives a small chuckle, enjoying her own bizarre joke. I force a polite smile. "I am agreeing with Miss Burimir," she concludes, the long, thin smile still on her face. "You two can be of using the springs to be mending yourselves."

She turns to direct us towards a long corridor that sits behind her. The corridor holds many doors that run down either side of the hallway. Each door is identical, aside from the number that rests at the top. "Follow me, please."

Damirius and I share a sceptical glance to each other. He raises an eyebrow to me. Reluctantly, I nod. We move. Slowly, we follow the peculiar woman down the long corridor.

Like the rest of the building, the walls of the corridor use the same white marble, as do the doors. We finally reach the end of the corridor, and stand in front of a door labelled with an ornate, silver one at the top. The door is pushed open for us, and a stunning, large room awaits ahead.

In the centre of the room sits a tub – the large rectangular pit sinks into the ground and benches sit around the edge of the room. The pool bubbles; spring water sloshes in from a marble spout that sits at the farthest end of the tub. Steam wafts upwards to the ceiling and dissipates, filling the room with moisture.

The organic, cyclical motion of water creates a ripple of waves in the tub. Gently, it sloshes over the edge of the tub and pools over the irrigated floor. The water seems to sparkle against the white floor. At closer inspection, I can see microscopic flecks of iridescent shards scatter through the water that pours into the tub. Odd.

Begrudgingly, my eyes peel away from the glistening water to take in the rest of the room. The walls are almost completely windowed, and the golden light of late afternoon saturates the room. The ravine the water pushes and pulls from flows through to a hollow inside one of the hillsides.

The highs and lows of the rolling hillside stretch as far as my eyes can see; the tumbling expanse seems endless from up here. The sky has become a painter's palette of yellows, blues, pinks, and lilacs; the clouds separating them in splotches of whites and greys. The scenery alone is enough to pull my body into a state of relaxation.

The woman turns to us, a pair of white cotton towels suddenly appearing in her hands. "A room for partners," she announces. My stomach drops. "I hope you are finding it comfortable and relaxing.

Here are the towels for you to be using. Please be enjoying your bath."

She rests the towels on a nearby bench, and rapidly exits the room. The door closes behind her, along with all hope I have of getting out of here. Stunned, I stay fixed to the floor, staring at the door. Something shuffles beside me. My head turns and immediately my hands fly to cover my eyes as I squeal. The image of Damirius in just his undergarments burns into my retinas. His laugh booms around the room.

"Never seen a naked man before, Tiny?" he snickers. I feel the heat rising in my cheeks. I want to claw my own face off.
 "No!" I yell, "No, I've never been near or with a naked man!" My face and neck feel like they're burning. Damirius is silent. Then, he panics.
"Oh! Oh, Gods! Oh no, I didn't think—I couldn't believe---!!" Within seconds, the splash of water fills the room. It sounds as though he dove into the tub. "Okay, it's safe. You can uncover yourself now."

Slowly, my hands peel away from my eyes. Though, it doesn't matter much, as they're scrunched tight anyway. He laughs again. "It's not funny!" I bellow. Embarrassment is not an emotion I deal with well, and this entire scenario is embarrassing.

"No," he agrees, "But, it is rather cute."
I grumble, my eyes trained to stare at my boots. They dart to the windowed walls, and my heart nearly bursts out of my already broken ribcage. There are no curtains. No way of shielding myself from the outside. No barriers to hide behind.

"I can't do this."
"Why?" Damirius looks around, "There's no one here. No one can see you."
I look at him, incredulous. His innocently confused face shows my greatest fear. He truly doesn't understand. We stare at each other; him in puzzlement, me in horror.

"C'mon, Tiny," he softly urges, "There's no one around. And the water is beautifully warm." A playful splash hits against my chest, and the warmth immediately soothes my skin. It's tempting. Fear keeps me still, but the temptation of a warming bath coaxes me closer.
"Tell you what," Damirius pipes up. "I'll turn

around. That way I won't see you, and I can keep an eye out to make sure no one else can see you. Deal?"

My fingers twist the hem of my tunic. My teeth chew at my lip. Everything about this makes me uneasy, but the promise of safety is horribly encouraging. Silently, I nod. My stomach flips rapidly. Immediately, he turns away so his back faces me.

Even with him facing away, I can't stop myself from turning as well. Old habits die hard, I guess. Slowly, I pull my tunic over my head. My movements are stiff. The aches and pain don't help. Lifting my right arm is a monumental task itself. Eventually, my shirt is removed and folded on one of the benches beside me. My boots follow. As do my trousers. I'm left in my undergarments, and I can finally see the extent of my wounds.

My skin is mostly discoloured; the caramel tint is swallowed in reds and purples. I should be used to seeing myself like this, but it's always jarring. Something about seeing the culprit of your discomfort seems to make the wounds more profound.

I risk a glance backwards to Damirius. His back still faces me. A wave of relief washes over me. Feeling braver, I remove my smallclothes and finally slide into the steaming pool. Instantaneously, the warmth sinks into my skin and I shudder in relief. The water rests around my shoulders, the steam sticking to my hair and face.
"You can turn around now," I say softly.

His body turns around, and his eyes quickly dart around to avoid looking at me. I glance down, and become painfully aware that the water doesn't obscure much. My arms immediately cover my chest. The heat of embarrassment rekindles my cheeks, but I can't help noticing that Damirius has turned a deep indigo.

"Never seen a naked woman before, Damirius?" I mock, laughter building as his skin deepens even more.
"Sorry," he mumbles. "Didn't mean to look." He goes to look down at the water, but quickly changes his mind and stares at the ceiling. I can't stop the quirk of a grin that pulls my lips. Watching him squirm is quite enjoyable, actually.

He stays still, almost statuesque, as his eyes stay pinned to the ceiling. My grin evolves into a quiet laugh as I watch his chest heave.
The awkward tension is palpable. I'm not sure whether to move, or laugh, or both. I decide to splash water at him instead.

The spray of water hits his face, and his intense stare upwards is broken. He looks at me, shocked, before he suddenly laughs and splashes water back at me. Our laughter fills the chamber as we finally relax in the presence of each other.

Steadily, a gentle, tingling sensation starts to grow over me. It's warm. Hotter than the water around me, but not hot enough to burn. Like the sun tanning skin instead of blistering it. I melt into the sensation, the heat becoming a soothing balm to my skin.

An unexpected sparkle catches my eye. I glance down, only to see my entire body scattered with tiny glittering particles. The incandescent lustre glistens from a viscous liquid that sticks to my skin. The globs almost resemble bedazzled slugs. I shudder.

My right arm begins to sting, and I turn my head to see the substance sink into the deep slice in my forearm. Wide eyed, I look to Damirius, who's inspecting a shimmering section of his thigh. The miniscule, coagulated blob slides from his thigh and slowly sinks to the bottom, out of view. He notices me watching, and smiles weakly.
"Scorned client," he explains. I don't ask.

Curiously, I pull an arm out of the water. The shimmering gelatin slides down my skin like translucent slugs, before they plop into the water again. Scar tissue begins to lift and lighten as more of the mysterious substance peels away from the wound.

My fingers probe along the scar, the jagged ridges now a much softer, smoother curve. A consistent, pleasurable heat permeates from the dip in my skin. I sink a little further into the water, content for the first time in a long while.

A sudden crack ricochets through the chamber, and a blinding pain erupts from my side. Within seconds I'm under the water, my screams silenced in bubbles. The heat is undescribable. My body is frozen from shock. I want to rip my ribs out of my skin, but my hands can't stop shaking. My head is spinning; I can't tell if I'm floating or sinking. Warm water suffocates me, pouring into my throat as I try to breathe. Another crack shakes the tub, and my vision is gone.

24

Damirius

In an instant, Nylani's out of view. I dive, panic rising as her lifeless body slowly drifts down. She looks almost ethereal; a beacon of light as thousands of glittering salves pour from her tiny form. I push further down. Finally, I grab an arm. I fight against the current, yanking her towards me. Both arms wrap around her – nakedness be damned – and I fight my way back to the top. The resounding booms of her bones breaking make me want to vomit.

At last, air fills my lungs as my head breaches the surface. I gasp, choking against the water that's determined to stay in my nose. My arms lift Nylani out of the water, cradling her to my chest as I move us to the edge of the pool. I hoist her out of the tub, and lie her on the floor. She remains lifeless.

"No no no no no!" I panic. Hurriedly, I scramble out of the pool and kneel beside her. Without a thought, I push against her chest. Once. Twice. A third time. A sudden, wheezing gasp comes out of her.

She splutters and gags, but I've never felt happier. She rolls onto her side and continues to rasp noisily. My hand claps against her back and she manages a deep, clear breath. Her face is covered in sparkling slime. My thumbs roughly wipe it away, allowing her eyes to finally open.

"You gave me a fright, Tiny," I pant. My fingers push her soaked hair away from her face. She continues to heave, her chest rising and falling dramatically. The bruising on her skin is minimal compared to before. Nothing is said, the only sound is our collective panting.

Slowly, I drag myself to the edge of the tub, dangling my legs into the water again. Nylani's eyes shut tight once she realises we're both still naked. I laugh. After everything we just went through, she's still worried about our bodies.

Shaking my head, I dip back into the pool. I turn to face her, and impulsively grab her in a tight embrace. She doesn't fight it.

Her hands are shaking, but she clings to my shoulders tightly. My heart surges; a wave of protective affection pours through me. My arms squeeze against her a little more. Her legs shift and dangle into the pool beside me. Her head rests against my shoulder. My cheek lies against her ear. We stay like this for a while.

The sun begins to vanish behind the hills as the moons slowly rise into the sky. Eventually, her erratic breathing calms, and we both pull away. Her face stays close to mine, and I find myself dazzled at how her long lashes flutter against her cheeks. And that her freckles look like a constellation against her skin.

Deep brown hair falls around her face with ease. Her beauty is effortless, and I'm starstruck. It isn't until I'm taking note of how the colour of her eyes contradict her tanned skin that I realise those gorgeous, silvery eyes are staring directly at me. I jump backwards, arms flying up. She laughs. My skin warms under her scrutinising gaze.

"You okay?" she asks. A devious grin lifts her cheeks, "You seemed lost in thought there."
"Yeah, I-I was just..." I stammer. My cheeks feel like miniature infernos. "Yeah, I'm okay."

She doesn't pry any more, and I'm thankful for it. We stay at the side of the tub - me submerged, her sitting - for a while, and gently push the remnant gel off of Nylani's skin. Though we seem more comfortable in the presence of each other, I still remain cautious as to where I lay my hands.

Most of my attention is on her back, peeling off what feels like thousands of thin strips. I can't fathom how many scars must have covered her back, but they're either gone or are partially healed now. The only ones that remain must have been vicious before. A deep, curved line curls over her spine and finishes at her left shoulder blade. I quickly look away from it, and notice the weak, yellowed bruise that nestles in her ribcage instead.

"Well," I quietly say, "at least the spring healed your ribs."
"Could've been less aggressive about it," she grumbles. Annoyance pulls her lips into a frown, and her fingers gingerly caress the dim bruise.

Unsteadily, she rises to her feet and my eyes squeeze shut as her ass fills my view. A ringing laughter echoes around the room. Gods, I wish the tub drowned me instead.

"You drag my unconscious ass out of the pool, and now you're suddenly shy?" Her laughter grows, and I want nothing more than to be underwater. "I presumed you, of all people, would be used to seeing the unclothed," she teases.
"It's different!" I whine. Another roar of laughter fills the chamber, and I sink further into the water. "My mind was a bit preoccupied while you were drowning in my arms."

"So, you admit your mind's occupied on my ass now?" I can hear the devilish grin in her voice. Oh, please pool, swallow me whole.
"There's no winning with you, is there?" I grumble, frustrated.
"No, so get used to it," she chuckles.

A towel smacks me in the face, and I have to quickly grab it before it falls in the water. I throw it back at her, and grin as it hits her face. I pull myself out of the tub as she scrambles to pull the towel away. She goes to throw it, notices I'm out of the water, and squawks in surprise. The towel falls to the floor as she covers her eyes, and I bark out a laugh.

"Shut up! Shut up! Shut up!" She squeals, which just makes me laugh harder. The fallen towel is scooped up and tied around my waist.
"Alright," I grin, "It's safe again."

She uncovers her eyes and scowls at me. My grin spreads wider. Shaking my head, I walk to the door. I swing the door open and bow dramatically, arm bending across my waist.
"After you, m'lady," I announce, voice teasing.
 She grimaces as she walks past, and I chuckle.
"Not a fan of honorifics?" I continue, "What about, 'My Liege'?"

She groans, and I cackle. Damp feet softly pad against the cool marble flooring, as we finally leave the wet room. The receptionist suddenly appears at the end of the hallway, forcibly reminding me that she exists. A potent air of enthusiasm emanates from her, and it makes me uneasy. She stands at the far doorway, unmoving, though her excitement is apparent.

25

Nylani

"I am assuming that the time for bathing is over, hm?" the woman's smile spreads thin. Her posture is rigid. She stays in the doorway of the long corridor, hands calmly clasped in front of her. But her head tilts awkwardly. Her eyes don't blink. I glance back at Damirius, unease rising in my chest. "Everything is being well, yes?"

An indescribable indignation fills me. Apprehension is replaced by outrage. "No, not everything is well!" I practically scream, "I nearly died!" My voice is much louder than I had meant for it to be, but I'm past the point of caring. I was screaming bloody murder, and she was nowhere to be seen. But she has the gall to stand here, mere metres away, and act as though nothing happened?

The woman's brows furrow, puzzled, "I am not understanding," she states. "The spring's healing cannot be murdering. That would be doing the opposite of the spring's magic." Perplexed innocence fills the bizarre woman's face, dark eyes wide in confusion. My temper rises. Her bewilderment isn't feigned, and for some reason that vexes me more.

"I nearly drowned!" I yell. The woman's face instantly falls. My voice lowers as I try to curb my temper. "The healing hurt, and when I screamed I got pulled underwater." She gives a deep bow, a sombre look on her face.

"I am sorrowful," she says, her soft voice low and solemn. "It was not of my meaning for you to be unprepared. I should have been explaining the spring's magics to you so it was not giving you a frighten." Her head doesn't rise as she apologises. She stays in a low bow, eyes focused on the floor.

I glance beside me to Damirius, who simply shrugs. I let out a frustrated sigh. I turn back to the woman, who hasn't moved.
"Alright," I finally concede, my rage simmering. "I can see you're genuinely apologetic." The petite woman's face lifts to look at me. "It doesn't seem like you get many visitors here, so I guess it makes

sense you wouldn't know." A shake of the attendant's head confirms my thoughts.
"Well, let's see this as a learning point, alright?" I remark, albeit pointedly. "Just... make sure to warn people next time, okay?"

The strange woman nods fervently, her eyes fixated on me. With my temper settled, the sinking uneasiness returns. The longer I look at her, the more inhumane she becomes. Her eyes are unblinking; pupils dilating and almost swallowing her irises whole. Her lips seem to stretch impossibly wide, the desperation of hunger clear on her face.

I stumble back, into Damirius' chest, and the woman seems to snap out of her trance. Her eyes dart behind us, glancing down the hall, before they settle on us again. I shift closer to Damirius.
"Would you be liking to be staying in a room for this night?" her cheery demeanour is back again, as if the previous conversation never happened.
Before I can even open my mouth, Damirius agrees. I glare at him. His head lowers to my ear as he whispers, "It's already dark, Tiny. We don't know where we'll be able to sleep out there."

I sigh, frustrated, but I reluctantly agree. The woman quickly skitters back to the front desk. Cautiously, we follow behind her. As we approach, she holds out a small key, dangling from her index finger.

"I am showing you to your room, yes?" she asks. "No, that's okay," I force a polite response. My nerves are wracking through me; everything screams danger. The key drops into my open hand.

"Ah, yes, that is acceptable." She smiles at me. Her teeth are pointed. "The room is being the first door you see at the top of the stair casing. Enjoy your restfulness." She chirps happily, watching us as we approach the staircase.

As we reach the bottom of the stairs, a wet thud behind us makes me pause. Slowly, my head turns to face the sound, just in time to see a jet-black, slimy tail slither into the corridor from which we had just exited.

Quickly, we scramble to the room. We stumble in, locking the door behind us. My back presses against the door, panting. Damirius leans against the wall beside me.

"You saw that too, right?" He whispers.
"The jet-black eel like tail?" I hiss back, "Or the fact it was going to the room we were just in?!"
"Both."
"Yes, I saw!"

Tension builds as we stay silent. My ears strain to hear movement, if any, but nothing is heard. Somehow, that stresses me more. My body presses against the door, ear almost merging into it. My eyes close, trying to focus my attention on anything beyond the door. Nothing. No movement, no sounds, nor any sense of anything past the immediate four walls.

A warm breath wafts over my back. I yelp, spinning to face the source. My fist collides with something solid. And something purple. Damirius groans, holding his jaw.

"Shit!" I shout, adrenaline pumping through me. I cradle my hand, soothing my sore knuckles, "What'd you do that for?!"
"It wasn't on purpose!" he retorts, "Some of us need to *breathe*, Princess!"

"Sorry," I mumble, head lowering. "You startled me."
"Yeah, I gathered," he grunts.

Shame fills me. Slowly, I lower to the floor, my knees folding up to my chest. I stay close to the door, pressing my ear against the marble again. A gentle grazing of fingers reaches for my elbow. I flinch away from his touch.

26

Damirius

My heart shatters. Slowly, my hand inches away. I sit beside her, at an arm's distance, my back against the cool marble wall. She looks pallid; eyes downcast, arms wrapped around her knees. My body yearns to touch her - soothe her somehow - but I fight against the feeling.

"Hey," I call to her softly. Her eyes flit up to look at me. "It's okay," I say, "I'm not hurt." I offer her a small smile. Her eyes soften, and I feel my heart skip. My smile grows and I relax against the wall. "I am, however," I continue, a dry chuckle underlying my speech, "amazed that we're in another weird situation already."

Quiet chuckling grows beside me, and I join in. The stress that holds the tiny woman tight begins to melt away. Her arms unwind from her knees, and her legs lower to the floor. She shifts closer to me,

the warmth of her skin tickling the hairs of my arms.
"And I'm annoyed," she quips back, a smile still evident on her lips, "Why do people keep assuming we're a couple?!"

Her arm gestures towards a large four-poster bed incredulously. It sits a few feet from us, smothered in multiple layers of blankets. It looks cosy. I walk to the bed, a cursitory hand pressing against it. Soft. Plush. I dive onto the bed, much to Nylani's amusement. My body melts into it, the fear of the monster within the spa melting away, too.

"I do have one request," I call out to Nylani, in my sanctuary of blankets.
"Hm?"
"I get to be the boyfriend." A pillow smacks against my nose, and I can't stop laughing.

Hours pass, and I'm woken by golden rays of light spreading across my face. Grumbling, I sit up, and my eyes blink the blurry vision of the bedroom away. Glimmers of early morning sun peak through the blinds, and bathe the room in a golden hue. The pearlescent marble twinkles in the light; it's almost heavenly. The white linen that pools around my waist is tinted in the ethereal morning light, and I feel rejuvenated. The trickles of warmth against my bare skin don't compare against my bedmate, however.

Despite being on the other side of the bed, the heat she produces still manages to reach me. I chuckle softly. Memories of her being terrified at the prospect of lying in bed resurface. It was only when we had decided to sleep that we realised neither of us had retrieved our clothes. And neither of us wanted to brave whatever resided downstairs to rescue them. So, Nylani devised a plan.

We take our share of blankets, and stay on one half of the bed. The only issue that she doesn't seem to realise is that she moves in her sleep. My night consisted of prying the elf off of me, fearing for my life that she would wake and freak out. I chuckle at the memory.

My eyes graze over the sleeping elf. If she were any further off the bed, she would fall out. I shake my head, amused. Then, something catches my eye. At the far right of the room resides a small, cyclical table. It's made of the same white marble that makes everything else here. What catches my attention, though, are the two neatly stacked piles of clothes that sit atop the table. Clothes that I am very certain were not there last night. Tentatively, I creep out of the bed, and am immediately greeted to cold morning air. I shiver. My foot makes contact with the floor, and I'm surprised that it's heated. Small graces.

As I approach the table, I spot a note that rests across both sets of clothes. It's a small, scrap piece of parchment. Blotches of ink scatter across the page, intermingling with the barely legible handwriting.

I am giving you sincere apologies for my behaviour on the yesterday's night. I was very hungry. But that is not giving an acceptable excusing. It will not be happening again. I am promising you.
Please be accepting of my gifting. I am hoping you are appreciating them.
I am wishing that this is not upsetting you,
Lady

The note creates more questions than answers. How did she get clothes? Where are our old clothes? Did she unlock the door and neither of us noticed? Did she see me naked? I tense at the thought. Being eaten, naked and asleep, is not the way I saw myself going.

I shake the thought away. She hasn't eaten me... At least, not yet. And she left me clothes. Very nice clothes, by the looks of it. Vibrant hues of purple and red catch my eye. And a simple pair of briefs in a light cream. I have to stifle a laugh. Here I am, stark naked in a spa, terrified of being eaten by a gigantic eel-like monster, and she bought me underpants.

Quietly, I pull the clothes on, surprised at how well they fit; a pair of deep burgundy, corduroy trousers that hug my legs; a shimmering powder-white shirt with loose sleeves gets pulled on; followed by a deep purple waistcoat, with a golden, floral design embedded into the bodice. Once I finish dressing myself, I wander towards the simple, oval mirror that's embedded into the wall. And I nearly faint at my reflection. The clothes fit me gorgeously. I stand, admiring myself, until a sharp cough from behind me startles me out of my transfixion.

Sheepishly, I turn to face her, smiling wryly. She sits upright, blankets covering her chest, eyebrow raised in quiet judgement. My cheeks burn. I point to the table.
"Looks like we got the premium package," I say.
"Apparently so", Nylani agrees, voice full of suspicion.

She rises from the bed, and wraps a linen sheet around her. Her eyes never leave the folded clothing, as if she's walking towards a wild animal. I have to bite my tongue to stop my laughter.

"They're just clothes, Nylani. They won't hurt you." It's getting harder to fight the urge to laugh. She looks like a threatened cat, hackles raised and on high alert. Finally, she reaches the table. Her thumbs and forefingers pinch the undergarments that rest atop the pile, and she holds them at arm's length, inspecting them dubiously. The flood gates open, and I roar with laughter.

27

Nylani

I shove the cackling tiefling, forcing him to face away from me. "Alright, alright. I get it," he giggles, covering his face with his hands. I silently shake my head and sigh. My back faces him, but I turn slightly to look. He stands obediently, face obscured by his hands. I relax a little. He may be an irritating imbecile, but at least he's kind.

I disrobe quickly, and pull the clothes on with haste. Despite their thin appearance, the materials carry a hefty weight with them. The simple, dark grey tunic fits my form like a glove, but it doesn't feel restrictive. The sleeves just pass my wrists, but don't obscure my hands. A pair of black, thick trousers follow after. The fastening rests higher than I'm used to, at my midriff. Though, it is comfortable.

A pair of boots sit beside the table. New, dark brown boots. Carefully, I lift them to eye level. A note is stuck to the heel of one.

Dearing Miss Nylani,
The old boots are being very damaged. Please be accepting of these new ones.
These should be of helping for you on your journeys.

I rip the note off the heel and pass it to Damirius. He reads it, and seems unphased. I regard him incredulously, and he shrugs.

"She's not wrong," he muses. "They were pretty beat up."
I sigh, exasperated. "This…" My hands wave around in frustration. "Just doesn't feel right."
"You mean to say that a creepy lady - who looked at you like a meal - suddenly giving us free clothes and leaving notes in our room isn't normal?" He retorts dismissively. "Wouldn't've guessed."

I flop back onto the bed, my frustration building. The bed sinks beside me. I don't lift my head. He leans back, hands behind him.

"Realistically," he says, breaking the silence, "If she wanted to eat us, she would've done so already. Obviously, she has access to the room."
I grumble an agreement, and Damirius chuckles.
"You're impossible, Tiny," he remarks. He nudges me. "C'mon, get your boots on."
"Well, it's these or nothing," I mumble, as I reluctantly sit up and pull them on.

I didn't want to admit it, but they really did feel a lot nicer than my old boots. He must've noticed my hesitation, as a wide, shit-eating grin plasters his face.
"Go look in the mirror," he says, not unkindly.
"No thanks," I scoff.

"Oh, come on," he laughs dismissively. Before I know it, I'm pushed towards the mirror.
Instinctively, my eyes look at the floor. Gentle hands urge my head up. Reluctantly, my eyes flit up to look at myself. And I feel tears threaten to fall already.

I'm much older now. I knew I was, but seeing it is unreal. Plump cheeks are now shallow. My smooth face is angular and jagged, much like the scars that once adorned it. It's like staring at a stranger; I don't recognise the woman in front of me.

My fingers gingerly brush against the bridge of my nose, expecting to feel the angry ridge that I had grown accustomed to. But all that remains is a small dip of a thin cut. Wide, pale grey eyes scan my reflection. The once rough, battle-scarred landscape of my face was clear. Hesitant fingers explore this new face – the only remaining scars rest across my nose and left brow. Droplets glide down my cheeks.

"I have freckles," I manage to choke out. "I never knew I had freckles before." This fact seems to make me cry harder.
Firm arms wrap around me from behind. Damirius' head rests on my shoulder. He stays silent as I finally break in his arms. We crumple to the floor together, his lanky body curling over mine like a protective blanket. I feel ashamed, crying like this, but I can't stop. I heave, desperate for breath, but the tears continue to flow.

"It's okay, Tiny," his voice whispers in my ear, "Let it all out." And just like that, the flood gates open. I weep; for the child I never got to be; for the woman I don't recognise; and the person I don't know how to become. This face isn't mine. It's gentle. Unmarred. Unburdened by years of pain. That face cannot be mine.

Tender hands turn me towards Damirius' body. Then, they cradle my head and back. He sways, humming a song I don't recognise under his breath. His fingers comb through my hair. My wails quieten to soft whimpers, and his arm squeezes against me.

"Shh, shh," he murmurs. "It's alright. I'm here." His heart beats softly against my temple, and my eyes flutter closed as I focus on it. Thump. Thump. Thump. The rhythmic drum is soothing. Finally, my breathing calms. My crying stops, as I slump against Damirius' chest, exhausted.

We stay on the floor for a while, my head pressed against his chest. His fingers card through my hair. His other hand rubs my back. I could sleep here, if I so choose. "Feeling better?" his voice rumbles from his chest. I nod half-heartedly, not wanting to move from my spot. His gentle chuckle jolts my head slightly.

"Ready to head out?" he asks softly. I grumble. I don't want to move, but I know we should.
"I suppose," I say, slowly inching away from him. I already miss the feeling of his arms around me.
"It's best to use as much daylight as we can."

He nods in agreement, slowly rising and retrieving our bags from beside the bed. The serpent woman - Lady - must have placed them there. The idea of her crawling around our room makes me uneasy. As Damirius moves away, the stains of my tears on his shirt are evident. My stomach tightens at the sight.

"I'm sorry," I muster, voice weak. He looks at me, confused. "For... For crying like that." He smiles, full of warmth and kindness, as he shakes his head. "It's alright, Tiny."
"It's just that – I – I just –"

He lifts a hand, cutting me off. "You don't need to explain, Tiny," he assures me. He flashes his smile at me, and the same feeling of comfort washes over me. I nod quietly, my apology dying in my throat. Finally, we shrug our bags over our shoulders, and head down the stairs.

The halls are eerily calm. The stagnant silence is not unusual for the reservoir, evidently, but deafening echoes of our footsteps set my nerves ablaze. The hairs on the back of my neck stand completely upright. The descent down the stairs is slow. I try to move as stealthily as I can, though the new boots make it near impossible. The tense leather creaks at each bend and crease of my feet. Damaged or not, at least my boots didn't make so much fucking noise. I grit my teeth, eyes scanning the room as the lobby comes into view.

'Lady' stands at the receptionist desk, her back turned to me. I let out a silent sigh of relief. If we manage to evade her, we can get out of here. We just need to be quiet. I crouch, grimacing as the boots squeak under my weight. She hasn't moved. I thank whichever gods are watching silently.

Tentatively, I creep across the lobby floor, sticking close to the wall. Damirius' breath rolls against my back. We pass the seating area. I glance at the doorway. Only a few feet left.

"Ah! Hello!" I nearly jump out of my skin, and tumble into Damirius. He falls onto his back, and my head collides with his stomach. Quickly, I find my feet and pull him up. My eyes turn to Lady, who simply looks at us with a blank smile. "I am seeing you are testing the new items of clothing. It is fitting your bodies good, I am hoping?"

28

Damirius

"Why?" Nylani demands, turning to face the bizarre woman. "Why did you give us clothes?" It was startling how quickly Nylani could flick between sobbing in my arms and glaring down an eldritch beast. It was almost terrifying. "Surely not every customer gets treated to such frivolities. So why us?"

The woman's brows furrow in confusion, "I am explaining to you my reasoning in the writing. You did do a reading of it, yes?" A small, unsure smile wavers on her thin lips, "I am apologising for my misbehaviour on the night of yesterday."

There's a pause. Then, her face pulls into a sorrowful frown. The line of her mouth almost encompasses her entire jaw. If it weren't so morbid, I'd feel genuine pity. "It is not taking a person of high intelligence to be knowing that you were seeing my natural form. I was hearing you running up the case of stairs." Our silence confirms her thoughts. She smiles weakly. Black eyes flicker to the floor, as if ashamed. "I was finding it very hard to be holding my hunger in. My hunger has been growing large for a long time." Lady explains, "So many Shimmers sitting in the pool, making my hunger growing in strength... I was not able to be having much control. I am sorrowful."

My eyes widen as realisation slaps me across the face. "So, you're not going to eat us?!" I blurt out. Nylani's face was enough to make me want to be sucked into the marble. I should not have said that aloud. Thankfully, Lady laughs. However, that also means I get to see the rows and rows of needle-like teeth that fill her mouth.

"No. My digestive tract would not be willing to have such a complex being within it," she explains, "Instead, I am eating pain. In many of the instances, the Shimmers are coming from a physical pain. But..." her eyes flicker over Nylani, "...there are some Shimmers that are appearing from an emotional or mental pain. Those can be becoming so strong that their Shimmer is very enticing to eat."

My eyes peek over to Nylani, her face unreadable. Stone eyes regard Lady impassively. But the tension between her shoulders tells me all that I need to know.

"The Springs are just to be washing pain away," Lady continues to explain, "I am just feasting on the remains - I am more of being the cleaning staff." She huffs a quiet laugh, though it's clear she's uneasy. She fiddles with her fingers. Her long, unnaturally thin fingers.

Nylani rolls the tension out of her shoulders. The ghost of a smile touches her lips, encouraging Lady to continue. A weak smile lifts the corners of her extended mouth. The intense politeness that holds Lady rigid slowly eases, her shoulders slumping slightly. "I am Wraith. Wraiths are eating things like Pain, Time, or Emotion; the things that are not being…" She pauses, looking around as if trying to find the right word. "That are not being… Real? Or not being physical, I am thinking."

Nylani's eyes light up, her entire demeanour relaxed. She seems to be studying Lady more thoroughly, her stance changing to one of morbid curiosity instead of hostility. My presumption is that she seems to have knowledge on Wraiths and their ilk. Which is great, because I haven't got the foggiest idea.

A small vibration of laughter builds in me. The ridiculousness of the past day finally surface and spill out. I double over, barking out a laugh. "By the Moons and Stars, Tiny. I wasn't expecting to get an education on our adventures!" I nudge her ribs, her bewildered amusement provoking a new wave of uncontrollable laughter.

Nylani begins to snicker. At me or with me, I'm uncertain. But I don't care. After the tumultuous turns we've endured, relief overwhelms me and flows out in bellowing chuckles.

Nylani's laughter grows alongside mine, and she tumbles into me. A harsh elbow drives into my rib, and I collide with the floor. Then the weight of a muscular elf drops atop me, and I groan in pain.

"Shit! Sorry!" She scrambles off me, before pulling me back to my feet. An unfamiliar, gentle laughter resounds beside us. The sound comes from the petite Wraith woman, needle-like teeth hidden behind thin lips.

"When I was first of meeting you," she manages to choke out, "I was being certain you were in relation of marriage." Her lithe body trembles as she tries to stifle her laughter. "But I am seeing I was being very, very incorrect! You two are most definitely in the relations of family."

29

Nylani

The laughter dies, as does the debate on whether I'd suffer more as Damirius' wife, or his sibling. My cheeks hurt. I'd not laughed like that for a long time... Or ever, really. As we settle, Damirius and I finally move towards the entryway of the springs. Rolling hills and plush meadows greet us, but there's little else here. By the looks of it, any towns that we'd be able to find work in were days, if not weeks, away. And even that is uncertain. I sigh.

"You ready?" I ask, nudging him softly.
"Where to?" His smile is dazzling in the morning sun.
"Well..." I think aloud. I glance around, trying to get some kind of bearing on where we are. The hills of the harbour sit on the horizon to the left of us. The sea stretches behind them. "If we go on water, we can pass the Isles, but there's not much there."

My face scrunches in thought. Shipwrecks and makeshift huts aren't worth a potentially dangerous trip. Especially now that I have another body to worry about. I turn right, trying to pinpoint a location on my mental map. It's hard when we're in the middle of nowhere.

"We could visit Dororra, but I'm not entirely sure how far away it is," I admit. "It's definitely at least a week's travel on foot, though."
"It's a busy town – it'd be worth the travel compared to islands no one really knows about," Damirius counters.

I hum an agreement. From what I can remember, Dororra sits north of the continent, alongside the neighbouring town of Ozmoor. Both cities are prolific in mining; though Ozmoor favoured its metals and jewels, whereas Dororra enjoyed clays and rockery. Dororra's large enough to house the entirety of Kohrmiir twentyfold and then some. There's definitely a high probability of getting work in a place that size.

"I am apologising for my dropping of eaves," Lady gently approaches, "but I am hearing you are wanting to go to Dororra? I am having a faster path there, if you are choosing to go."

I glance up at Damirius, who gives me the same quizzical look. I shrug. We might as well go. He grins, and we follow Lady back into the building. We walk through the foyer and into the familiar corridor that holds the array of spa rooms. However, as soon as we enter, Lady makes a sudden turn to the right. She gives a quick glance over her shoulder.

"We are moving this way," she says. We quickly follow behind her, down the narrow hallway. Eventually, she stops and motions towards a small broom cupboard on the left. I peer in, and see a mop and bucket. I turn to face Lady, perplexed. She nods eagerly, ushering me into the miniscule room. A large painting of a luscious forest pathway hangs on the wall beside me. It's large enough to completely cover the wall it hangs from. I step towards it, uncertain. Lady's enthusiastic nodding encourages me to continue. I gently push the painting aside, revealing a large, cavernous opening.

"You know…", Damirius starts, his head appearing over my shoulder, "of all the things we've seen recently, I still never considered a secret tunnel to be an option."

Lady's head leans into the room, a wide, toothy smile on her face, "That is being the idea!" She giggles, "It is being a much more pleasuring experience, moving in my natural form. It is also being a straight line to Dororra."

A weight settles in my stomach. Apprehension prickles my nerves. No one would just give away such a valuable secret for nothing. "What the catch?" I turn to Lady, squaring my shoulders as my eyes bore into hers.
"No catching," Lady assures me. Then, she pauses. Her brows furrow gently as she thinks. "Actually, I would be wanting a promise, please."
"...A promise?"

"A promise, that is all I am wanting." She insists, a genuine sincerity resides in her face. Her eyes are wide; easy to read the blatant openness that pours out of her. "I am wanting a promise from you that you will be returning."

The request surprises me. It must have been evident, as Lady curls into herself, bashful. "It is getting very lonely in these mountains... and you are seeming so nice." Her voice is soft - softer than usual. She chances a glance up at me, and I notice

the tears that slowly fill her black eyes. Her thin, elongated smile quivers and threatens to fall. Instantly, I'm at her side and enveloping her into a tight hug. She's unsure where to place her arms, and shakes in my embrace. My heart yanks in my chest.
"I promise," I whisper. Lady's arms wrap around me.

Slowly, she pulls back, giving me a solemn smile. She looks like a completely new person to me, now. More human. Her hair's dishevelled, eyes are watery and her face is reddened from embarrassment.
A tiny elven child replaces her. Wide, grey eyes stare up at me, full of tears. Anguish and dirt covers their face. The child's elaborate braids are loosened. Someone has been pulling them. Bruises and cuts cover the child's face and body. A truly pitiful sight, indeed.

"Nylani?" Lady's voice pulls me from the void. My eyes focus on her face. "Are you feeling well?" Concern pulls at the woman's face. Her face shifts between her own and the memory of the child. Both are looking at me pitifully. Long, cold fingers caress my temple, and my eyes close. I sink into the touch. The image of the child fades into the darkness of my eyelids.

"I'm fine," I manage to mumble. My eyes open, and all I see is my reflection in the large black orbs of Lady's eyes. I focus my eyes upwards slightly. I force an apologetic smile at the tiny woman. "Sorry for spooking you like that."
Lady shakes her head softly, a sad smile replying to my false one. Of course she would know. Her entire existence is to divulge in pain, after all. Her finger strokes against my cheek, wiping away a tear I didn't realise was rolling down my face.

A white-hot sting blossoms over my cheek. I swallow my scream, but the tears continue to fall. "Stop crying, girl, or I'll give you something to cry about!" Hot breath bellows in my face. I bite my lip, begging my tears to dry. They don't stop. The metallic tang of blood blooms from my lip. Knuckles find my jaw. I'm on the floor now, with his body looming over me. Still, I remain silent. But water still pours from my eyes. And that's unacceptable. Another hit. And another. My face is hot. My eyes are heavy. Blackness envelops me.

Cold fingers brushing the back of my hand force me out of the memory. I bite back the impulse to scream, but that doesn't stop my body flinching away from Lady's gentle caress. My face is warm. Salty tears flow freely down my cheeks. I use my sleeve to roughly push them away.

"I am sorrowful," Lady whispers, her voice heavy. Dark, doe eyes search mine, a silent understanding settling between us. My head gives a miniscule nod. A rueful smile strains my cheeks.
"Me too."

30

Damirius

"Let's go," Nylani says quietly. I can barely hear her anymore. Her shoulders sag; heavy lids are rubbed raw. She looks defeated. Hollow. I make no remark on it - I fear she'd collapse from my voice alone. I simply nod, instead. Her arms are braced around herself. Her nails dig into her shirt.

She passes me silently. Her eyes don't even flit upward to regard me. She looks like her mind is a thousand leagues away. An unnatural pull drives me to walk impossibly close behind her. I want to hold her - comfort her, somehow - but I deny the urge. One wrong move, and the brittle glass of Nylani's composure will shatter. And I would never forgive myself if I caused that pain.

We slowly start our descent in the mouth of the tunnel, when suddenly, a hand grabs my elbow. I whip around, coming face to face with Lady. Her large ebony eyes are full of worry.

"Please," she whispers, "Be taking care of her."

I nod silently, eyes darting over to Nylani. Her pace is slow. Catching up to her will be no issue. For some reason, that unnerves me more.
"Is she going to be okay?"

"I am thinking the springs were healing of pain in her mind." Lady explains in a hushed tone, "But now it is coming back and hurting her again."
She pauses, watching Nylani intently. "The mind is hard of healing. It can be lessening the memories for a moment, but it will always be coming back." Her wide eyes turn back to me, hardened with intensity. "She will be struggling. Be kind."
I nod fervently, swallowing the lump of uncertainty in my throat.

"Good. When you are ending the tunnel, you will be meeting my brethren, Atticus. He will be helping you."

Suddenly, she hugs me. Despite her scrawny appearance, her arms hold me tightly. I return the hug. For an eldritch being that looks like something from a nightmare, she's actually a sweetheart.
"You should be going now. I am wishing you the best luck."

I catch up with Nylani, my arm gently bumping against her shoulder. She jumps; wide, timid eyes staring at me. My chest constricts at her fearful expression. I look away, keeping my focus on where we tread instead. The silence is deafening, but I don't know how to break it.

We walk in silence for what feels like hours, though it's probably closer to just a few minutes.
The mouth of the tunnel disappears from view the further we go. We're slowly encapsulated in darkness. I stay close. My arm continuously brushes against hers, reassuring me.

"So," my voice punctuates the tense air. She doesn't seem to react to my voice. I can't even see her face to try to gauge if she's even hearing me. "How long do you think it'll take before we're in Dororra?" There's a heavy silence. We continue to walk.

"Two or three days, maybe," she replies. Her voice is barely above a whisper. If we weren't in a tunnel, I doubt I would've heard her. "Why?"

"Just wondering," I counter. I try to keep my voice casual. "Looks like I'll have plenty of time to learn about different types of dirt in the meantime, right?" I force a smile, before remembering she probably can't see it. I keep it there, just in case.

A small huff of a laugh sounds from beside me. But then we're quickly thrown back into our silence. My skin itches in discomfort. I feel like a fish, floundering out of water. Stress creeps into my throat. I want to keep her present. Keep her focused on anything than what her mind is conjuring. Frantically, my eyes are searching for something - anything - to discuss. But all that surrounds us are the sloped, dirt walls of this never ending tunnel. Until I catch the faintest glow a few metres ahead of us.

"Hey, look at this!" I grab her hand and pull her along to the weird source of light.
A scattering of pale-yellow mushrooms climb up the wall. A luminous green glow ebbs beneath the caps. The bioluminescent light has become our sconce in the depths of the underpass.
"How weird are these things?"

Finally, I can see her. The glow of the fungi carves the outline of her face, and luminates her curious, child-like eyes. She leans closer, and I can make out her face in better detail. Her brows seem tense. I watch her inspect the mushrooms. Delicate fingers swipe the underside of a cap, and the luminous spores spread across her fingertips.

"Hm." Her thumb rubs against the affected fingers, the glowing matter spreading further across her hand, "How odd."
"Right?!" I'm grinning, excitement builds as I watch her focus on the plant. "And it's just growing here in the middle of nowhere, of all places!" Who knew mushrooms would have me this excited?

Her face tilts to examine the wall, then she turns her attention to the rest of the tunnel. She steps away from the light, and I can just make out her outline as she shifts and turns. She seems to be studying the entirety of the passageway.
"It makes sense," her voice muses. "It's cool, damp, and dark here. That's perfect for fungi to grow." She pauses for a moment. "Though, I don't understand why it's glowing."

"Maybe to attract insects or whatever to it?" I suggest, unsure. "Help the spores spread?"
"I didn't even think of that." I can hear the surprised bemusement in her tone.
"I do tend to have ideas now and again, you know," I tease.

An unexpected chuckle bubbles from her. I can't help but join in. There she is. My Tiny.
"It's not that hard to believe, Tiny," I chuckle. We continue to walk.
"Stop calling me that!" She grumbles, though I can hear the smile in her voice.
"Would you prefer a different name, then?" I gently taunt, voice thick with exaggerated affection. "How about 'Darling'? Or perhaps 'Sweetheart'?" Her grumbling fuels me and I amp up the dramatics. My hands hold my chest as I gasp out, "Or maybe even 'My love'?"

She shoves me away, and my backside collides with the dirt. She groans, but an undercurrent of a laugh is evident. "Gods you're infuriating," she whines. "Fine, Tiny can stay," she grumbles, "It's better than any of the others."

Jokes and jibes spread between us as we continue our excursion. Many jabs are tossed between us about Nylani's height or my apparently incessant need for a bedward companion – or lack thereof, as she constantly teases. Shoves, pokes, prods, and laughter fill our day as we walk. Though, there's no way to tell for certain how long we've actually been walking.

I don't mind, though. It's nice to simply be in the moment with her, hearing her growing laughter - even if it's at my own expense. Another jab at my rumoured promiscuity elicits another wave of giggles out of her. So I decide to strike. Wiggling fingers catch her throat and relentlessly tickle against her skin. She screams, and topples to the floor. I fall with her, my hands assaulting her sides as she screams a shrill laughter.

"How rude!" I jeer, laughter erupting out of my mock anger. "How unbecoming of such a young lady, talking of others bedfellows!" Her legs kick under me, but to no avail. She writhes and squirms under my weight.

"Please!" She squeals, "Please! I can't breathe!" Her laughter booms around me, and I finally relinquish my attacks, allowing Nylani to breathe again. Her chest rises and falls heavily; I stay straddled atop her, catching my own breath. It's only once we're calm that I realise just how intimately close we are. I'm glad she can't see my cheeks right now.

The outline of her silhouette is all I can make out. My hands gingerly place themselves into the soft earth beneath us, my skin brushing against a shoulder and her hair. Her heavy breath helps to locate her mouth. I could kiss her. I want to. My head leans down, and I can almost smell her. A subtle sweetness lingers in her hair. It's intoxicating. Shallow breaths flitter against my cheek. She's facing me.

I regain my senses and pull away. She doesn't need my nonsense. Especially right now. I hoist myself back onto my feet.
"Sorry about that," I mumble, shame filling me.
"If it gets it out of your system, you can do it," she replies. "I don't mind."

My cheeks flare up at the thought. Soft lips against mine. Entangled in each other's arms. The thought makes my heart soar.

"Did you want to?" I ask. My voice is trembling. My stomach flips in knots.
"...Huh?"

My stomach drops like a brick in water. I can feel the colour rapidly leaving my face. I'm so glad the visibility here is next to non-existent.
"Did you want to kiss me, Nylani?" I ask, struggling to keep my voice level.

"I... I don't know?" She sounds confused. "I didn't think I had to want it." The silence lasts for just a second, but it feels like eternity. "I was... People kiss each other to show they care for them, right?"
"Only when both people want to kiss, Nylani." My voice is hoarse. A shaky breath gets drawn in from the tiny woman.

"What if... What if someone didn't want to, but the other person did?"
"They can say no, Tiny." I don't even know if my voice can be heard any more. Another pregnant, tortuous silence fills the space between us.
"...I can say no?" Her voice is barely above a squeak. Before I know it, Nylani collapses onto the floor in a flood of tears, and screams in pure, heartfelt anguish.

Guttural, heart-wrenching sobs wrack the tiny body. Her lungs rattle as she tries to gulp in air, but all she can do is continue to cry. I feel helpless. I feel guilty. Cautiously, I crawl to her. My hand gently touches her arm. She doesn't move away.

As softly as I can, I pull her onto my lap. I wrap my arms around her, allowing her sobs to soak my shirt. Heavy cries die into muffled whimpers. The weight of her head sinks into my shoulder, as she slowly exhausts herself to sleep.

The ringing of her screams still pound my ears. An anger sits in my chest. What kind of evil bastard would take advantage of someone so delicate? A nauseous feeling stirs my stomach. I nearly did. I want to vomit.

Her gentle snoring pulls me out of the thought. I may have wanted to, but I didn't. And she feels safe enough to sleep in my arms. That must mean something, at least, right? I'll at least let the thought soothe me for now.

She shifts in my arms, mumbling discontentedly. She continues to shift and turn, and I begin to wonder if she's uncomfortable. Suddenly, a nail scratches my face as she thrashes and I drop her onto the floor. She jolts up screaming, and scurries as far away as possible. I clutch my cheek. Her breathing is erratic.

"Sorry," she whimpers.

"I'm sorry, too, Tiny."

31

Nylani

The walk for the next two days is in near silence. We trudge along until we're exhausted, we rest, and then we continue. I want to break the silence, but I can sense his discomfort. After the incident, he kept his distance. The only time he comes near me is after my nightmares.

His arms wrap around me protectively while I cry, but as soon as I stop, he lets go. I'm almost craving nightmares, because it means he will be near me. The forced separation is just as torturous. Maybe even more so. Blindly, my hand ventures through the dark and my fingers brush against his hand. He stops.

"Hm?"
I didn't think this far ahead. My throat swallows my voice. I can't see his eyes, but I can feel them watching me, curiously.
"I–" My voice falters. "Tell me about your family." Silence. "Please." My fingers coil around his, pleading for something - anything.

Gently, his hand squeezes mine. "What do you want to know, Tiny?" His voice is gentle, soothing. "Tell me everything," I plead. And he obliges.

We walk hand in hand, as Damirius talks animatedly about each member of his family. I lean into the memories he shares so freely with me, picturing the ragtag family on a solitary farm. Warmth fills me as he describes his siblings in detail. I can almost imagine them - and the havoc they wreak. I chuckle at the thought.

Before I know it, Damirius divulges me with tales of his childhood. He reminisces on his upbringing; how his father was rarely home - and if he was, he was asleep. He helped his mother raise his siblings, but it wasn't until he was older that he realised that his family didn't have much money at all. He talks in depth about how he desperately wanted to change that. How he wanted to be useful.

I listen intently, basking in the pure delight that pours out of him as he recalls his home. Though, with all the joy that I soak in, a hole still carves its way into my chest. The hollowness makes my heart heavy. I try to push the feeling away, but it persists. A gnawing, nagging, relentless ache of...

envy? I scowl at myself. I refuse to spoil this moment of reprieve.

His voice pulls me away from my inner reprimand, and I dive headfirst into his memories again. A lush landscape fills my mind's eye, full of the oranges and pinks of autumn. His words create the image of goats skittering around me, as multiple siblings run past. I can almost smell the fresh air that he remarks brushing past his face.

"Despite the havoc all the animals - children included - made, I couldn't help but feel relaxed amongst it all, you know?" His voice pops the scenery, and I'm pulled back to the present. His voice is wistful; probably lost in his own memories. I smile.
"I can see why," I say. "I'd love to visit, one day." I blurt out, surprising myself. My cheeks flare in embarrassment.
"I'd like that, too, Tiny." I'm sure my head is producing steam.

We continue our walk. Thankfully, a lot more relaxed than we have been for the last few days. Our fingers stay interlocked, though neither of us mention it. He gives a gentle squeeze each time I go quiet. When I squeeze back, I feel him relax. When I don't, he gently probes me with questions or memories of his life of travelling. Sometimes I deliberately don't respond, just so I can hear him talk.

His talent for storytelling is far better than I could do. And it helps with staying out of the silence this damned tunnel pushes us in.
"I'm surprised I haven't bored you with my stories, yet," Damirius' voice clips through my thoughts. I must have been too quiet again. "What about you, Tiny? Any memories of your family?"

Fire. Thick, billowing smoke. Flashes of lightning carve through the ground around me. A body. Two bodies. A man and woman, face down in the dirt.
"Not really," I say, my voice nonchalant. "They died when I was young."
"Oh," he tenses a little against my fingers. "I'm sorry."

"It's okay, Damirius." His fingers squeeze my hand, despite the reassurance. I squeeze back, batting the image of Mother's smile away.

Eventually, the tunnel ends. A ladder stands ahead of us, illuminated by the faint light that filters through the ceiling. Looks like this is our exit.

"Ladies first."
"If you're nervous to go first, just admit it," I retort.
He snorts dismissively.
"I am *not* nervous."
"Then, by all means, you go first."
"No, no, you can go first."

I roll my eyes and laugh. He huffs. The thin streams of light are just enough to outline his scowl. I relent and begin to climb, stifling my laughter as I ascend. The climb is slow - even more so without any indication on how high we're climbing. Finally, my head brushes against the top.

Gingerly, I raise a hand and feel around, waiting for a spot to give way. My hand runs along the surprisingly smooth top, anticipating any kind of change. Nothing. I press my hand firmly against the ceiling, pushing upwards. Finally, the ceiling gives and I shove the area above as hard as I can. The ceiling flies open and light floods into the tunnel.

It takes a moment for my eyes to adjust to the sudden influx of bright lights. I feel blind as I crawl out of the tunnel and shuffle across the smooth, cold floor. Slowly, my vision starts to clear.

Aged, cracked tiles surround me. My eyes lift, and I realise we're in a storage room of some kind. Boxes cover the floor, all in various stages of disrepair. Shelves of vials clutter the walls. Torn, raggedy wallpaper hides in the spaces between the multitude of shelves. The pinstriped design is barely visible.

Damirius finally appears out of the hole in the floor, looking as confused as I feel. I slowly rise, clattering against empty vials that roll around the floor. But it's a shelf of full bottles that catch my attention.

Purple smoke rolls endlessly in one flask; whereas, a deep, navy liquid rests within another. I pick one up, trying to decipher the scratchy penmanship on it's label.

"Naah-vaah.... Nah-vah.... Nava-core-uhm?" Damirius is squinting at another container. A sparkling, fizzing liquid pops against the glass vial he holds.

"We're... at an alchemist's?" I question, aloud. My eyes dart around the room, a disarray of vibrant colours blurring my vision as I look at the thousands of concoctions that surround us.

" 'A fizzing elixir to bubble up joy'," Damirius continues to read from the label. He scoffs, "For a healing potion, it doesn't look very healer-y."

"That's because I'm an unconventional healer, my dear chum," an unfamiliar voice responds. My head whips to the sound, looking at a face that peers down from the top of a doorframe behind us. An elongated, curled grin greets me. Tiny, framed spectacles obscure the pitch black eyes that study us.

All of a sudden, a large, thin hand appears from behind the door. Elongated fingers curl around the vial Damirius holds, plucking it out of his hands with ease. "And I would appreciate it if my potions were not manhandled, thank you."

The owner of the hand ducks his head into the room, leaning closer to the pair of us. His long, angular nose obscures his face, which looms above me. His smile is unwavering, gleaming against the light from the sconces.

"The name's Atticus," the spindly man continues, "I'm assuming Lady sent you to me?" His dark eyes glance over to the open hatch.
"Yes," I say. He regards me with curiosity. "She wanted to give us a quicker way to Dororra." He nods, understanding.

"Well, a friend of Lady's is a friend of mine." His smile stretches further - if it were possible. He gesturs for us to follow, before scuttling along the hallway with ease. His body was unnaturally long, and remarkably thin. The top of his head brushes against the ceiling as we walk behind him, his arms and legs continuously shifting from the floor to the walls like a spider. The easiness of his movements make it clear he has lived here for quite some time.

"I must say," he remarks, bemused, "For my darling sister to allow you to use her tunnel, you must have left a decent impression on her." His head pivots to look at us as he talks, his body still moving forward.

"Sister?" Damirius' faint voice questions, "But... you don't–."

"--Sound like her?" Atticus intercepts. A pointed grin is aimed at Damirius, and I can feel him shrink beside me. "Unfortunately, it's a side effect of mingling with common folk for too long; you start to sound like them."

"And you don't want Lady to integrate with us common folk?" I question, earning his lingering gaze.

"Gods, no. One or two visitors is fine, but surrounding her with swarms of people?" His eyes widen, incredulous. "It'd be cruel. She's far too..." He stops, contemplating for a moment, "She's too kind for the reality of people." I nod, agreeing with his sentiment. Her sweet demeanour would be crushed once people realise they can exploit her desire to please. He relaxes; hunched shoulders slack, and he continues to guide us through the labyrinth of his abode.

We walk through winding, narrow hallways; left, right, another left – it's hard to remember where we came from. Everything's the same; the same white walls with the same tiled floors. It feels like we're hardly progressing at all. The longer we walk, the more jittery Damirius becomes.

His eyes are fixated on our spidery guide. I offer my hand to him, which he immediately holds. His fingers turn into vices, holding my hand hostage in a terrified grasp. I have to stifle my smirk. After everything we've seen already, a harmless Wraith should be a walk in the park.

Suddenly, we're bathed in sunlight. The mid-morning sun stings against my eyes, but I'm grateful to feel the warmth against my skin. I glance around. We seem to be standing outside a shop front for an apothecary. But instead of a simple street ahead of us, a canopied lounging area fills my view.

It's full of chairs and oversized pouffes, arranged erratically; a few patrons have pulled chairs together in a tight cluster. Elaborate pipes with ornate, silver bases sit atop tables throughout the enclosed shelter. The lingering patrons are sharing a pipe, a multi-coloured smoke drifting lazily between them. The smoke shimmers, bedazzling the kaleidoscopic smog in the daylight. A deep inhale from beside me draws my attention, and I watch as Atticus breathes in the lazy tendrils of vapour.

Now that we're outside, Atticus has unfurled to his true height. He easily doubles my own height, even with his natural slump. His neck is as elongated as his arms, like a vulture's. His amusingly miniscule spectacles sit at the bridge of his crooked nose, barely of any aid to the menacing, black eyes that are watching me intently. He swoops down, his face a mere few inches to my own.

A cloud of orange hair surrounds his emaciated face, obscuring the world from view as he fills my vision. I can't help but notice how flat it is at the top of his skull - probably from years of brushing against ceilings. His eyes glisten; probably aware that I'm studying him just as much as he's studying me.

"I sense a lot of pain in you, little one," his voice breaks my concentration. There's no sympathy in his voice. It's the bored recounting of someone simply stating a fact. It's refreshing. "You're welcome to use my wares, if you'd like. They're far more capable than Lady's springs."

A snort of amusement escapes me before I can stop it. His constant lean into his unnerving appearance does nothing for his marketing skills. A ginger brow quirks upwards, his beady, black eyes alight with a similar mirth. Damirius looks between us, befuddled.

"No, thank you," I finally say to the towering man in front of me. "I think I've had enough healing over the last few days."
"Ah," Atticus muses. "Well, in any case, my services are always open for such a... filling meal." His eyes glaze over me, his hunger evident.

A thin tongue flicks over stretched, cracked lips. My eyes roll, unphased to his antics already. For an eldritch being that's lived amongst humanity for years, you'd think he'd have more ways to convince the populace. I begin to walk towards the exit of the extravagant tent, pulling Damirius alongside me. Atticus trails behind us.

"A quick puff before you go, ma'am?" He asks, his eagerness overtaking any sense of unease he tries so hard to cultivate. "One for the road, so to speak?" His smirk has eased; it no longer pulls at his cheeks uncomfortably, but rests in the divots of his shallow skin.

"Just directions to the market, please, Atticus." He relents, raising his large hands in a mock defeat. "Okay, okay, you win." He chuckles darkly, shaking his head as he shows us out of the seating area. He points a long finger to the left. "Follow the path until you see the postal office. Then turn right."

"Thank you, Atticus," I pause for a moment. "And if you see Lady before I do, please tell her I intend to keep my promise." He nods, smiling much more warmly than when we first arrived. Slowly, he slinks back within his canopies, and disappears from view. I look at Damirius, whose eyes are close to popping out of his skull.

32

Damirius

"How do you do it?"
Nylani raises an eyebrow, "Do what?"
"You don't show fear, even when there's a creepy looking guy that wants to devour you."
She scoffs, "He didn't want to eat me. He just wanted my pain."
"Alright, a *part* of you, then," I stress.

She continues walking down the street, like she hadn't just been face-to-face with a horrifying, twelve-foot-tall man that's older than time itself. Even his smile was sinister.

"He's harmless," she remarks nonchalantly. I almost feel the gravel scrape against my jaw.
"Are you joking?!" I manage to squawk. "He was looking at you like a roast dinner! He even called you a 'filling meal'!"

She finally stops walking, and faces me. Her eyes lock onto mine, her face serious. "He's a wraith. Wraiths can't physically hurt us unless he was willing to pick me up and throw me. And I highly doubt javelin is his preferred sport." She stares at me, as if expecting a response. I can't think of any. "Just because they look monstrous," she continues, "doesn't mean they are. The most terrifying people I've met are also some of the most appealing." The ferocity of her tone keeps me silent. We continue to walk.

Silence consumes us, and I feel my mind plunge into the darker crevices of my mind.
Memories of clamouring hands bruising my skin intrude my thoughts, despite me fighting against the images. Scowling faces pierce my mind, just as their sharp insults hurtle through my ears. I feel nauseous; the reminder of humanity's depraved nature is unwelcome. Maybe Nylani does have a point, after all.

"So, Mr. Not-Monster-With-A-Winning-Smile said this way, right?"
I can almost hear her eyes rolling, but that makes the awful joke worth it. Bad jokes are always a remedy for awkward pauses. Moving on from tense conversation was just an added bonus. Her jaw relaxes, and her eyes soften, as we continue our walk.

The simple path morphs into cobblestone as we pass the postal office, and head for the heart of Dororra. The further we walk, the more people we encounter; muscular miners bumble past with heavy loads, a mother with three sproglets pulling her in different directions, and multiple busybodies that dart past in quick succession.

The familiar sense of eyes watching me creeps up my spine. Of course, a tiefling is still a commodity - even in a place as busy as this. I touch my horns instinctively. Still there. Unfortunately. Though my curls do obscure them a little, at least. The familiar brushing of Nylani's head against my shoulder catches my attention. I turn to face her, only to find her scowling. Her eyes are downcast, staring at the floor as we walk.

"Not a fan of busy places?" I ask, innocently.
Her eyes flick up to notice me. "No."
"I'm surprised," I say, noncommittally. "I thought you'd like it, since it's so much like Kohrmiir."
"Didn't like Kohrmiir, either."
"Really?!" My jaw is agape. She looks confused at my surprise. "But you were so nice!"
"I needed work," she states matter-of-factly, "No one gives you work if you're not nice."

Suppose that makes sense. I give a small hum of agreement, and the conversation dies. We walk in silence - a comfortable silence, this time - as the residents of Dororra run past.

A gentle bump against my shoulder gains my attention, and I'm pleasantly surprised to see Nylani cozying up to me. My arm instantly wraps around her, pulling her close. But her startled expression makes my brain falter. Shit. I need an excuse.

"It's, uh..." my voice waivers. Gods damn it. "It's getting hectic," I manage to get out. "Stick close. Don't wanna lose you, Tiny."
Thankfully, the populace of Dororra follows through with my lame excuse, and the streets are suddenly bustling with people. Nylani curls into my torso. Her tiny hands cling onto me like a life-line. My hand holds onto her shoulder as we march through the swarm of people to get to the heart of Dororra - the Palderra Bazaar.

A sea of colourful banners assault my eyes. Large, bold lettering decorates the stalls that fill the town square. The plaza is packed with people; shoulders bump as people push to look at the wares of each stall. The smell of baked goods wafts through the bazaar, and my mouth waters instantly. Bright, fresh produce adorn multiple carts, each with their own tempting bargain signs. I have to stifle a chuckle at the sight of balding men furiously scribbling new prices on their signs to attract more customers. I don't get to see how their silent battle concludes, as we're pushed further and further into the bazaar.

Small tables of crafts appear in glimpses before I'm moved to another stall. Flashes of handmade paints, blankets, and clothing come and go as the crowd continues to undulate through the scattered arrangement of the bazaar. Nylani has cemented herself to my side, and we stumble in tandem through the current of Dororra's tide. Finally, her arm swings out and points ahead of us.

"There!" She yells above the chattering of the marketplace. "There's the notice board!" I follow her finger, and spot the wide multi-panelled board that heads the market on a raised seating area. I grip her tightly, holding her to me, as we push against the natural flow of the people.

The air feels lighter the second we're out of the bustling crowd. I take a large gulp of air, and release my hold on Nylani. She approaches the board, and I follow behind.

33

Nylani

A familiar face stares back at me. Familiar, but not quite right. These grey eyes are too bright - too happy. Her dark hair is in beautiful, elaborate braids, not my singular, plain one. And her olive-tan face is too young and rounded. But, the name is definitely mine.

Cecilaena Uvalaar.

It's written in bold, black ink, just under my portrait. Large enough for the entire market to read it. Under that, smaller scripture follows:

'*MISSING!*
*50,000 gold reward upon her safe return.
In mid-twenties. May have scarring. Bring our heiress home!'*

My stomach plummets. I rip the poster from the board and shove it in my bag, my heart pounding in my ears. How is that name here? *Why* is that name here? The people of Dororra normally don't have any interest in the politics of Ula'Rae. That must mean...

"Whatcha found, Tiny?" Damirius chirps, and my heart nearly leaps out of my throat. I quickly regain my composure, hoping that the shaking in my bones isn't visible. My heart rattles my ribcage. Blood pounds in my ears.

"Nothing," I manage to force out. I hope I sound calm. "Just loads of posters that are out of date." Damirius' eyes linger on me for a moment, before his attention turns to the board. "These are from last winter!" He grumbles, ripping the outdated posters off.

I feel like I'm going to deflate. Adrenaline rushes through me, the thundering beat in my chest slowly subsiding. I scrunch the paper into a tight ball in the bottom of my bag; my eyes are fixated on the posters, but I'm not reading anything.

The familiar grumbling of the tiefling beside me pulls me out of my head. I turn to look at him, only to find his honey-coloured eyes already staring at me, expectantly. I practically jump out of my skin.

"Lost in your own world, huh?" He laughs. I feign a smile, which he accepts.
"Yeah," I mumble, "Sorry."
"Guess you're not getting much luck either, then?"
"Hm?"

He points an exasperated hand at a bunch of flyers in front of him. "It's all lift-and-shift stuff." He grabs a few and reads from them, " 'Deliver a parcel to the other side of town', or 'Move carts for miners'. There's nothing interesting!" He sulks like a petulant child, and I chuckle.

"Not everything can be as exciting as a golem."
"I know, but…" He sighs. "When I was whisked away on an adventure, I didn't think I'd be lifting clay and carrying it to a shop."
I snort out a laugh, which grows at his bewildered expression. "That's the reality of being a wandering mercenary." I remark, though not unkindly.

"You gotta find a way to survive, even if it means lifting clay and moving it for a week. Besides," I add, "I don't think I could stomach another fight just yet." His familiar smile returns, and I feel my own grow. We lean closer together, musing over which requests sound best out of our very limited pickings.

All of a sudden, a muscular arm forces itself around my neck, and I'm hauled away from the safety of my lavender-tinted friend. I go to scream, but a dark hand covers my mouth as we plunge into the shadows of a secluded alleyway. I'm forced against a wall, and meet the face of my abductor. A face I presumed long dead, and very far away.

"Oh, moons above!" the older, elven woman cries, "Cece, you're okay! You're really okay!" She moves her weathered, battle marked hand away from my mouth.
"Ayda, what are you doing here?!" I whisper, incredulous. The last I had seen of her was the night I escaped. The last thing I had heard was her yells of pain as she was found not long after I slipped away.

Her hair has streaks of grey running through it, now. Her face has aged, and a long deep scar runs down her cheek. My heart aches.
"I could be asking you the same, missy!" she mockingly scolds me. She engulfs me in a tight hug, and I instantly feel like a small child, wrapped

up in her loving embrace again. Calloused fingertips stroke against my cheek; the sensation as soothing as it was all those years ago. I sink into her, just like I had before. She was a mother to a motherless child, though she would always claim she never had a maternal bone in her body.

"I'm so glad you're okay," I mumble into her shoulder. Her hands cradle my head. I can feel hot tears threaten to swell. I grab her shirt, and her fingers stroke my hair.
"Same here, kid," she responds. I can hear the emotion break her voice. My tears bleed into her grimy shirt. I don't care. "After you got away," Ayda continues, her voice faint, "it inspired us grunts to run for the hills, too." She chuckles.

Her deep, hearty laugh reverberates in her chest. I finally pull away, looking up at the darker, older, woman before me. She looks so different, yet still the same. A melancholy happiness settles deep in my gut. She got away; but I know it must have cost a lot. My eyes drag over the scar that sinks into her cheek. It always costs.

Ayda's dark brown eyes dart out of the alleyway, as if she's suddenly remembering something. Her face falls. She looks back at me, her eyes slowly widening. Her body hunches over me, her face a mere inch from my own.

"Of course..." She mumbles, "I should've known." Her breathing picks up, panic filling her features. "You gotta go, Cece. He's here, somewhere." My stomach twists and convulses uncomfortably. Her eyes bore into mine, her panic seeping into me. She glances over her shoulders, her grip tight on my arms.

"He's had spies everywhere, trying to find you. Been at it since you left." Her voice is barely a whisper, but she's a foghorn in my head. "Cece, focus. You need to go. He will stop at nothing to get you back."

My mind whirls. My stomach is so tight I feel like I'm going to hurl. She's talking but I can't hear a word she's saying any more. Suddenly, the sun hits my face and I'm on the street again.
"Go," Ayda whispers in my ear, "Before he finds you."

I want to face her - to memorise her face before I run again - but I know she won't be there. Ayda was always quick on her feet. My heart is pounding, and my mind is spinning, but my legs are numb. I'm frozen in place as terror cements my feet in place. I have to go. But where? Somewhere safe. Where's safe? Damirius. Damirius is safe. And just like that, I'm in a full sprint to the bazaar.

The blurs of people dart out of my way as I carve a direct path to the marketplace. Some yell, but their complaints are drowned out by the perpetual pumping in my ears. My chest is aching, and I'm heaving for breath, but I can't stop. I won't stop. Not until I know we're safe. If he knows I'm here, then he definitely knows I'm not alone.

The lavender man sticks out like a sore thumb, and for once I'm grateful. Relief hits me like a tidal wave as I charge towards him. But the feeling quickly dies as I realise he's screaming my name. The name he knows, at least. Shit!

I dive at him, heads colliding as I try to silence the bellowing that comes out of his mouth. It takes a moment for the racing of my mind to register the softness of his lips against mine. Everything happens so fast, but it takes another moment for me to feel his arms tighten around me and pull me closer. My nails sink into his shoulder, desperate to not fall. We're spinning, and my eyes are trying hard to focus. Finally, we stop, and my eyes fall to something deep in the crowd behind us.

The burning, blue eyes of my master.